Praise for *Deranged*

"A complex web of interconnected events,
similar to *Gone Girl* or *A Time to Kill* keeps readers engaged.
Deranged may be Netti's eeriest thriller yet."
—Timothy Gene Sojka, the author of
#1 Thrillers *Payback Jack* and *Politikill*

DERANGED

Chapter 1

Everyone is a moon and has a dark side,
which he never shows to anybody.
–Mark Twain.

Maddy Reynolds, 1978, Utica, New York
"Is Mr. Beretta feeling hot today, Maddy?"

"He's boiling, Jake."

The old sergeant laughed. He always asked the same question and got the same answer, but Maddy didn't mind. She knew a range master at a police shooting facility was a lonely job, and she understood lonely.

Each day, after her daughter got on the bus for school, Maddy would stop at the range to run through routines before heading in to work. Shooting started when she was fourteen, and for her, it was as essential as eating and sleeping.

Placing the black case on the same table as always, she retrieved the Beretta 9-millimeter and walked to lane three. She popped in a magazine. Feeling herself step out of the personality known to her family, friends, and coworkers, she became a very dangerous person. Few people knew that person, but Jake was one. She had sworn him to secrecy about her shooting skills.

It was a day for holster, long-range draw-and-fire drills. Fifty or one hundred yards, it didn't matter. Maddy was a High Master Shooter, and her scores were always off the charts.

When she finished and was packing up her weapons, Jake sauntered up. "Do you have time for a cup of coffee? I've got a fresh pot brewing."

"Love to, but not today. Maybe tomorrow."

"Okay, but I'm going to hold you to it. By the way, rumor has it you've made detective."

"That's a true rumor," she said. "I start next week."

"Nice. The first woman detective in the Oneida County Sheriff's Department is nothing to sneeze at."

She smiled. "Thanks."

"Well, congrats. Will you be working under Captain Zepatello?"

"Yep, he's the one who hired me."

Jake nodded. "He's an awful hard ass. Ex-military. He runs the place like a combat unit but takes good care of his people. In the long run, you'll be better for it."

The old man handed Maddy a clipboard to sign. As usual, hers was the first name at the top of the sign-out sheet. "You have a good one," he said as he took it back.

"See you tomorrow, Jake."

Chapter 2

I'm so glad it's Friday. Maddy pulled up to her house, grabbed a pizza box from the back seat, and plodded up the stairs with keys clenched between her teeth. A cool fall breeze brushed up against her face, reminding her that winter was on its way. *There's so much I need to do around here before the snow flies,* she thought. She tripped on a broken piece of concrete and thought how the old place was too much for a divorced mother living on a cop's salary. She shook her head, thinking of the old house. *If Grandma hadn't willed it to me, I'd sell it.*

She opened the front door. "Hey, kids," she said, maneuvering past Amber and Samantha to the kitchen with arms full. "My God, it's seven thirty? Sorry I'm so late. Who's winning?"

"Amber is killing me, Mrs. Reynolds."

"I just bought a hotel," Amber said.

"You two must be starving."

"Naw, we've been snacking on chips." Amber held up a bag of Doritos.

"Can you stay for pizza, Sam?"

"No, I better go. My mom has dinner waiting."

"Take a couple of slices for later. Before I forget, let me get your money. Thanks for helping me out tonight. I needed to get my reports to the D.A."

She returned from the kitchen and handed Sam an envelope with money in it and two pizza slices wrapped in tinfoil.

"Thanks, Mrs. Reynolds. How do you like your new job? I read that you're the first woman detective in the Oneida County Sheriff's office. How cool."

"She loves it," Amber said. Maddy tried not to interrupt the flow of conversation as she hung up Amber's coat, put her book bag in the hallway, and carried empty glasses from the living room to the kitchen. "Every night since she made detective, she comes home, puts on sweatpants, eats, pours a glass of wine, and reads reports. How boring!"

Maddy laughed. "Yeah, I do like it. It's what I've always wanted to do. But I still have a lot to learn. It's only been a couple of months."

After Samantha left, Maddy and Amber sat at the kitchen table and dug into the pizza.

"So, what are your plans for tomorrow?" Maddy asked.

"Dad wants to take me to the zoo, but it's not his weekend, so he has to ask you."

"Do you want to go?"

"Only if I can bring a friend...I think Abby's around tomorrow. What about you? What will you do if I go with Dad?"

Maddy laughed. "Well, I'm going to be the laziest person in the neighborhood. No reports. I might sleep in, eat junk food. I might not even take a shower. And maybe I'll make progress on my new puzzle. What do you think of that?"

"I'll believe it when I see it," Amber said with a giggle.

When they finished, Maddy put the leftovers in the refrigerator. "Let's go up early tonight, pooch. I'm exhausted. I can read to you for a while."

"No, that's okay. I have a magazine."

Lying in bed, Maddy tried to focus on her latest Stephen King novel, but her thoughts hung on her daughter. She tiptoed down the hall, cracked opened Amber's door, and inched her way over to the bed. Amber lowered a magazine and smiled.

"What are you looking at?"

"Just *Teen Magazine.*"

"Anything interesting?"

"Not really."

Maddy put her hand on Amber's arm. "Honey, I'm sorry I haven't been around as much lately. I just don't feel like I'm doing a good job of keeping all the balls in the air."

"What do you mean, Mom?"

"You know. I missed your school concert a few weeks ago, and I rescheduled your dentist's appointment for the third time, things like that. We don't have time together the way we used to."

"It's okay. Don't worry so much."

Maddy tussled her daughter's hair. "I miss our talks. I don't want my job to take the place of us." She hugged her daughter, snuggled her head up against her shoulder, and said, "Nothing is more important to me than you."

When she returned to her room, she plopped onto her bed and took a deep breath. Reaching over to her nightstand, she picked up a leather-bound book and opened it to a blank page. After a moment of thought, she wrote, "Dad, I wish you could have known your granddaughter. She would have made you so proud." She closed the diary, returning it to its placed next to her father's Chicago Police Detective badge, and switched off the lamp.

***

"How about bacon and eggs this morning?" Maddy asked.

Amber pulled up a chair at the table. "No, thanks. I'll just have Cheerios. Do you know what the weather's supposed to be like today?"

Her mother opened the newspaper to the weather page. "Let's see. It says overcast, then sunny, and then, oh crap, snow."

"Snow! Really?"

"That's what it says. I guess I better get the storm windows on this weekend."

"Dad said he'd help with that."

"Tell him thanks, but I can handle it."

The phone rang. "I'll get it," Amber said. "It might be Abby." She pulled the long cord over to her chair. "Hello. Just a minute." She covered the receiver and handed the phone to her mother. "It's for you. It's a man."

"Hello."

"Hi, Maddy. Sorry to bother you on the weekend, but I've got something I'd like you to handle. Can you meet me at the office?"

"Sure, Zep. I'll be there in an hour." She hung up. "I guess you were right; it doesn't look like I'll have a relaxing Saturday after all. It's a good thing your dad wants to take you to the zoo."

"What do you have to do?"

"Zep said he wants me to handle something, but he didn't say what."

"Your boss?"

"Yes."

"Why is he called Zep, anyway? That's a weird name."

"It's short for Zepatello, and you should only have nice things to say about him. If it wasn't for him, I wouldn't be where I am."

"I know, I know. Amber rolled her eyes. You're the first female detective. It's a big deal. I get it."

"Come on, let's finish up and get dressed. I'll drop you off at Dad's on the way to work."

"Aww, Mom. I like to relax on Saturday mornings."

"Sorry, honey."

Chapter 3

"Sit down, Maddy." Zep put his feet up on his desk and took a sip of coffee from a Styrofoam cup. "Thanks for coming in. I know it's Saturday, and you've been putting in a lot of hours, but something's come up I think you're ready for." He picked up a folder and handed it to her.

"An eleven-year-old girl has gone missing. Her name is Sarah Benning. Over the last few years, we've been to the house several times. Domestic disputes, runaway issues, but no violence."

He put his feet down, folded his hands on the desk, and said, "The kid usually shows up in a day or two, but this time it's been six nights, and the mother is beside herself. She's an alcoholic and gets ornery when she drinks. Shit has hit the fan since the husband moved in with a woman half his age. According to the interview conducted yesterday with the mother, Sarah's been acting out worse than normal ever since the father left. It's all in the report," Zep said as he pointed to the folder in Maddy's hand.

"Trick Diaz, did the interview?" Maddy asked when she saw his name on the report. "I thought he transferred into the K-9 unit."

"Do you know Trick?"

"We partnered last summer for a few months."

"Well, say nothing, but we've accepted him. It's just a matter of paperwork. Do you have questions?"

She glanced at the folder one more time and said, "Nope, got it."

"That's it, then. Just do your best and keep me posted."

Maddy walked out and thought, *My first actual assignment.* She reached into her jacket pocket, felt for the brass Chicago Police Department badge she always carried, held it in her hand, and whispered, "I did it, Dad."

***

The Benning place was on the county line. As Maddy drove, a gray October sky set off by orange and red trees brought back memories of fall in Chicago when she was a kid. But the beauty ended when she pulled up to the house. *I can't believe anyone lives in this shithole.*

Yellow paint flaked off wood clapboards, and a piece of lumber propped the side porch. A woman in her fifties with long, gray, stringy hair came to the door. She wore dirty overall jeans, and a faded green flannel shirt with holes in the elbows.

"Are you here about Sarah?" the woman asked.

"Yes. I'm Maddy Reynolds from the Oneida County Sheriff's. You must be Martha."

The woman looked at her and twisted her face. "You're a detective?"

Aww geez, here we go with that female cop shit again. "Yep," Maddy said.

"Oh well, come in." She opened the screen door and nodded to Maddy.

Maddy sat in an old, cushioned chair. Worn-through fabric exposed stuffing on its rounded arms, and an empty bottle of vodka rested on an end table next to her. "I know you explained everything to Officer Diaz yesterday, but would you go through it again one more time for me?" Martha cleared her throat, sat up, and brushed the hair from her face.

"Last Monday after school, I told Sarah she had to come with me to Herkimer to help get a load of firewood. With winter coming, I can't afford oil, so I try to heat with wood. But Hank, the asshole — excuse me, my ex-husband — told Sarah that he and his bitch girlfriend wanted to take her to the movies to see Cinderella. Of course, Sarah wants to go with them, and I end up being the bad guy. So, Sarah gets all pissed off when I say, 'No,' storms out of the house, and I haven't seen her since."

"Do you have any idea where she might have gone?"

"She has a few friends from school, but none of them have seen her. Sometimes she runs to her daddy, Hank, when she's in a snit, and sometimes she'll go to Mary Thompson's. She lives just down the road. But Hank ain't seen her either. When I called Mary, she said Sarah stopped by that day for a little while, then left. The only other place she's been that I know of is Utica. That's where she went last time. She hitchhiked there and stayed for three days."

"Do you know where in Utica she went?"

"Nope. She wouldn't say. But I hope she didn't go there again. That's no place for a child."

Maddy spoke as she wrote in her notebook. "Has Sarah talked about meeting any new people? You know, teachers, friends, neighbors?"

"Nope."

"Have you noticed her acting differently in any way?"

"Other than being a little shit, not really."

"Can I look at her room?"

"Oh, she's not in there."

No shit, Maddy thought to herself. "I just want to look around. We might find something that'll give us an idea of where she's gone."

Martha balked, put her fingertips together, and appeared pensive, as though she was about to choose one of three doors on a game show. Finally, she said, "I guess it'll be all right."

She led the way to a room off the kitchen. *Oh my God,* Maddy thought when she walked inside the bedroom. *This place isn't fit for a dog.* The room was damp and musty. It reeked of mouse droppings. Broken windowpanes covered with plastic and water stains on faded yellow walls painted a picture of neglect. Maddy recoiled at the sight of a sleeping bag draped over a twin bed, half lying on a filthy floor. *Poor kid.*

On a pillow lay a small photo of two adults and a child with their heads together, smiling. "Who's this?" Maddy asked.

"That's me, Hank, and Sarah, six years ago. It was all different back then. We had jobs. But when GE moved out, everything hit the shitter."

A plaque of a girl kneeling with her hands clasped in prayer, looking up to heaven with a tear running down one cheek, lay next to the photo. The inscription on the bottom read, "Dear God, I know you are always with me. Please comfort me and make my sadness go away. Amen." *This kid sounds depressed.*

Maddy walked over to Sarah's dresser and rummaged through odds and ends scattered on top. She held up small scraps of paper, flyers, notes from teachers, gum and candy wrappers, ballpoint pens, hair clips, combs, and even arms and legs from broken Barbie dolls. She pulled open the dresser drawers and found two empty—one with pants and tops and another with a few pairs of underwear and socks. "It doesn't look like there's anything here to go on. Can you give me Sarah's description, as well as the addresses of her father and the Thompson woman?"

"Well, Sarah's about four foot seven and weighs about ninety-five pounds. She has brown eyes and dirty blond hair."

"Can you remember what she wore?"

"Hmm, let's see. She wore black pants and a purple dress down to her knees. Over that, probably her black sweater-coat that zips in the front. She always carries a purple-and-white beaded bag with a rag doll inside."

When they walked back into the kitchen, Martha grabbed a utility bill from the top of a breadbox. On the back, she wrote the addresses. As they left the kitchen, Martha kissed her fingers and gently placed them on a picture of Jesus taped on the refrigerator.

She's going to need his help, Maddy thought.

***

"Are you Mary Thompson?" Maddy stood in front of a black woman sweeping leaves off a porch.

The old woman straightened up and smiled. "I am the woman. Or at least what's left of her." She leaned back, rested her weight on the broom, and eyeballed Maddy up and down. "You look like the law."

"I'm Detective Reynolds from the Sheriff's Department. I'd like to speak with you about Sarah Benning."

The woman's lips curled sadly. As she paused, her cheeks drooped, and the light that had beamed from her eyes faded. "I was just about to have a cup of tea. Why don't you come inside and join me?"

They walked through a dining room with uneven floorboards and burgundy wallpaper that someone had scrubbed clean. An old Stickley table and chairs, perfectly kept, gave Maddy the impression that Mary once knew the more beautiful things in life. Mary gestured to Maddy to take a seat as she walked to the stove, poured the tea from an already hot kettle, and placed two cups on the table.

"What is your relationship with Sarah?" Maddy asked as Mary sat down.

"Well dear, sometimes Sarah needs a mama, and every once in a while, God asks me to be that mama. You know, just for a few hours, to help her through a bad day. Last Monday was one of those days."

"Can you tell me what happened?"

"Sarah walked in about six thirty and said little. I offered her some warm apple pie that just came out of the oven. Her eyes lit up. She sat right where you're sitting now, took Jenny from her bag, and leaned her right there." Mary pointed to a sugar bowl. "Jenny's the old rag doll I gave her a long time ago."

"Then Jenny and I watched Sarah eat her apple pie and ice cream. You'd think the child hadn't eaten in a month. When she ate it all up, she took my hand, held it in hers, and asked if I'd pray with her. I nearly cried. She looked at me with those big, sad brown eyes, and I said, 'Sure, honey.' She bowed her head and said, 'Please God, make Mom and Dad love each other again.' That was all. She got up, put Jenny back in her bag, and walked out the door."

Mary's account was so absorbing that Maddy forgot to take notes.

"I've watched the Benning family grow over the years, and then, over the last few, fall apart. It happens all the time around here. Once, they were a happy family. But when the jobs go, troubles come. First, the alcohol, then the bickering about money, and before you know it, there goes the car down the road to the watering hole, sometimes staying away for days. It doesn't take much of that before the marriage goes too, and with it, the little family. Finally, comes the broken child. That's Sarah."

Mary had set a hook in Maddy's heart. "Where are you from, Mary?"

"Now, you didn't come here to ask about me, did you?" Mary said with a laugh.

"No," Maddy said sheepishly.

"Well, I don't mind. I grew up in South Carolina. I married the man of my dreams when I was nineteen. Ben was smart and went all the way through high school, which is rare for colored folk where I come from. His best friend was a white boy who convinced him to take a job at the General Electric factory in Greenville. Eventually, Ben got transferred to the Utica plant. By that time, we had three children, now all grown up and doing fine. But Ben got sick ten years ago and passed. Now it's just me here with my letters to the grandkids, all far away, and my memories. There's not much more to it than that, dear."

In less than an hour, Maddy felt like she had known Mary her entire life.

"Would you like more tea?" Mary asked.

"Oh my God, it's getting late. No thanks. I have to go."

When Maddy walked out on the porch, clouds had cleared, and the sun beamed down from a blue sky. The scent of fall filled the air, and a soft yellow carpet of birch leaves lay beneath her feet. Before she got in her car, she looked back and saw Mary on the porch, sweeping leaves again. "It's a beautiful day," Maddy shouted.

Mary stopped and looked over. Her white teeth stood out against her black face as she said, "Every day the Good Lord makes is a beautiful day. You find that child, Miz Reynolds, you find her."

Chapter 4

I can see who got the best of that divorce, Maddy thought as she drove up to Hank Benning's house. *No wonder Martha's so bitter.* Sarah's father lived in a sprawling ranch house, surrounded by trimmed lawns and expensive landscaping.

"Can I help you?" an attractive woman asked when she came to the door. Maddy introduced herself and asked for Hank Benning. "I'm Cindy Featherstone, Hank's fiancé. He's up at his hunting lodge. Can I be of help?" She was in her late twenties, slender, had long black hair, and wore a burgundy workout outfit with spotless white sneakers.

"Maybe," Maddy said. She stepped into a large, ornately decorated room. *Someone has money, and I don't think it's Hank,* she thought. She sat in an oversized white leather chair and marveled at hand-painted murals of dancing ballet figures in tutus and oblong wood carvings of African warriors. *Holy shit, this room is worth more than my house.* She opened her notebook and asked, "Did you know Sarah left home Monday and hasn't returned?"

"Oh, dear! I didn't. I was afraid something like that might happen. Hank wanted to take her to the movies, and I thought there might be trouble over it."

"Martha said an argument about Hank and you taking Sarah to see Cinderella is what led to Sarah walking out."

"Martha hasn't done well since Hank moved in with me. She's bitter and takes it out on Sarah. I wasn't in favor of the whole Cinderella thing. I knew Martha would react badly, but Hank insisted."

"Does Sarah come here often?" Maddy asked.

"Hank has visitation rights every other weekend, but since it's only a twenty-five-minute walk from Martha's house, Sarah comes and goes all the time during the week. She has her bedroom and a key to the house. Sometimes we'll come home to find cookie crumbs in the kitchen and know she's been here."

Maddy jotted down a few words. "When did Hank go to the lodge?"

"After Martha told Hank he couldn't take Sarah, he got agitated. When I came home from my class, there was a note saying he'd gone up north. That was a little after six o'clock."

"Is there any chance Sarah is with him now?"

"I suppose it's possible," Cindy said, tossing her hair back. "He might have seen her on the road and picked her up. There's no phone up there, but I can give you the address and directions."

Maddy tore a piece of paper from her notebook, handed it to Cindy with a pen, and asked her to write the address.

"If Hank took Sarah with him, would he have let Martha know?"

"Probably not," Cindy said. "He was furious with her."

"Well, if Sarah doesn't show up by tomorrow, I'll be back," Maddy said, taking the directions.

The weather had turned bad while Maddy was interviewing Cindy, and when she opened the door to leave, a blast of cold air blew in her face. As she drove down the road, snow fell, and within minutes, she could barely see a car's length ahead. While she focused on keeping the car on the road, in the back of her mind, thoughts of Sarah lingered.

Here's a kid living in poverty with an alcoholic mother at one house, and right up the road, her father is living high on the hog with a woman half his age who looks like she belongs in Hollywood. The kid probably doesn't know which end is up.

The phone rang as she was about to turn onto the expressway. "What ya got, Maddy?" Zep asked.

"I just left the father's place. He took off to his hunting lodge on the afternoon Sarah was last seen, so I spoke with his girlfriend. I also interviewed the mother and a neighbor. Nothing new came out of it, except the possibility that Sarah was with her father. The lodge is up in St. Lawrence County. There's no phone, but I have an address."

"I'll contact the sheriff up there and ask them to check it out. It's nearly five. There's nothing more for you to do right now, so why don't you go home? Al Ramirez is working tonight. I'll have him call if anything breaks."

As they hung up, the snow intensified. *I hate this weather. One minute the sun's out, and the next, you can't see your hand in front of your face.* She pulled into her driveway, and snowflakes pelted her face as she pushed her way to the front door. She stepped inside, turned up the thermostat, and kept her coat on as she stood near an old, cast-iron radiator to warm herself. The phone rang. She rushed into the living room and picked up the receiver.

"Mom, you won't believe what I saw at the zoo today." Amber's voice was high and shrill.

"Tell me."

"A new baby elephant. Today was the first time that people got to see her. She's so cute! I want one."

Maddy laughed. "You're too funny. It sounds like you had fun."

"Abby came with us, and it was a scream."

"Any plans for tonight?"

"Abby's staying for a sleepover, and Mom, did you see the snow? Do you think maybe we won't have school on Monday?"

"You never know. You guys have a blast tonight. Let me talk with Dad, please…. Love you."

"Hey, Maddy," Jack said.

"Jack, I'm investigating a missing kid, and I might have to work tomorrow. Can you keep Amber if need be?"

"Not a problem. She's been a peach all day."

"Thanks. I'll let you know what's going on tomorrow when I know more."

After she hung up, she finished a dish of leftovers from the fridge and trudged her way upstairs to the comfortable chair next to her bed. She grabbed her book and snuggled up to read, but her mind was on autopilot, analyzing everything she'd learned about the case.

That plaque on Sarah's pillow worries me. Maybe she killed herself. God knows she has a reason to be depressed. She could have jumped in the river. Shit, we might never find the body. I've heard of kids her age hanging themselves. Maybe we should search the woods around her house.

Her mind raced as she went down to the pantry, pulled out a bottle of Merlot, and poured a glass. Sitting in the only chair at the dining room table, she emptied nine thousand pieces of her new jigsaw puzzle, *Tempest on the Sea.* She propped the empty box's cover on an easel in front of the table where it was visible from every angle and scrutinized the picture.

A lone ship faltered in a storm, its masts tilting to nearly forty degrees. Waves crashed over its bow. Black, ominous clouds swirled overhead. In the far distance, a slight break in the clouds let streams of light through that rested on the smashing sea. *There's something very odd about this,* Maddy thought as she tried to pinpoint what disturbed her about the puzzle. Then she recognized it. Barely noticeable, in a window of the ship, stood a silhouetted figure of a man. His features, almost indistinguishable from the shadows of the room he was in, gave

Maddy the feeling that he enjoyed all the chaos, and maybe had even caused it.

What the hell is he doing there?

She sorted through the puzzle pieces but couldn't find the one with the man. "Ahh, I see. Your creator has made you difficult to find."

Maddy then focused on cloud pieces. Selecting and sorting, she organized them into piles by shades of black, white, lavender, and gray, then placed them where they'd likely belong. When the wine muddied her thinking, she knew it was time to quit. Before she went up to bed, she stood before the easel and said to the mysterious man on the ship, "I will find you."

Chapter 5

Sunlight burst through the bedroom window. Rolling over, Maddy shaded her eyes, squinted, and looked at the alarm clock. It was 12:10. *Wow, I can't believe I slept that long.* She threw the covers back and felt cold air on her body. *Damn, I should have let Jack put on the storm windows.* Wrapping herself in a robe, she walked to the window and gazed out. The reflection of sunlight glistening off several inches of newly fallen snow pained her eyes.

She went downstairs, put on a pot of coffee, and grabbed the Sunday paper from the porch. Scanning the headlines, she sat at the kitchen table, but her mind was on Sarah Benning. Her curiosity got the best of her, and she called Zep.

"I hope I'm not bothering you."

"Not at all, Maddy. What's up?"

"Have you heard anything more about the Benning girl?"

"No, still no word. Until we hear from St. Lawrence County, all we can do is sit tight. I'll call you if anything changes."

With Amber still at Jack's and nothing more she could do on the case, she thought about taking care of the storm windows. *No way am I doing that now.* With her mind racing, she eventually lay on the living room sofa, covered up with a quilt, and drifted off into an afternoon nap. The phone rang, and she picked it up.

"Maddy?" Zep said, sounding excited.

"Yeah, I'm here," she said groggily.

"They reached Sarah's father at the hunting lodge, and she's not been with him. Hank will be back at his house soon. Can you get over there and interview him before it gets too late?"

"Sure thing."

"Let me know how that goes."

Maddy scrambled to get dressed, brought along a cup of the cold morning coffee, and started for Hank Benning's. She knocked and waited at the door for a long time before a bearded man with long hair finally opened.

"Are you Hank Benning?"

"Yes," the guy said nervously. Before she could get a word out, he snapped at her. "Do you know where my daughter is?"

"Can I come in?" she asked.

"Oh…oh, of course."

As she stepped into the hall, Cindy walked in from another room with her hands clasped. Her calm demeanor from the previous day was gone.

"Mr. Benning, I don't know where Sarah is," Maddy said. "I'm hoping to get information from you. If you don't mind, I have a few questions." Hesitantly, he agreed.

Sitting in the same chair as she had the day before, Hank and Cindy sat across from her. "What time did you leave for your lodge on Monday?" she asked.

"A little after seven p.m."

"Which route did you take when you left?"

"Route 5 West." Hank's face tightened, and his lips curled, obviously irritated.

"Sarah left a house up the road about 7:05 p.m.," Maddy said.

"What are you getting at?" He snarled with his fists clenched.

Surprised, Maddy took a moment to compose herself. "It seems you should have driven right by her."

"I didn't see her!" he shouted. Cindy put her hand on Hank's shoulder.

Maddy remained quiet and looked at her notebook for a few minutes to give him a chance to calm down. Then she asked to see Sarah's bedroom.

"Sure," Cindy said.

They walked through the house to a room off a long hallway. A neatly made bed with a yellow comforter that had designs of orange butterflies resting on green plants stood in the middle of the room. On a desk, a goldfish bowl with blue pebbles contained two giant angel fish gracefully swimming. A poster of the Marx Brothers with silly faces hung on a wall, and the bed frame matched the oak desk and the headboard.

"Does Sarah keep a diary?" Maddy asked.

"Not that I know of," Hank said.

Opening the dresser drawers while asking questions, she shuffled items around, looking for anything that might give a clue to Sarah's whereabouts. "Do you know where Sarah has run away to in the past?" Maddy tried keeping the conversation alive while continuing to look.

"Once she tried to hitchhike to New York City on the Thruway," Cindy said. "But the troopers picked her up and brought her home. Another time she went to Utica for a few days."

"Do you know where she stayed in Utica?"

"No, she just ended up coming home."

A small bookshelf with knickknacks and books lined a shelf and caught Maddy's attention. She thumbed through *The Box Car Kids*, and a valentine fell onto the desk. It seemed vintage and appeared to her to be from the nineteen-thirties. A naked cherub stood on a heart with a bow and an arrow ready to be released. The inside read:

My lady fair at Valentine,
When lovers pledge anew,
I send to you, to have and hold,
A loyal heart and true.

Someone signed it 'Mark.'

"Do you know who gave her this?" Maddy asked as she handed it to Hank. He looked at it and passed it to Cindy. They both shook their heads.

"As far as I know, she doesn't know anyone named Mark," he said.

An alarm went off in Maddy's head. *Child predators groom their victims*, she recalled. *They give them little gifts and ask them to keep secrets.* She turned to Hank and Cindy.

"We need to go into another room. I have to call in a forensics team to go through this room with a fine-tooth…" Before she finished the sentence, Hank exploded.

"What the hell is this all about? Do you think I had something to do with this?" His face was red, and his hands shook. Cindy put her arm around his waist, trying to console him.

"I didn't say that, Mr. Benning. Someone with bad intentions may have given the valentine to Sarah, and there might be other clues. That's what I meant." Hank stormed out of the room.

"He's not normally like this," Cindy said. "It's just that he's so upset about Sarah."

"Of course," Maddy said. Monitoring Sarah's room from the kitchen to make sure Hank and Cindy stayed out, she called Zep.

"I don't think we can rule out foul play," she said.

"What do you have?"

"I found a Valentine in Sarah's room that was signed, Mark. The father and his girlfriend hadn't seen it before, and they don't know a Mark."

"Did you find out where she went in Utica the last time she took off?"

"No one has any idea."

"Okay, I'll send forensics over, but make sure you keep them out of that room. We don't need Hank Benning washing it down with Clorox right under our noses."

By the time the forensics team finished with Sarah's room, it was almost nine thirty. Maddy smoothed things over with the Bennings as best she could before she left. It was after ten thirty when she finally walked in her front door, and she called Jack to say goodnight to Amber.

"Sorry, Maddy, she's asleep."

"Shit! Tell her I'll call tomorrow."

Maddy put on sweats and her favorite black sweater, the one with the holes in the sleeves, and a pair of loose-fitting wool socks. She went downstairs, poured a glass of wine, and sat at the table with the *Tempest on the Sea*. But when she looked at the thousands of puzzle pieces, her mind said no. It wanted to analyze the case, so she let it.

Martha has a lot of pent-up rage. Is it possible under the right circumstance, she might harm her child? And Hank is so tightly wound he might explode over anything. How is it he didn't see Sarah on the road? I need to know more about that guy. I'm not sure about Cindy. She'll probably cover Hank's ass no matter what. But the question is, just how far will she go? Then there's Mary, sweet Mary. She has no motive and is as kind as they come. But it's the valentine that's scaring the shit out of me.

Her thoughts became heavy from the wine. She walked up to the bed, pulled a journal from her nightstand drawer, and wrote. *Sarah wanders the streets tonight, her whereabouts unknown, and I'm worried about my child too, here within my home.*

Chapter 6

The next morning, Maddy wanted to pick up cinnamon rolls for the people in the office on the way to work. She pulled up to the Friendly Bean, a boutique-style bakeshop and restaurant. It always put her mind at ease.

Rusty, the owner, was the heart and soul of the Bean. He kept it lively with humor and witty chitchat. Headquarters was less than a block away, and each morning, cops filled the place. "Did you see what our brilliant mayor is up to now?" or "When will they ever fix those potholes on Main Street?" were typical conversational topics that lightened everyone's spirits before heading in to work.

When Maddy opened the door, a tapestry of aromas—cinnamon, fresh bread, and newly brewed coffee—greeted her.

"There she is," Rusty said. "Seeing you just makes my day." His loud voice rang through the restaurant from the front counter, where he sat with a few customers. "How are you doing, Maddy?"

"Doing well, Rusty. How about yourself?"

"As good as expected for an old fool." He chuckled as he walked over.

"What's good today?" she asked as soft reggae music played in the background. It felt like valium to her soul.

"Well, let's see, besides our world-famous cinnamon rolls, today we have a raspberry tart, cheese Danish, blueberry muffins, and apple pie, just like mama used to make." He smacked his lips.

"Hmm, I'm afraid I'm going to be an old fuddy-duddy and go with the cinnamon rolls. I'll take a dozen." Artie, who worked behind the counter, filled her order.

"Why don't you have a seat and chat a bit?" Rusty asked.

"I have a few minutes, sure." She sat at his table, and Artie placed down a cup of coffee for her.

"So, how is Amber doing these days?" Rusty asked.

"She's entering the boy stage, and it scares me."

"We all went through it, Maddy. Does she have a particular boyfriend?"

"Not yet, but there's a boy named Ben that she talks about all the time."

"It reminds me of Tennyson's words," Rusty said. 'Deep as love, deep as first love, and wild with all regret.' "So true, aren't they?"

Maddy grimaced at the thought of her daughter being in love, but she remembered how it was when she was Amber's age, and indeed it was beautiful.

"Well, I guess I'll just have to muddle my way through it," she said. She glanced at her watch. "Oh, my God, I really have to get going." Reaching for her purse to pay for the coffee, Rusty put his hand on her wrist.

"The rolls and the coffee are on me today."

"You're too kind, Rusty." As she walked out of the restaurant, she felt like she was leaving a great movie. Startled at the sight of Al Ramirez rushing to his car as she pulled into the department parking lot, she asked what was going on.

"Zep will fill you in. You had better get upstairs. He's waiting in his office." Seeing Al's unshakably calm demeanor disrupted, Maddy left her placid feelings from the Friendly Bean in the parking lot. When the elevator door opened, she stepped into a room of deadly serious people rushing around the office.

What the hell's going on? She dropped the cinnamon rolls on her desk as she hurried to Zep's office. He stood with his arms folded and his coat on.

"They found the body of a girl that fits Sarah Benning's description at a construction site," he said. "Come on, let's go. You drive." Maddy felt sucker punched. Her heart pounded as they rushed to the car. On the way, Zep asked, "Have you ever been involved in a child murder case before? It can get the best of even the most seasoned detectives." It was not the time to open childhood wounds, so Maddy remained silent.

When they pulled up to the construction site, the scene screamed of a tragedy—flashing lights, squad car doors left open, and men in hardhats from a construction crew racing in the same direction. It looked like something out of *The Blob*, but it wasn't. It was real. Maddy's thoughts ran wild. *It's not a car accident; it's not a fire – it's a dead kid. Can it be Sarah?*

She lost Zep among a sea of men in hardhats. Their necks stretched, trying to look above the person in front. Their heavy work boots sloshed in the mud as they seemed to dance for a better position to get a peek at the spectacle.

"Sheriff—make way. Sheriff—make way," Maddy shouted. The further forward she moved, the stronger the foul smell of urine, feces, and disinfectant grew. She saw a small opening in the crowd just ahead and edged her way into it. A man down on one knee looked into the mud, vomiting. Another stood near with a hand on his shoulder, trying to console him.

As she neared the front of the mob, a middle-aged worker on her left nudged her. She turned and looked into his tear-filled eyes. He outstretched his glove-covered hand with a pair of little girl's underwear soaked in blood, with the crotch ripped open. "I found these," he said. Maddy's body stiffened, and her eyes widened. She backed away, too stunned to say or do anything, then turned and forced her way forward until she finally broke through.

The naked body of a girl lay on the floor of a portable toilet. Her skin appeared waxed white, and a streak of dried blood, reddish-brown, ran from her buttocks to the floor. Toilet paper, strewn about like streamers in the aftermath of a New Year's Eve party, was everywhere, and a cake of urinal disinfectant soap leaned up against the girl's head. A rag doll lay nearby, and a muddy, torn purple dress spread out several feet away. *That's Sarah Benning, and that's her doll, Jenny.*

Maddy's arms and legs lost all strength, her insides shuddered, and her core became as cold as winter as she kneeled next to the child. A feeling of unreality shrouded over her, and for a moment, she forgot where she was. The stink of the portable toilet gathered in her throat, and she gagged. Suddenly aware of dozens of men gazing on like vultures eyeballing roadkill, she got up, turned to the crowd, and screamed, "Somebody cover her."

The men jolted back at the shrill of her voice, and a few looked away in shame. She ripped a blue plastic tarp from a worker standing nearby, shook it open, and gently floated it down over Sarah's body. She lowered herself with the tarp and then looked down into the mud. The touch of a hand on her shoulder startled her. Jerking around, she saw Zep. Feeling the muscles in her face contorting and tears running down her cheek, she bolted to the car.

After he gave directives to bring the scene under control, Zep came over to Maddy. Like a coach encouraging his star quarterback to get back on the field after throwing an interception, he said, "Come on. There's a lot to do now. These guys will take care of the scene. I need you to complete your report with as much detail as possible and get it out to law enforcement in the area. When you finish, get back over to Mary Thompson's and find out if there's anything more she can tell us."

The humiliation Maddy felt for running from the scene disappeared. Her thoughts moved to following orders, and it was what she needed. Implicit in Zep's words was the notion that all cops are human and break sometimes; when they do, they must get back up and keep moving.

By the time Maddy left the construction site, the sky had darkened. As she drove back to the office, she struggled to fight off images of Sarah on the floor of the portable toilet. She finished her report and headed back out to Mary Thompson's. As she arrived, snowflakes swirled around in the wind. Mary sat on her porch, wearing a heavy black coat with her hands buried in the pockets. Gazing far away, her face appeared etched in stone. Before Maddy uttered a word, Mary spoke. "I know why you're here. I know nothing more than what I told you yesterday."

Maddy stopped. The wind blew snow in her face, and flakes attached to her eyelashes. "How did you hear?" she shouted over the sound of rustling leaves.

"News travels fast around here, especially when it's bad."

"I'm sorry," Maddy said. "I know you cared a great deal for Sarah."

"They say to harm a child is to make an angel cry," Mary said. "Today, there is a host of angels crying for little Sarah. Although I must say, the poor thing is happier now with the Lord than she could ever be in this world."

Maddy looked down, turned, and walking back to the car heard Mary behind her shout, "Be careful. I have a feeling things are going to get a lot worse before they get better."

Chapter 7

Nigel, 1954, London

Nigel's room was his sanctuary — the only place he felt safe. His friends were his rock collection because rocks didn't talk back. He felt protected in his private place, but when he ventured out too far, dragons appeared, spat fire, and attempted to devour him. He often spent his afternoons joking with Green Opal, but after a beating, the only one who could comfort him was Jade.

"You're ugly," or "What a fat pig you are," were the insults he endured from Mother and Gertie. For the longest time, he ignored them, believing they didn't really mean it, but eventually, he realized they hated him.

Gertie was only eight, but made Nigel feel small. She possessed the power to bring Mother's wrath down on him, and whenever she lurked about, he grew fearful, because she always drew blood. Although he was big for fourteen, Nigel paled compared to his mother. She had the punch of a heavyweight, wore a massive ring with a blue stone on her right hand, and wasn't afraid to use it. *I'd rather get kicked in the balls by a mule than hit by that baby,* he once told Green Opal.

"Someone's at the front door. Answer it, Nigel!" Mother yelled from her room.

"Can't Gertie get it? She's right downstairs."

"You do it! Now!" Nigel set aside his rock collection, jumped down the steps to the front room, and, as he passed by Gertie playing on the floor, asked, "Is that a new toy Mother bought you?"

"Yes, it's a tea set. She gave it to me yesterday." Her haughty tone added to his irritation. *Mother showers her with gifts for no reason.*

When he opened the front door, Paul from down the street stood on the step. Freckled-faced, a smile like a broken fence, Paul always looked ridiculous in Nigel's eyes. "A few kids are going to the playground. Wanna go?"

"Sure. Hang on; I'll be right back." He ran up to Mother's room, but her door was closed. "Mother," he said through the closed door, "can I go with Paul to the playground?" A faint moan grew louder until, like an orchestra, it reached a crescendo, and ended with a deep voice grunting out, oh baby.

Shit, she has a man in there again. Nigel turned in disgust, walked back down, and forced a smile on his face as he cracked open the front door. "Sorry Paul, but Mother is taking Gertie and me to the zoo today. I completely forgot. Thanks for asking, though." He closed the door quickly, leaned his back against it, and stared at the floor. The words his father spoke the night he left drifted back into his mind: "Get out of this place, boy, before they kill ya."

Gertie's mocking voice sailed in from the next room. "Mother is taking Gertie and me to the zoo. Why would she do that when she just took me last weekend? And oh, by the way, it was terrific."

Nigel's boiler was at maximum pressure, and Gertie's words blew its gasket. A torrent of energy propelled him toward his sister. He wanted to explode her face with his foot, but at the last second, an ounce of reason nudged him off course, and instead he kicked the ceramic cups, saucers, spoons, and a teakettle into pieces. Realizing what he'd done, he tried to tone down Gertie's train-whistle scream.

"Quiet, Gertie, please," he begged. She looked at him, unable to hide the glee in her eyes as she howled even louder.

Mother's door slammed, and Nigel's heart stopped as he watched the stairs. A fat man leaped down from the risers with his shirttail outside of his pants. He stopped, and raising an eyebrow, stared at Nigel and Gertie. Shaking his head, he turned and walked out the door. Gertie resumed her feigned hysteria, attempting to draw Mother's attention.

"I'm sorry, Gertie," Nigel begged. "I'll give you my piece of chocolate cake if you stop screaming." The door upstairs slammed again, and this time Nigel knew it was Mother.

Her feet pounded on the stairs as she ran down with her loose-fitting nightgown flowing behind, breasts bouncing, hair spiked as though she'd been in a wind tunnel. Her eyes searched for her son. Glaring at him, she said, "You're a no-good piece of shit, just like your father. I should have put a coat hanger up my twat and gotten rid of you when I had the chance."

Stunned, Nigel stood in disbelief. Mother lurched at him with her fists clenched. When she smashed his face, the blue stone of her ring penetrated his cheek. Lightning bolts flashed, and a hundred screaming freight trains echoed through his head. He fell into murky darkness, and when he opened his eyes, Mother was halfway up the stairs with her arm around Gertie. Blood and tears dripped from his face. It felt like the time Mickey Jennings flung an ice-ball, clobbering his jaw. It hurt just as much, except Mickey said he was sorry.

Each whimper added to Nigel's physical pain, but it didn't compare to the pangs of abandonment that twisted in his gut. *It's one thing for her to hate me and another to punch me*, he agonized. *I wish she had killed me before I was born.*

Deeply shaken, he felt the emotional glue holding him together coming undone. A steel door within him opened, and a river of vague memories flooded into his consciousness. Finding himself drifting back in time, he stood in a cage, alone in the darkness. The smell of a dirty diaper rose from his wet, cold crotch. Screaming for someone to come, no one did. Eventually, dropping and rolling to his side, he put his thumb in his mouth and gazed into the black, empty room.

A flash of light startled him, and a glowing speck moving up and down, captured his attention. Plumes of smoke made his nose itch, and when the red speck glimmered brightly, he saw a hand, a ring, and a blue stone. Excited, he stood up in the darkness, held the wooden bars, and called out, "Mummy, Mummy!" But when she didn't come, he cried himself into exhaustion and collapsed. The steel door slammed shut, and Nigel left his dream-like state. Looking around at pieces of pink ceramic spread out on the floor, he wiped the blood and snot from his face, stumbled up to his bed, and fell into sleep.

Chapter 8

"Ouch." Nigel winced as he pulled the bandage off the hole Mother made in his face. "God, that's ugly," he said out loud, looking in a mirror at the bloody mess. He gently touched around the edges of the wound, and fearful it might get infected, pulled out a bottle of distilled water and washed it.

Remaining hidden in his room all night, the next morning, the popping sound of a VW engine sent him to the window to look outside. Mother's car sputtered down the street, and he thought, *This is my chance; I have to get out of here.* He ran to the kitchen, stuffed a handful of Cheerios in his mouth, and took off on his bicycle to Paul's flat.

"Oh my God, what happened to your face?" Paul's mother shrieked when she opened the door.

"I fell off my bike."

"Oh, poor dear. Step inside, let me put something on that," she said. Reluctantly, he walked in and let her put iodine and a fresh bandage on the wound.

"Stay for lunch, Nigel," Paul's mother said sternly. "We're only having tuna sandwiches and tomato soup, but I insist."

Famished, Nigel agreed. A bowl of peanuts on the kitchen counter caught his eye, and Paul's mother noticed him gazing at it. "Go ahead, help yourself." He took a hand full, put some in his mouth, and the rest in his pocket.

"I never get to have peanuts at my house because my sister has a peanut allergy," he said.

"That's very dangerous," Paul's mother said.

"What do you mean?"

"Well, a person with that kind of allergy can die with just the smallest amount of peanut."

"I knew peanuts could make her sick, but I didn't realize they could kill her."

"It's true, so be sure to wash your hands before you leave."

The woman peppered Nigel with questions during lunch. "What does your father do? How is it I never see him? Which church do you go to? I see your mother leave the house late; does she have a night job?" *What a pain in the ass*, he thought.

Slugging down the last of his milk, Paul asked if he wanted to play chess. "Now, Paul, that's not fair," Paul's mother interrupted. She turned to Nigel. "Paul's won the regional chess tournament for his age group three years in a row. He's been playing for a long time. Why don't you boys go outside and ride your bikes? It's a beautiful day."

"I'd like to learn how to play chess," Nigel said.

"Great. Come on; I'll show you how," Paul said.

In the den, two thickly padded black leather chairs stood up against a table with inlaid gray and white marble squares. White and black chess pieces, nearly the size of billiard balls, lined up facing each other, looking like two armies about to face off. Paul explained the concepts behind chess as he held each piece and described its movements on the chessboard.

"It's a game of strategy, Nigel. The goal is to keep your king safe while you figure out how to entrap your opponent's king. When you play well, you think several moves ahead and expect your opponent's moves before he makes them. If you have a response planned, you'll crush him. Come on, let's play," he said.

Paul looked at Nigel like he was about to devour an ice cream sundae. Nigel knew Paul was eager to beat him but would take a licking to gain the knowledge of strategy, the hallmark of chess.

The match progressed slowly, and Paul thought a long time before each move. But for Nigel, it was like returning a serve in a ping-pong match; he responded quickly. Nearly an hour and a half had gone by when Paul's mother stuck her head in the door. "You boys are quiet in there." She looked at her son and said, "Are you okay, Paul? You don't look well." He didn't answer.

After several minutes of contemplating a move, Paul reached out, picked up his Queen, hovered it over Nigel's king, and said, "Checkmate!" He slumped back in his chair, let his hands fall to his side, and appeared relieved to have averted an embarrassing loss to a novice.

The second game went differently. "Shit!" Paul shouted in frustration several times. Nigel knew what Paul was thinking: *This isn't supposed to happen. I should kill this guy.* When the game ended in a stalemate, Paul yelled, "Damn!"

"Paul!" his mother shouted from the kitchen. "That's enough chess for today."

The next week, Nigel spent afternoons at the library reading up on chess strategy. He couldn't believe how much there was to know. When he met Paul for another match, it lasted nearly two hours. Although Paul won, Nigel did not see it as a setback, but as a mark of his progress. It wasn't the game itself that mattered, but the ability to manage situations strategically and achieve the outcomes he wanted.

Within a few weeks, Nigel defeated Paul. He reached over, grabbed his queen, held it over Paul's king, and said, "Checkmate." In Nigel's head, however, he said, *Checkmate, motherfucker*, deriving pleasure from Paul's misery as he watched his eyes glare, and his face turn pink.

He believed he attained a new weapon—the power of thought unencumbered by feeling, and its application went far beyond the game.

***

The sun descended behind the houses as Nigel rode his bike home after his victory. But it wasn't chess that was on his mind; it was Mother and Gertie. *I wonder if they're in there.* He leaned his bike up against the back-yard fence, stuck his head in the kitchen, and found the house eerily quiet. He crept upstairs, opened the door, and in shock, seethed as he gazed at his ransacked room. Torn out pages from his journal strewn on his desk, gems from his collection scattered on the bed, and the lapidary polisher left running pointed to Gertie as the culprit.

"Where's Jade?" He said out loud. "You just couldn't leave things alone, could you, Gertie?" He started for the door, then paused. The words, "Think chess," popped into his head. He realized he was in a chess match with Gertie. *She made the first move. Now she wants me to respond by blowing up. Sure, that's what she wants. Then Mother will get involved, and I'll get a beating. Well, I will not take the bait.*

Nigel sat on the floor, put his hands over his face, closed his eyes, and took deep breaths, repeating to himself over and over, *Don't take the bait.* His anger eventually subsided, and he began a search for Jade. Thinking strategically, he imagined the carpet was a chessboard and searched each square before moving to the next. Within minutes, he found the beloved stone under the bed.

Harnessing the power of thoughts over feelings gave him a sense of control he had never had before. *I can accomplish things I never imagined.* Then it hit him: *I could even kill Gertie!* He mulled the thought over throughout the day, but by the next morning, when he saw kids riding their bikes in the sunshine, the idea left him.

Maybe Paul's up and would like to go riding. He headed to the yard to get his bike, but Gertie's shrill voice came from inside the house and caught him off guard. "Mother, Nigel ate my Cheerios and left the box open. Now they're stale." He froze. Mother's bedroom door slammed, and he heard the sounds of feet thudding down the stairs.

"I'm going to kill that bastard," he heard her say. "Where is he?" she asked when she reached the kitchen.

Nigel bolted for his bike, hopped on, and went for the street. He pumped the pedals as fast as he could, but it felt like he was barely moving. Mother screamed, "Get back here!" He looked over his shoulder and saw her running behind him in her bare feet and in a nightgown. He stood on the pedals and pushed with all his weight, and when he was finally at a safe distance, he heard her scream, "Wait till I get my hands on you."

Tears and snot blew back in his face as he pulled away. He turned in to an empty wood lot, dismounted, and walked his bike back to where no one could see. He got off, kneeled, and retched. It felt like the time he had food poisoning, but nothing came out. He wished he were dead.

Rolling to his side, he stared past the trees into nothingness. *What am I going to do now?* He closed his eyes, with his mind drifting back to the dark place within himself. *Mother hates me and wishes me dead.* The door inside him blew open again, and feelings that smelled as rank as dead animal carcasses overwhelmed him.

"It's not fair," he wailed. "I did nothing to deserve this."

The door, which had opened only slightly before, blew off its hinges as pent-up rage poured out. *I can't keep on this way. I have to do something. If I run away, they'll only catch me, send me back and it will be worse.* He remembered to think strategically, like in chess, and killing Gertie returned. *But will that make any difference?* He answered his own question. *Gertie is at the bottom of every beating I get. If she's not around, I'll just stay out of Mother's way. She'll probably leave me alone.*

The sun cast long shadows in the patch of woods. He found a candy bar in his jacket, sat up, and ate it. Listening to the breeze blowing through the treetops, he wondered how he might kill Gertie and not get caught. Every possibility that he thought of pointed right back to him.

This is stupid; it can't be done. He felt like he was drowning and needed someone to throw him a lifeline. In a flash, he realized that someone had, and of all people, it was Paul's mother. *Peanuts!*

For several weeks, Nigel made himself invisible in his house. He recorded observations about Mother and Gertie's daily rituals in a notebook and tried to identify patterns in their behavior. *I think I've got it;* he concluded one night. *Breakfast, that's the best time to get peanut powder into Gertie.*

After researching allergic reactions to peanuts at the library, he determined it would take ten minutes for his sister to die by asphyxiation once she ingested the crushed-up nuts. Critical to his plan were the calculations of time. *Gertie eats breakfast in the kitchen at 9:00 while she watches Howdy Doody. On certain days, Mother goes into the bathroom about 8:45 to take a shower and comes out about 9:15. That gives me enough time to get the powder in the milk before Gertie goes into the kitchen. The problem is, Mother is inconsistent about the days she goes in the shower.*

He studied Mother's showering habits carefully. He recorded her routines before and after a shower and hoped to predict the days she went in by eight forty-five. *That will give me enough time.*

After gathering all the data and analyzing it thoroughly, he realized *Midnight Matinee* was the key. *On mornings after Mother stays up late to watch a late-night movie, she enters the shower about 8:45. Now I have everything I need.*

Chapter 9

Nearly asleep, a television commercial in Mother's room woke Nigel. The clock read 11:57 p.m. *This is it!* He jumped out of bed, put his head to the door, and listened to the Midnight Matinee theme music. Running to his dresser, he grabbed a vial of powder he ground from the peanuts he'd taken from Paul's house. Reaching under his bed, he pulled out two empty milk bottles.

Quietly, he crept down the stairs to check the refrigerator for milk. *There's more than enough*, he thought, then returned to his bedroom and waited for the television to turn off. *Perfect. Now to be patient and wait until morning.* He couldn't sleep. His mind raced, and as he stared at the ceiling, he thought about turning back. *But if I do, I'll just be a punching bag again for Gertie and Mother. I have no choice but to do this.*

When light gathered outside his window, Nigel got up to look at the street below. A soft rain fell, and he wondered where he'd be by the end of the fateful day. At a little past six a.m., he went down to the refrigerator with the two empty bottles and poured a cup of milk in each, then returned to his room. Just a tap on the glass vial slid the peanut powder into one of the milk bottles. A few stirs and shakes, and he was ready to go.

Right on time, he thought when Mother walked into the bathroom at 8:52. The sound of the shower water running allowed him to move to the next step in his plan. Gertie played in the living room, and as he thought she would, she went to the kitchen and turn on the TV before 9:00. *Perfect!*

Slipping the bottle of tainted milk under his loose-fitting shirt, Nigel walked down to the kitchen, opened the refrigerator door, and swapped the peanut milk for the untainted milk as his sister laughed at a commercial. She ignored him. Returning to his room with his heart pounding, he waited.

Okay, Gertie, now fill your bowl with Cheerios and watch Howdy Doody. Listening from the staircase, Gertie seemed to follow his commands. A tingling sensation in his abdomen turned into exhilaration.

Expecting to hear death sounds, he instead heard only the TV show. *Shit. Maybe I didn't use enough peanut powder.* When the shower water stopped running, his stomach dropped, and he ran back to his room, fearing Mother would discover what he was doing.

The air in his lungs felt thin, and it was hard to breathe. He didn't have a plan for things going wrong. But then a loud crash, a thud, and the tinkling of silverware hitting the ceramic floor restored his revelry. *That was Gertie!*

Nigel's thoughts went to mother.

Please stay in the bathroom. If Mother came out at that moment, she would hear Gertie and save her, exposing his scheme.

"Mother! Mother! Nigel! Someone help me," a muffled, raspy voice cried out.

Stay in the bathroom, Mother, stay in the bathroom, please, Nigel thought. The fan in the bathroom was loud and always drowned out other sounds. *I don't believe Mother can hear her.*

Waiting ten minutes, he peeked out and was relieved to find Mother still in the bathroom. He ran down to the kitchen with the untainted milk in his hand. Gertie was lying face up with her eyes bugging out, mouth open and vomit smeared around her lips.

Stopping and gazing, he was surprised to feel no emotions at all when seeing his dead sister—no sympathy, no remorse, not even hatred. He didn't understand the void within him but had no time to contemplate what that meant and moved on with his plan.

Taking the tainted milk from the counter, he put it in a plastic bag and replaced it with the untainted container. Snatching up the cereal bowl and the silverware off the floor, he put them in a separate plastic bag and replaced them with untainted items. To make Gertie's breakfast appear consumed as usual, he rinsed out the cereal bowl with water, and poured in some good milk and a little cereal from the box.

Fear struck him when he heard the bathroom door open and Mother's bedroom door close. *Don't panic, Nigel, just follow the plan; just follow the plan!* He took the bags with the contents to the back garden and shoved them behind a loose clapboard on the house.

The rain had stopped, the sun shone, and Nigel casually walked to the front of the house and sat on the step. He pulled a handful of rocks from his jacket pocket and began polishing them with a rag.

Time dragged as he waited for Mother to discover Gertie. He scolded himself to stop looking at his watch and to act naturally. As the minutes passed, his stomach tightened, and he had to fight the urge to go back in the house, discover the body himself, and call out to his mother. Then Mother's shrill voice shrieked, "Help, help, help, help!" It brought him both relief and fear. When he went inside, he tried to act genuinely panicked, but Mother didn't seem to buy it and did not look at him.

"Oh my God," he said, as he tried to stay in the role.

With her face turned away from him, she held Gertie, moaning, "My poor baby," over and over.

"I'll call an ambulance." He dashed to the phone and said something that he wished he hadn't. "Poor Gertie." With her eyes fixed wide, Mother lifted her head and glared at him. *She knows.*

As he waited at the front step for the ambulance, the tingling sensation again grew in his abdomen, then moved to his genitals, made them throb, and he ejaculated. *How did that happen?* He felt his face grow warm, and he looked down to check for evidence on his trousers, but there wasn't any.

When the ambulance arrived, two medics got out. Nigel pointed to the inside of the house and they rushed in, and he followed. One put an arm around Mother, lifted her to her feet, and said, "Come, let us work on her," and helped her to the next room. The other cleaned vomit from Gertie's face and tried to revive her.

It's way too late for that, Nigel thought, quite satisfied that he had waited for the required amount of time. His greatest challenge at that moment was to hide his delight. He walked back to the front steps where he was less visible, sat with his face buried in his hands, and pretended to cry. When Gertie was in the ambulance, Mother told the medics that she wanted to go along.

"What about your son? There's not enough room for both of you," a medic said. Mother grimaced, said nothing, and hopped in the back before the ambulance sped off.

Nigel went back to the living room, trying to think of anything he might have forgotten. It hit him that peanut residue may be on the kitchen floor or in the sink. He checked the front window to be sure the coast was clear, ran to the kitchen, and hurriedly washed down the counters and table, then cleaned the sink.

After he mopped the floor on his hands and knees, he put all the rags in a plastic bag, went to the yard, grabbed the evidence behind the loose clapboard, and included it with the other evidence. Shaking, he stuffed the bag under his coat, jumped on his bike, and rode to the next neighborhood, where a house was under construction. As he passed a truck-size dumpster, he tossed the bag inside.

Rounding the corner to his street, he grew cold at the sight of an unmarked car in front of his house, but when closer, he saw the vehicle belonged to a neighbor. *I'm really getting paranoid,* he thought, leaning his bike on the side of the house.

Now what? Nigel had no plan for what came next. A sense of anticipation slowly faded into monotony as he waited in the living room. Feeling like he should do something, he wracked his brain wondering what someone else would do in his situation.

Geez, I need to call the fucking hospital and check on Gertie's condition.

A woman with a smooth voice came to the phone when he asked about Gertie. "My sister came to the hospital this morning, and I'm really worried about her."

The woman said, "I'm afraid your sister didn't recover. I'm so sorry. We've been trying to sort things out here with your mother, and well," she hesitated, and stumbled over her words before she finally said, "someone will be out to speak with you soon. Please be patient."

Sort things out, he repeated to himself. *What the fuck does that mean?* Half an hour passed before Nigel saw a brown Ford with two people inside pull up to the front of his house. He tried to look despondent when he answered the door. A man and a woman dressed in plain clothes stood outside. "Can we come in?" the woman asked. Nigel brought them into the living room, where they sat down.

Feigning a cracking voice, he said, "I called the hospital, and they said Gertie died. I just can't believe it."

The woman detective waited for him to compose himself, then asked, "Can you explain what you were doing at the time of the tragedy?" He put his hands to his head and propped his elbows on his knees. "I was polishing some rocks on the front stoop when I heard Mother scream."

"Your mother said you hated your sister," the male detective said in a harsh tone. Nigel looked at him, and a surge of anger bubbled up inside.

"We had our disagreements, and she was an awful pesky eight-year-old, but she was my sister, and I loved her."

"Can we look around?" the woman asked.

"Sure."

The man went to the car and brought in a box labeled "Sample Collection Kit." The detectives spent a long time in the kitchen while Nigel waited anxiously in the living room. The sounds of cupboard doors and drawers opening and closing made him question himself. *Did I forget anything? I can't remember if I replaced the towel I used to wipe the floor.* On and on, his mind raced. He reviewed each step of his plan until interrupted by another knock at the door.

"Hi. I'm Diane Green, and I'm a social worker." She asked to come in, and they sat across from each other in the living room. She tried to strike up a conversation. "I'm very sorry for your loss, Nigel."

Nigel looked down with as sullen an expression as he could muster.

"I have been with your mother, and she is beside herself with grief."

I'm sure she is, Nigel thought.

"Strangely, and I am sorry to say, she doesn't want to see you."

He looked at her, faked surprise and hurt, then put his face in his hands and pretended to cry. The woman got up, sat next to him, and put her arm around his shoulder. "I don't know what was happening among the three of you, but the death of a family member can bring out feelings that we don't know we have. That must be what is happening with your mum."

With his guts in turmoil, Nigel thought, *Get away from me, lady.* Finally, she walked back to the other chair, opened her briefcase, and pulled out a folder. "Except for your father, who lives in the United States, you have no family nearby to stay with. Until we can sort things out, you'll have to live with a foster family."

"Can't I stay here?"

"You're only twelve, Nigel. We can't leave you here alone. You'll have to go into foster care where we can begin family therapy and start working you back to living with your mum.

Bullshit, he thought.

That evening, after several hours in the social services office, they took Nigel to the Nelson family for temporary foster care until they addressed a permanent solution to his circumstance. Tim and Brenda Nelson were the foster parents and seemed okay to him. They asked little, only that he was present at mealtime and respectful to the rest of the family. They had three kids of their own and made a temporary home for three others, all younger than Nigel.

So, this is how a typical family operates? he thought after a few days at the Nelsons'. It was enlightening to see family members getting along respectfully with one another. Ten-year-old Eric took a liking to him and would ask to play checkers. He accommodated, but deep down, he was envious that Eric had it so much easier than he did.

One morning, Brenda came to his room and said he had a visitor. In the living room, a man in a leather coat stood with his back to him, looking out the front window. Brenda left them alone.

"Hi Nigel, remember me?" the man said when he turned around. Nigel felt a vague sense of familiarity, but he could not place him.

"I'm your father. It's been a long time, I know, but I'm here to take you with me to live in Chicago." Nigel didn't know what to say. His emotions bounced around like a pinball, reacting to rejection, anger, warmth, and excitement.

"A lot has gone on behind the scenes that you don't know about," his father said. "Your mother thinks you killed Gertie and has tried to have you prosecuted. The police haven't found enough evidence to support her claim, so you're out of the woods. Gertie died of an allergic reaction to peanuts. The police concluded that someone must have contaminated the cereal at the factory." Nigel felt an air of unreality flow into the room.

"The thing is…well, your mother wants nothing more to do with you."

Nigel thought it was odd that he felt pain when his father said that. He knew Mother hated him, but the words hurt.

"I know I left you behind in that awful situation when you were little, but I couldn't take you where I was going. You were too young. If you want to come with me now, I have airline tickets right here in my pocket. It's up to you."

"Yes. Yes, I'll come."

"All right then, get your stuff and let's blow this popsicle stand."

Later that afternoon, as they flew over the only city he had ever lived in, Nigel looked down from the plane at the houses below. A feeling of elation overcame him. *I did it,* he said to himself, and at that moment, felt he could do anything he put his mind to.

Chapter 10

Maddy, 1978, Utica, New York

"Are we almost ready to eat, Mom? I'm starving," Amber whined when she walked into the smoke-filled kitchen, drawn by the smell of hamburgers sizzling on the stove.

"Almost." Maddy tried to carry out the motions of normalcy for Amber's sake while images of Sarah's body intruded into her thoughts.

"Are you okay, Mom? You don't look well."

"I'm fine, just a little tired."

The stench of feces and urine that lingered in her olfactory neurons caused the ground meat to smell spoiled, and all of her movements required extra effort, as though she had a hangover.

"Mom, tell me what's wrong!" Amber insisted.

Maddy knew she couldn't fake her feelings for long. "When we finish eating, help me with the dishes, then we'll talk." After they ate and put away the last of the silverware, they walked into the living room and sat across from one another.

"So, what is it, Mom? You look like you did the day you told me Dad, and you were getting a divorce."

Maddy spoke from her gut. "Remember the other day when I told you I was investigating a runaway girl?"

"Yes."

"They found her dead today. Her name was Sarah, and she was about your age. Someone murdered her, and I believe she experienced immense suffering before her death."

Amber got up without saying a word, walked to where her mother sat, kneeled, and put her head on her lap. "That must have been terrible. I can't imagine what it must have felt like."

Comforting one another, Maddy started nodding and noticed Amber had already fallen asleep. "Come on, honey. Let's go up." Once Amber was in bed, Maddy came back down to the pantry, grabbed a fresh bottle of wine, and brought it to the living room. She sat in the dark.

Filled with guilt, she played prosecutor against herself, as though she were on trial. *You missed something in your investigation, Ms. Reynolds. Why didn't you stay with the case 24/7? Why didn't you request roadblocks around the area? Maybe they could have stopped a car with the child, and she would still be alive today. You should have followed up further on Sara's trip into Utica. Your first case and look at what happened. Are you sure you're cut out for this job, Maddy Reynolds?*

The phone rang, interrupting her self-flagellation. *I'm not in the mood to talk with anyone right now.* She let it ring. It kept ringing until she finally picked up the receiver.

"Maddy," she heard a familiar voice.

"Is that you, Sherlock?" she asked.

"Yes. I was just sitting here working on my puzzle, and you popped into my mind. How's it going?"

Maddy had met Harvey at an international puzzle conference years earlier. He was an avid puzzle enthusiast like herself, lived in San Francisco, and although he was considerably older, they had a lot in common and became friends. He was the most analytic person she'd ever known and nicknamed him Sherlock after Conan Doyle's famous sleuth.

"I've had better days. How about you?"

"I'm okay. Have you started that new puzzle yet? What's it called? 'Stormy Sea'?"

Maddy laughed. "*Tempest on the Sea.* Yeah, and it's bizarre."

"How so?"

She described the ship and the shadowy figure. "I've seen nothing like it before. The man looks like he's controlling the storm from within his cabin. It's weird."

"That is odd. I wonder what it means."

"Okay, Sherlock, what do you think it means?" she said in a slightly sarcastic tone, sensing his analytic mind kicking into gear.

"Well, are you involved in anything nefarious?"

His words sent a chill through her body. It was as though a window had opened, and a cool breeze entered the room. Surprised, she asked, "Why do you ask that?"

"Sometimes, a puzzle finds its way to me for reasons beyond my understanding. If you ask me, that shadowy figure is symbolic of a diabolical force."

Shit! Maddy thought. *How does he do that?* Her voice cracked as she spoke and she said, "Sorry, Sherlock, I'm tired, and I have had too much wine. You caught me on a bad day."

"Would you like me to call at another time?"

"No, no. It's just that there's so much happening that it's hard to know where to start."

"Try the beginning."

Like a truth serum, the wine did its work, and although she knew she shouldn't discuss the case, she opened up.

"They gave me my very first assignment the other day. An eleven-year-old girl had run away. I was supposed to track her down. This morning, someone discovered her dead and brutally raped. Someone treated her body like garbage." Maddy's tone increased in intensity as she spoke. "Harvey, she was just ten, almost Amber's age!" She sat on the couch, elbow on her knee and a hand propping up her head, and she strained to pronounce each word as tears flowed down her face. Harvey remained silent.

"I'm sorry, Sherlock," she said painfully. "I guess I'm questioning whether I'm cut out for this."

Harvey finally spoke. "Evil is all around us, Maddy. The worst day of my life was when I sent a squad of men on a mission of questionable importance to check out a village." Harvey was a major during the Korean War, one of only a few black men to reach such a rank. His wounds put him in a wheelchair, though the circumstance only seemed to make him wiser.

"They tortured the men to death. I was there when they found the bodies, and until that moment, I didn't realize that human beings could do such things to other human beings."

Maddy could hear Harvey's voice lower. It became raspy as he talked. "Once you see with your own eyes what evil can do, you're never the same." A long pause followed. "Listen to what I am going to tell you, Maddy. You must do the work you're doing. Shake yesterday off and keep pursuing this monster."

In a tired voice, drained of all energy, she exhaled a heavy breath and said, "Thank you, Harvey." After several moments of silence, she added, "I need to get to bed—nice talking to you. I'll be in touch. Goodnight, Sherlock."

"Goodnight," Harvey said. "And Maddy…"

"Yeah?"

"Beware of the man on the ship."

***

Maddy lay on the sofa with the lights off after she and Harvey hung up. With her mind too wired to sleep, she drifted back in time to a Halloween night when she was twelve.

The scent of wood burning in a bonfire filled the air, and kids laughed as they paraded up and down her street in costumes. A strange, odd-shaped moon hung above.

"Hey, Maddy," a voice called out to her as she sat on her front step. Janet, her best friend, dressed as Athena, the Greek goddess, broke away from a group of goblins and ghosts and ran up the steps to where Maddy sat holding her stomach.

"What are you doing here? I thought you were trick-or-treating with your dad."

"He's not coming."

"Does he have to work late?"

"No. He's injured."

"Gosh, I'm sorry." Janet reached into her bag of loot, pulled out a handful of chocolate kisses, and handed them to Maddy. "Want some? They're your favorite. They'll make you feel better."

Maddy took a few pieces and opened one. "I'm worried about my dad. He's in the hospital. Someone's on their way to get me."

"He'll probably be okay, Maddy. The doctors here are excellent. Try not to worry."

"Yeah, I hope you're right."

A pair of headlights pulled up. "I've got to go, Janet." The two friends hugged, and Maddy ran to the car. She hopped in and turned to her father's partner. "What happened to my dad, Uncle Bob?" Bob Bennett was also her father's best friend, and Maddy expected honest answers, but he hesitated and stumbled over his words.

"Your dad? Umm, he's injured."

"What happened?" she screamed in frustration.

"Someone stabbed him."

Maddy gasped, and for a moment she couldn't breathe.

"Will he be all right?"

"I don't know," Bob said sheepishly.

"You don't know? Where was he stabbed?" She watched Bob's face strain as he wrestled with his words.

"In the back of his neck."

Maddy thrust her face into her hands, whimpering, "My poor daddy." Turning to Bob, she added, "Why didn't you stop it? You're his partner!"

"I was on a special assignment today and wasn't with him. Another detective went in my place. He died. I'm so sorry this happened. I wish I had been there."

After a long silence, she spoke.

"Did they catch the guy?"

"No. He got away."

She turned toward the window in a daze, watching buildings and people zipping by. Trick-or-treaters swarmed the neighborhood streets as Bob drove to the hospital. One, dressed as the devil, looked right at her when they passed by. As he followed her with his eyes, goosebumps ran up her arms like droplets of ice. She had heard stories about evil spirits that came out on Halloween night and wondered if that devil was one. Spooked, she looked over her shoulder into the back seat to make sure it was empty. Her thoughts turned to what might have happened to her father.

"Why was Dad after the man in the first place?" Bob's lips tightened, and again he seemed to struggle to find the right words.

"You're upset right now," he said. "Maybe we should talk about this later."

"I want to know, Uncle Bob. Please tell me." He pushed himself back in the seat and took a deep breath.

"He killed little girls…at least two. Maybe more."

The words ricocheted around in her brain like a cue ball on a pool table. She fell back in her seat, and with her mouth opened and thought of the devil who had stared at her. *Maybe he stabbed Dad and wants to hurt me, too.* Aware she was becoming unraveled, she tried to calm herself and remained silent the rest of the way.

Arriving at the hospital, they stopped to check in at the front desk. "James Reynolds is in the ICU," they were told. "Since you are an immediate family, you may visit him." Bob led the way to the Intensive Care Unit, and when they reached the double doors, Maddy stopped dead in her tracks.

"What's wrong, Maddy?"

"That's where Mom went the night of her accident. She died in there."

"You don't have to go in if you don't want to." He put his arm around her shoulder.

"I need to see my father," she said. They walked in, and as though expecting them, a nurse waited.

"I'm Sally. I'll bring you to your father." A sicky-sweet disinfectant smell filled the air of a large, brightly lit room. They passed by ten or twelve patients lying in beds, connected by wires to machines that buzzed and beeped. Sally stopped at a bed and began reading a chart, and after a minute, Maddy grew impatient.

"Can we hurry? I really want to see my dad."

"Honey, this is your dad."

"This is my father?" she blurted out. A body with white, waxy skin lay before her. The man slept on his stomach with a bandage around his neck. Maddy felt lightheaded and grabbed the bed rail, as Bob reached over and held her arm, helping her into a chair.

"Put your head between your knees," he said.

Sally rushed over. "Are you alright, honey?"

"I'll be okay."

Finally, she looked up and began rubbing her father's arm, placing her head on his shoulder. Although he was unconscious, just touching him comforted her. She felt something rough just above the back of his wrist and, inspecting it, saw dried blood that had crusted around an open cut. Concerned, she got up to see if there were other wounds. She found a red spot on the bandage around his neck the size of a quarter. Realizing it was blood, she called out to Sally to come and stop the bleeding. When Sally finished, the red spot was gone, and Maddy felt relieved.

"We need to prep your dad for surgery now," Sally said. "But you can have a few more minutes." Bob, who was standing nearby, walked away. Maddy pulled her chair closer to her father, leaned over, and began whispering.

"I love you, Dad. I'm wearing your dress blue uniform for Halloween. I was going to tell you when we went trick-or-treating tonight that I plan on becoming a detective someday, just like you." She felt Sally's hand on her shoulder, stood up, and rubbed his arm one more time. She leaned over and kissed him.

Sally directed Bob and Maddy to the waiting room and said the surgeon would find them when it was over. The room was a large, brightly lit place, cheerfully decorated in soft shades of mauve and blue with landscape paintings on the walls. *It would be better if they painted it black,* Maddy thought to herself, as she felt darkness growing inside her. A half dozen families whispered among themselves as they sat clustered together. One by one, doctors came to the waiting room and spoke with a family. Sometimes the members would smile and laugh, but a few times, they appeared upset by the news and comforted one another. In time, all gathered their things and strolled out. After four hours, only Maddy and Bob remained.

Negative thoughts haunted her as she stared at the clock. She wanted to be optimistic, but with every passing minute, her longing for her father grew, and she feared that she'd never see him again. As she stewed, a short, stout man with blue scrubs walked in and shuffled over. "I'm Dr. Black," he said and looked away as he spoke. Maddy's heart sank. His voice was low and barely audible, as if avoiding something. "Your father's wound was very severe. The weapon severed nerves critical to sustaining life functions." He looked at the floor. "We did everything we could. I'm sorry, but we couldn't save him."

"That can't be!" she screamed.

"I'm sorry, I'm very sorry," the surgeon said as he seemed to dance in place nervously. As she wailed, Dr. Black looked at Bob as if to say, "Do something."

With his face contorting, Bob looked at her and said, "There is nothing anyone can do now, Maddy. Your father is with God."

She felt betrayed. "How can you say that, Uncle Bob? You're his best friend!"

"Yes, I am, and I love him. And I know what he would want me to do right now. He'd want me to help you understand what has happened, and I am going to try. But you will have to let me help you."

Maddy cried uncontrollably and fell into Bob's arms. Her agony found new depths until her body, drained of all strength, barely stood. Bob helped her into a chair. She saw the surgeon turn and walk away with his head hanging low, as if defeated by an opponent far more powerful than himself.

As Maddy sobbed, a woman dressed in street clothes came over and sat next to her. Waiting for the right moment, she said, "My name is Sheila. I'm a social worker. Would you like to see your father?"

Looking up, Maddy wiped the tears from her face, and said she would. *Maybe he's sleeping, and they just don't realize it,* she thought. *He's a very sound sleeper.*

Sheila led them to an empty room with a high ceiling. All lights dimmed except the one shining down on a body. She edged her way close and gazed at a man on an examination table lying on his back, covered up to his neck with a white blanket. Sheila walked out and left Maddy, Bob, and the man alone. The body resembled her father, she thought, but also it didn't. The skin was tight and shiny, and something seemed fake about it.

Sitting motionless next to the table where the man lay, and gazing in its direction, she did not look directly at the corpse. She took her father's patrolman's hat off and held it as she rested her hands on her lap. Flaccid and hunched over, she felt as if she'd been waiting hours for a bus that never came.

Finally, Maddy stood, walked to the body, and looking down, blurted, "This isn't my father!" She ran out of the room and Bob followed, catching up with her in the parking lot. They got in his car without a word as he drove off.

As the vehicle climbed the entrance ramp to the highway, Maddy looked for the moon, but didn't see it. A clock on top of a tall building read 3:23 a.m.

How strange, nothing will ever be the same again.

"Your grandmother from Utica will be here in the morning," Bob said. "You'll stay with Marge and me tonight, but first, we'll pick up some clothes at your house."

All the houses on the street, except hers, were dark. Scattered pieces of pumpkins left by mischievous boys, seemed odd, as though the world had gone on without her. The address book she used to call her father's work lay face down on the couch when they walked inside.

"Do you want me to wait down here while you get your things?" Bob asked.

"Can you wait just outside my room?" She tried hiding her fear.

When she finished and they walked downstairs, Maddy stopped at the front door, turned and looked into the house's darkness. It was the only home she'd ever known. *Oh my God, I'll never live here again.*

Gazing out the window on the way to Bob's, she wondered what might become of her. The enormity of the thought was too much, and she pushed it from her mind.

Later, as she lay in a strange bedroom, she wondered what had happened to her dad. She didn't believe the corpse at the hospital was him. Wrestling with her thoughts, her brain grew unbearably heavy, and she fell asleep.

The next day, her grandmother arrived, and all that followed passed in a blur. Maddy couldn't wait until the funeral was over. Looking back, her only memory was when she was to place a white rose on her father's casket. When her turn came, she could not do it. It felt too much like goodbye.

Wrapping the flower in a tissue, she shoved it in her pocket. Kneeling, touching her forehead to the casket, she whispered, "I promise, Dad, I will become a detective and, like you, I'll stand up and protect innocent people."

Within days, Maddy was to move to Utica to live with her grandmother. The Saturday after the funeral, they drove to meet movers at her house. Passing familiar places—schools, stores, churches, and playgrounds—her only thought was, *This is so unfair.*

When they walked up the steps of her house, the pumpkins that she and her father had carved still sat on the porch. They had shriveled into scary monsters. Inside, someone had shoved furniture together, and the place reminded her of a used car lot. Someone had marked boxes stacked high in the living room labeled "silverware," "bathroom," "breakables." Rolled-up rugs piled along a wall looked like cut tree trunks waiting to be hauled off by loggers. Her house mirrored the disruption in her life, and a sinking feeling in her stomach grew.

After selecting the items that she wanted to keep, she went to the front stoop and sat waiting for Bob Bennett. He arrived, walked up, and sat next to her.

"How are you, Maddy?"

"Okay," she said as she looked down.

A silence settled over them until finally she spoke. "Uncle Bob, I'm sorry for the things I said that night." Bob put his arm around her shoulder. "Do you think I can come to visit you sometime?"

"Of course," he said. "We can write and talk on the phone, too."

"I'd like that," she said. "And Uncle Bob, will you let me know when you catch the man who injured my dad?"

"I will."

When the movers finished loading the truck, they came to the porch. Her grandma put the key in the door, the lock clunked shut, and Maddy felt something end.

After reliving the saddest and scariest night of her life, she drifted back to the present. That night shaped all that followed and haunted her teenage years with fear and anxiety. Fighting hard to overcome, she ultimately attained the courage she relied on as an adult.

The deranged killer popped back into her head, and she thought of what he had done to Sarah Benning. It was hard to fathom the depth of such depravity. She shuddered at the thought of having to face the man alone and hoped she wouldn't have to.

Over an hour had passed since she hung up with Harvey, and it was late. She finished the last of the wine, stood up, and slowly trudged upstairs to bed.

Chapter 11

Maddy waited in the lobby for the elevator. *Boy, that wine kicked my butt last night. I've got such a hangover.* The sledgehammer pounding in her brain had receded to a dull ache, although everything around her still seemed fuzzy.

"Hey, Maddy," a voice called out. Allison Van Dyke walked up, smiling.

"Oh, hey Allison. I hear you're going to be the second woman detective in the Oneida County Sheriff's," Maddy said with a smile.

"Okay, go ahead, rub it in," Allison said. "You beat me."

"So, when will you finish training?"

"Just a few more weeks, so you better get those old fogies prepared for me." After the two stopped laughing, Allison said in a serious tone, "I heard you were at the scene yesterday when they found Sarah Benning's body. It must have been awful."

"Indescribable," Maddy said. Briefly closing her eyes, the image of the child lying in filth flashed before her.

While they chatted, Maddy noticed Bud Renshaw and another old-timer detective looking over and smirking. Bud had a reputation for disliking the notion of women detectives. Zep had forewarned her about guys like him when she took the job. He said changing the culture was one of his top priorities, and Maddy's coming on board was an essential first step. She ignored Bud and turned to Allison. "Let's go shooting again, soon," she said.

"I feel a little out of my league going shooting with you," Allison said. "And besides, I'm not a member of that fancy club you belong to."

"We can go to the department range," Maddy said. "Jake's there every morning."

"Do these people know you're a High Master shooter?"

"No, and please keep it under your hat." Maddy looked at her watch. "Oh shit, it's almost eight thirty. I have to get to a meeting." As the elevator door closed, before leaving Allison in the lobby, she added, "I mean it; let's get together soon."

Detectives swarmed like bees around a table of pastries and coffee when she arrived. Wanting the caffeine, but not the calories, she grabbed a cup of high-test before taking a seat.

"Okay, people, listen up." Zep stood in front of the room waiting for the chatter to die down, then started an overview of the Benning situation. He finished with a stern warning. "I don't have to tell you the reaction this is going to have in the community. I want all inquiries by the press directed to me. That's an order. Anyone who violates it will look for another job." Then, to Maddy's surprise, he said, "Maddy Reynolds had already been investigating the case before we found the body. Maddy, can you give us a rundown on what you know?"

All heads turned. Unprepared to speak impromptu in front of a group of over twenty men, she felt her heart race and struggled to catch her breath. Taking a slow, deliberate sip of coffee to give her heart a chance to calm down, she called upon a few old tricks she'd learned as a teenager struggling with anxiety. She imagined everyone was in their underwear, kept her eyes focused on the clock in the back of the room, and took three deep breaths before starting in.

She spoke slowly, and like a stenographer reading back testimony at a trial, she described every detail of the case, from the moment it was called in as a "Missing Persons," to the time the body showed up in the portable toilet. Nearly finished, she glanced at Zep, and he was smiling. Two other detectives, however, glared at her. One was Bud Renshaw.

Before dismissing the meeting, Zep directed the detectives to pick up their assignments in the back of the room. As Maddy moved with the crowd, Zep pulled her and Al Ramirez aside.

"See me in my office in ten minutes," he said, before rushing off.

"What do you suppose he wants?" Maddy asked.

"I think we'll be working with him directly," Al said.

Zep wasn't particularly close with any of the detectives, Maddy thought. He seemed to treat them all about the same—except Al.

"You seem pretty tight with Zep," she said as they waited in Zep's office.

"War does that to people," Al said. "We were in Nam together."

Zep walked in with papers in his hand and sat at his desk. "The FBI is checking into cases that involve valentines. They have Sarah's information, but the search will take a few days. Ditto on the lab samples from her body." He thumbed through a spiral notebook on his desk. "Al, you know what you have to do, right?" Al nodded. "We also have a guy at the construction site who has a criminal record. Maddy, interview him, and when you finish, come back and give Al a hand."

Zep said he had a meeting and started for the door, but before he left the room, he stopped. "Oh, Maddy, we set up an appointment for you to meet with Dr. Sidney Myers tomorrow morning. He's a criminal psychology professor at Syracuse University. He's a little weird, but good at what he does. We need a profile of our guy." Maddy and Al remained sitting in the room when he walked out.

"So, what does Zep want you to do?" Maddy asked.

"What I do best—research. My new home will be in the basement file room for a few days, so when you get back, that's where you'll find me."

Walking to her car, Maddy thought, *Al's a strange character, but I kind of like him.* Clouds covered a blue sky, the wind kicked up, and cold air found its way into the vehicle as she drove. *It's going to be an early winter; I can feel it.* She turned up the heat as she headed back to the construction site.

The sign in front of a trailer read, Briganti Construction—Site Superintendent. Stopping before she walked up the steps, she looked over at the portable toilets. Her mind flashed back to the sights, sounds, and smells of the previous day's nightmare, remembering its terror and sadness.

A heavy-set man with a white hardhat and gruff voice sat, arguing with someone on the phone when she stepped inside. "I don't give a good goddamn," the guy said. "You gotta send me another guy." He waited, then said, "Not my fucking problem. Your union promised me the men I need. One of your guys didn't show up today, so you have to send me someone to take his place." That got Maddy's attention. "That's right, the guy's name is Hawk Jenkins. He didn't even call in." The boss listened, and said, "Okay then, have him here by noon," and slammed down the phone.

"Oh, I didn't see you come in," the guy said.

"I'm Detective Maddy Rey…"

"I know who you are," he interrupted. "How can I forget yesterday?" Maddy said she'd like to discuss Billy Spires. "But I heard you mention this Jenkins guy who didn't show up for work today. I'd like any information you can give me on him, too."

"Spires is on the iron crew. You can find him on the west side of the site. As far as Jenkins goes, I have nothing. Most of these guys just come here to work. I don't ask questions."

"You must have some payroll information on him."

"If we have an address back at the main office, it's probably fake, but I'll check. Ask Billy about Jenkins; I see them eating lunch together sometimes." Maddy put on a hardhat and set out for the west side of the building to find Billy Spires.

A crane roared as it lifted iron beams five stories into the air. Its black diesel fumes poured through a long pipe that rose behind a man in the small glass cab operating the monster machine. Men on the highest beams walked back and forth as though they were on the ground. Each time a beam reached them, they caught it and guided it into place.

"Where is Billy Spires?" she asked a man nearby. Unable to hear her, she repeated herself much louder: "Where is Billy Spires?"

He shouted back, "Up there," and pointed to the men working above. "Why?" he asked.

"I want to speak to him."

The guy looked up, cupped his hands around his mouth, waited for the right moment, then screamed, "Hey, Billy. Someone wants to talk with you."

All the men on the beams looked down at Maddy. One whistled, and another said, "Whoa, Billy, way to go." The man who Maddy had stopped apologized. "Don't mind them. They're not used to seeing a pretty woman out here."

Her face flushed. It had been a long time since anyone told her she was pretty. When Billy climbed down, they walked to a quieter spot. She introduced herself and said she had questions about what had happened the day before.

"Why are you talking to me?" he said defensively. "Do you think I had something to do with it?" Billy leaned back, stretching out his hands with his eyes wide opened.

"I have no reason to think that. We're just checking anyone with priors. I noticed you had some trouble with the law a while back."

"I did, but that's all in the past. Or maybe it's never in the past," Billy said with resignation in his voice. "I went through a crazy time when I was nineteen after my father died. I went wild, stole a car, and got a DWI. But I've been off probation now for over five years, and there's been nothing since."

"I can understand how losing someone when you're young can knock you off course," Maddy said empathetically. "Where do you live, Billy?"

His facial muscles softened as he pulled out a pack of cigarettes from his shirt pocket. He offered one to Maddy, and when she refused, lit one up and took a drag. "I live at the St. Regis Reservation. I'm a Mohawk."

"Do you have family there?"

"My whole family's there; wife and three kids."

Maddy smiled. "How old are your kids?"

"Twelve, eight, and three…all girls."

"I have a twelve-year-old girl too…quite a handful, aren't they?

"Yes, ma'am. They take after their mama, that's for sure."

"Look, I just have a few questions, so bear with me." Billy leaned back on a steel beam and lifted a foot against it. "Your boss said you eat lunch with Jenkins sometimes. What can you tell me about him?"

"He's a strange one…a lot of bullshit."

"What do you mean?" She opened her notebook.

"He likes to talk big. But a lot of what he says is pure bullshit. Just last week, he said he was going to bring in his new Colt pistol to show me. But the next day, when I asked him where it was, he acted like he didn't know what I was talking about."

"Do you know where he lives?"

"He's been staying at the same motel as me when we're here, but I don't know where he calls home."

Writing quickly, she asked, "What's he like?"

"He keeps to himself most of the time and doesn't talk with anyone except me, although I don't know why. He's up and down like a roller coaster. One minute he'll be all happy, whistling and joking around, then something sets him off, and he gets all pissy. One time when we were working near each other, we talked, and everything was fine. Then, for no reason, he got up, took a hammer, looked at me like he wanted to cave my head in, and hurled it at the shithouse door. I swear I do not know what I said to piss him off." She wrote it all down. 'Mood swings; explosive temper, potentially violent.'

"What else can you tell me about him?"

"That's pretty much it, other than I heard him peel out of the motel parking lot in the middle of the night." She wrote the hotel name and said she might have more questions later.

Within minutes, she pulled up to a white building with several doors that opened to a parking lot. A sign read: Sunrise Motel, Vacancy, Rooms from $19.99. A short, heavy man sat at an old, beat-up desk in the office.

"Need a room?"

"I'm Detective Reynolds. I'm looking for Hawk Jenkins; have you seen him?"

"I'm Ben Crabtree. I own this place. Jenkins took off in the middle of the night, and in quite a hurry, too. But at least he paid me — slipped the money for the room under the door."

"What room did he stay in?"

"Number eight."

"Did he leave a forwarding address?"

"No, they never do."

Crabtree walked Maddy to the room, unlocked the door, and apologized for not having cleaned it.

"You'll have to stay outside while I look around," she said.

The room smelled like the toilet of a dive bar. Body odor stench, spilled beer, and cigarette smoke made her queasy. Empty Black Label beer bottles littered a nightstand and beer stains, still wet, spotted the rugs. Two empty pizza boxes on the floor next to the bed with partially eaten slices were open, and damp towels lay strewn on the bathroom floor.

Maddy's eye glimpsed something under a bed. She walked over and picked up a magazine filled with photos of prepubescent girls engaged in every sex act with older men.

This might be our guy, she thought. Before contaminating the room any further, she walked outside and marked it off with yellow crime scene tape. Crabtree gawked out the window of his office like a pervert trying to get a cheap thrill. She walked back and asked if Jenkins had anyone with him since he'd been there.

"Does this have something to do with the girl they found dead yesterday?"

"Just answer the question."

"No, I haven't seen him with anyone."

She called Zep from her car and told him Billy Spires was clear, but another guy didn't show up for work and took off in the middle of the night. "He also had child porn in his motel room."

"I'll send the forensic guys over," Zep said. "Stay there until they arrive and make sure no one gets in that room. Then head back to the construction site. Someone will meet you who can put together a facial composite of Jenkins."

Maddy arrived back at the construction site a little past noon. The person she was to meet hadn't arrived, so she looked for volunteers to help develop the sketch. When she returned to the trailer, a middle-aged detective named Tony DiCarlo sat in his car with the engine running, eating a sandwich. Rolling down the window, he said, "Let me finish eating and we'll get started."

DiCarlo interviewed a half dozen volunteers and masterfully used his skills to put together a sketch of Jenkins. As the face emerged, it was so ugly and scary that Maddy questioned DiCarlo about its validity.

"Are you sure you haven't dramatized this?"

"Listen, detective; I put them together according to the way they tell me."

Maddy scrutinized the face. Dark, curly hair hung down over a sizeable square forehead that had deep wavy wrinkles above bushy eyebrows. With the whites of bulging eyes, set off by black pupils, the appearance was one of unrelenting hatred. *The son of a bitch looks like he wants to leap right off the page,* she thought.

The jaw was broad and square, protruding beyond all other attributes on the face, except for a large, round, full nose. A six-inch scar traversed the right cheek from ear to chin.

"Jeez-Louise, we can't put this in the newspaper. Kids will have nightmares for a month," she said to DiCarlo.

"Sorry, Lady. Not my problem."

The face reeked of violence, volatility, and chaos. Maddy told Zep that if the sketch made it to the front page, they'd have a public panic on their hands. He agreed, and didn't release the image to the press, only to law enforcement.

When she left Zep's office, she headed to the basement to look for the file room where she was supposed to meet up with Al. The below-ground portion of the old building was like a dungeon from the Dark Ages. Brick walls and stone floors lined the long corridors. The walls, recently covered with glossy light-blue paint, gave Maddy the impression that the color was somebody's idea of a joke, a misguided attempt to make the place look cheerful, or a great deal from a going-out-of-business sale.

The oil-based paint smell was so strong, she thought she'd be high or dead by the time she found Al. After several left and right turns; she popped her head into a room where Al was sitting at a long table, reading reports.

"Where's the torture chamber?" she asked.

Al looked up and laughed. "This is the file room," he said. "And yes, they may have had a torture chamber down here at one time," Al said in such a serious tone that Maddy wondered if he might be right.

"Just kidding," he said.

She smiled, thinking, *There's more to this guy than meets the eye.*

Al proudly explained the library. "Records of cases going back to the eighteen-hundreds are still down here," he said as he went on about the method used to categorize files and how the old, yet efficient, indexing system worked. It seemed to Maddy that Al knew the file room like an auto mechanic knew a slant-six engine. *No wonder Zep picked him to do this work; the guy should have been a librarian.*

"Have you found anything?" she asked.

"Of the men in the area that are known child molesters, three are possibilities. They are all on parole or probation. One has fled. I need to do a little more digging, but I should have a report tomorrow."

He's in his mid-forties and good-looking, yet there's no ring on his finger, she thought. *He must have a girlfriend, or maybe he's gay.*

As it approached time to go home, she helped put boxes of files back on shelves. "I think my daughter is getting sick of pizza for dinner, but she's going to have it again tonight because I don't feel like cooking. How about you, any kids?"

"No, never been married."

Shit, he is gay. Maybe I offended him.

"I didn't mean to pry," she said.

"No offense taken. I have a strange background for a cop. I used to be a Catholic priest."

"Holy shit! Oh, sorry, I mean…"

Al laughed. "Don't worry; you won't go to hell. And besides, I haven't been one for a long time."

"How did you end up becoming a cop?"

"I joined the army as a chaplain. After discharge, I returned to the states, and my life turned to scrambled eggs. The war did a job on my head. I lost my faith for a while, then my reason for living. I left the priesthood and was hitting the bottle pretty heavy, and almost ended it, until one night, Zep saved me. He came down to Scranton, where I'm from, and stayed until I got through the worst of it."

It was unusual to hear such honesty from a man she had just met, but Al's authenticity helped her feel at ease.

"How did you end up here in Utica?" she asked.

"When Zep became captain, I'd been sober four years. He offered me a job as an analyst, and I took it. After that, I moved up in the ranks to detective."

"Do you live with someone?" she asked. *Oh my God, why did I say that?*

"My mother is frail and can't care for herself anymore, so I moved her up here a few years ago. We live together. She makes good company," Al said, paused a moment, then added, "and great chili."

I like this guy, Maddy said to herself. "Thanks for sharing, Al. It helps me. To be honest, I haven't exactly felt welcome around here since I made detective."

"That will change in time, Maddy. Be patient. Zep is determined to make it change. That's why he picked you to be the first woman detective. He carefully followed your work as a cop. He believes you have enough courage to tough it out, and he'll have your back when shit hits the fan. So will I."

Maddy felt warmth talking with Al. Being with him was like standing next to a wood stove in a cold room. It was the first time she had felt accepted since starting the job. Feeling more comfortable, she shared something that had bothered her all day.

"Shouldn't we be doing more to catch the murderer?" she asked. "It feels like we're not doing enough."

Al smiled. "I used to think like that, too. It took me a long time to trust the process. I learned that from Zep in Vietnam. If one of our units suffered heavy casualties, my immediate reaction was to pursue the enemy. But as captain, Zep had responsibility for the lives of the men. He never backed down from a fight, but hated to put their wellbeing at risk unnecessarily. He'd say, 'We respond, we don't react. Reacting gets you killed.' He'd think things through, come up with a plan, then execute it to a T. A lot of us are still alive today because of it." Al had Maddy's undivided attention.

"Zep planned our response to the murder before we met this morning. Each detective has an assignment. It's our job to carry it out as best we can and trust the process."

She walked with Al to the elevator to leave for the day, looking forward to getting home and away from the dark cloud of the investigation. When she stepped outside, a bitter October wind whipped into her face. *Damn, I don't think I'll ever get used to this.*

Chapter 12

Maddy was to meet with the criminal psychologist in his office at Syracuse University. About to leave Utica for the hour's drive, Dr. Myers's secretary called.

"Would you mind changing the location to *King David's* restaurant," she asked.

"Sure, I love Middle Eastern food," Maddy said.

As she approached the city, a huge hill standing out against the deep blue sky shone with buildings shining in the sun. The sight of the university on the hill appeared outstanding.

Medical centers, dormitories, lecture halls, fraternity and sorority houses, and people and cars moving about created a bustling display.

Snaking her way in and out of one-way streets, Maddy found an alley, and a sign that read *King David's*. Parking and stepping into the comfortably chilly fall air, students walking to classes reminded her of when she was young and without a care. When she entered the restaurant, a man with a red goatee sat at a table near a window, eating while looking at the street.

"Excuse me, are you Dr. Myers?"

"Yes. You must be Detective Reynolds."

"I am. Thank you for taking the time to meet with me."

Maddy stood next to the table, and Myers rudely said, "Well, don't just stand there, sit."

What an asshole.

Myers wasted no time cutting to the chase. "I understand you want a profile of a suspect. The murderer of Sarah Benning, I assume. I read about it. There wasn't much detail." Appearing annoyed, he took a sip of his soft drink.

"That's correct," Maddy said.

"Your secretary didn't tell me who you wanted to talk about," Myers said. "It would have been nice if you people had told me in advance."

"Sorry you weren't better informed." Myers frowned and didn't accept her apology.

A server came to the table and asked Maddy if she'd like to order. With her stomach in knots from her rude interaction with Myers, her craving for hummus and tabouli was gone. "Just water, please."

"What's been your involvement in the case?" Myers asked sharply.

"I was investigating it as a 'missing person' and was at the scene yesterday."

"Not a pretty sight, was it?"

"No, it was not."

"So, now you're here looking for a profile of the perpetrator and think it will help you find him?" he said sarcastically. "Am I right?"

"Yes."

Myers took a few bites of his falafel sandwich and another sip of soda. He took his time chewing as if Maddy wasn't there and, after he swallowed, didn't speak or make eye contact for a minute or two.

What a dick! She fumed inside.

Finally, as though he had just remembered her presence, he said, "Have you ever been involved with a child killer case before?"

Maddy wasn't about to share the story about her father with such a person, and said, "No."

"Why did you become a detective, detective?"

"I'm keeping a promise," she said.

"To whom?"

She wanted to say, 'None of you fucking business,' but just smiled.

After a long silence, Myers dropped the question-and-answer session and said, "Tell me what you know about what happened to Sarah Benning." With that, she pulled out her notebook and pen.

"Sarah was eleven and from a home with a great deal of turbulence: estranged parents, mother, an alcoholic. After an argument with her mother, she stormed out of the house, which was common behavior for her. Normally she'd show up again within a day or two."

"But not this time," he interrupted.

"No, not this time. We are waiting for the lab and medical examiner's reports, but someone raped, sodomized, and strangled her."

"Where did they find the body?"

"On the floor of a portable toilet at a construction site."

"Poor thing," Myers said, put his sandwich down, took off his glasses and rubbed his wrinkled forehead. "Did he leave a calling card?"

"A calling-card?"

"Some killers will leave something behind to claim responsibility."

"We found a vintage valentine, signed Mark, in Sarah's bedroom. Her family does not know how Sarah got it and didn't know who Mark could be."

"Either the card is unrelated, or your boy is extremely cunning," Myers said. "Getting that card in possession of the victim before the murder requires a highly crafty person." He paused and asked if there was any sperm.

"We won't know for sure until the lab report is back."

"Did they find prints or tracks or evidence of any kind?"

"No," Maddy said.

Stroking his goatee, he said, "Off-the-cuff, I'd say your killer is a male between thirty and forty-five, very intelligent, raised by an abusive mother, and has complete disdain for women. He is probably not originally from this area and has done this before."

"Why do you think he's done this before?"

"Because he's too good at it. A lot of practice is required to leave no clues. Your boy seems to have already fine-tuned his skills somewhere else. Right now, he is right where he wants to be, feeling very safe in his anonymity, and in total control. He enjoyed reading the headlines this morning about what he did and relishes listening to the ladies in the checkout aisle at the grocery store talk about how they're going to keep their kids locked up from now on. He loves all the chaos." The man on the ship in Maddy's puzzle popped into her head.

"But most of all, he enjoys waiting."

"Waiting? Waiting for what?"

"To do it again."

"How sure are you of that?"

"One hundred percent."

Dr. Myers turned his attention back to his sandwich. Maddy wanted to leave, but thought she better wait for him to finish and sat quietly. Then, as if he'd snapped out of a coma, Myers said, "This guy you're after, he's not your ordinary impulsive killer. A lot is going on in his head. He has a plan or a strategy of some kind and enjoys executing it to perfection." She asked what he meant.

"It's like he staged a performance. He put the gruesomely violated body of a child in a place where he knew everyone would see it. If he had buried her in the woods, the body might have remained undiscovered. But that's not what he wanted. It's showtime. He's making his debut and saying, 'I'm here.'"

Maddy knew what Myers meant. She felt it at the construction site when they found Sarah. It was as if everyone present was the audience, and a control choreographer was standing somewhere behind a curtain, watching their reaction to his creation.

When Myers finished, she thanked him, left the restaurant, and, as she walked to her car, wondered how the old blue-collar town was going to respond to a vicious serial killer lurking around in its backyard.

Chapter 13

Trying to calm down after her annoying interaction with the criminal psychologist, Maddy drove the back roads home to Utica. The sun shone brightly, and the countryside was alive with fall colors. She hoped nature's beauty might revive her spirits.

Apple orchards, one after another, appeared beneath fiery hills. A produce stand stood alone on a long stretch of road, and she stopped. Bushel baskets filled with different colored apples lined the walls when she stepped inside, the scent of cinnamon filled the air, and two large kegs of apple cider sat on an old picnic table. *Oh, I want some of that;* she said to herself.

Someone with a great deal of patience and an artistic eye had arranged pumpkins and gourds on the dirt floor. Old snowshoes, plows, fishing poles, and two double-barrel shotguns hung on one wall. On another, black and white photographs of people from the past reflected a proud family tradition. The apple stand seemed frozen in time.

"Can I help you?" a woman dressed in denim overalls asked.

"How about a jug of that cider?"

The woman reached for a jug but seemed distracted by a bald man in his fifties. He was talking to a young girl of about fourteen at another display table. Unshaven and with tattoos of spiders on the backs of his hands, the man seemed more like a cult member than someone out looking to buy apples. The girl, who looked like the woman and was probably her daughter, leaned over a bushel to fill a bag with apples as the man tilted his head to look beneath her shirt.

"Excuse me," the woman said to Maddy, and walked over to a tall man with long hair. She spoke a few words, and he looked over at the girl. *That must be the father.* He stopped stacking pumpkins, turned to his daughter, and said, "Go help your mother while I take care of this gentleman."

The man with the tattoos stepped back, turned his head like he just got caught stealing, walked out, and drove off. *If Sarah's parents had been looking over her like that, she might still be alive today,* Maddy thought.

On her drive back to Utica, Zep called to ask how the interview with Myers went. "He thinks the murderer is probably not from the area because he's too good at what he does to be new at it," she said.

"I thought about that, and he's probably right," Zep said. "What else did he say?"

"He said that he's sure he'll strike again."

"Shit, he's probably right about that too." Before they hung up, he gave her an assignment for the next day. "Tomorrow, I'd like you to take the Jenkins sketch to the people you interviewed before we found the body. Maybe we'll get a hit."

By the time she got home, it was after six thirty. Amber had already eaten leftovers with Samantha while doing homework. That was fine with Maddy because she wasn't hungry and wanted to make an early night of it.

After tidying up the kitchen and saying goodnight to her daughter, she walked to her bedroom, changed into a nightgown, and crawled under the covers. Before she turned off the light, she pulled out her journal and wrote, 'I'm falling into a valley of darkness and can't find my way out.'

The depth of Maddy's funk weighed on her the following morning. She had missed a few days of shooting practice, which was a red flag for her, so she stopped by the department range before work. Except for Jake, the place was empty.

Setting up her weapons, a voice behind her said, "Do you mind a little company?" It was Allison.

"Not when it's good company," Maddy said.

Allison pulled up a stool across from her and checked her revolver, but when she saw Maddy's three handguns, two of which were semiautomatic, she said, "You know, I've wanted to ask how you got to be such a good shooter."

Maddy rested her hands on the table, looked out at the empty range, and reflected on her childhood.

"When I was a kid, I lived in a prison of fear. At night, I saw faces in the shadows of my bedroom and called them 'Shadow Faces.' I'd stay awake until the morning light drove them away. Sometimes I'd run into Grandma's room and jump in bed with her."

The more she talked, the more she remembered. "One summer afternoon I sat in Grandma's yard writing in my journal. I must have been about thirteen. Everything was fine until I noticed the sun getting low in the sky, and I shook. Long shadows from trees stretched out across the lawn toward me, and I couldn't move. All I could think was the Shadow Faces would come soon."

She remained quiet for a few minutes. "Maybe my fear had to do with my parents dying in separate tragedies. I'm not sure. Poor Grandma. She didn't know what to do with me. That day she covered me up with a blanket and stayed with me until morning."

Staring at the floor, she continued, "Living in constant fear is a terrible way for a kid to exist. Unable to do the things other kids did, I stayed home. I never went to dances, sleepovers, or summer camp. Fearing someone was coming to take my life, the gun became my protector."

She took a deep breath and paused. "Yes, guns. My favorite TV show was Honey West. She was a detective and had a gun. It was her equalizer against the bad guys, and I wanted one."

Amazed that she readily shared parts of herself she'd never discussed with anyone, except Harvey, she continued. "I became obsessed. Having a weapon would give me power over death. I begged my grandmother to let me join a gun club. I'd say, 'You can take me, and I can learn to shoot.' That's how it began. Grandma gave in, and from then on, I virtually lived at the club."

Allison seemed enthralled with Maddy's story. "To see how you handle yourself so confidently now, I would never have thought you went through all that as a kid."

"Learning how to shoot was the beginning of controlling my fear. It helped me feel safe. In time, I kept a weapon in a drawer in my nightstand next to my bed. Still do. Finally, I could sleep in my room alone. Shooting wasn't a sport for me; it was medication."

Leaning over, saying nothing, Allison put her arms around her. Maddy felt a deep bond with a woman she barely knew. As they were about to leave after finishing their shooting routines, Allison said, "Let's do this again soon."

Smiling, Maddy said she'd like that.

***

Late in the morning, as she arrived at the Benning home with Hawk Jenkins' facial sketch, the thought of showing the monster to Sarah's mother seemed cruel. She pensively walked to the front door, knocked, but there was no answer. Peeking through the window — empty beer bottles scattered on tables and no sign of Martha probably meant the woman was sleeping off a hangover. She headed to Hank Benning's.

The sun showed in the distance, but darkness grew inside, as Maddy rang the doorbell. Cindy answered. "Can I speak with Hank?"

"Sorry, he is in town making funeral arrangements for Sarah."

Hanging her head, Maddy said, "Of course. How are the two of you holding up?"

"Hank is taking it real hard," Cindy said. "He hasn't slept since it happened, and I'm worried about him." Although seemingly disingenuous when they first met, Maddy felt Cindy's phony air was gone.

"How about you? How are you doing?" Maddy asked, empathetically. Cindy looked away, and Maddy put her hand on her arm. Turning back, the bereaved stepmother rested her head on Maddy's shoulder and wept.

"I thought nothing like this would ever happen to someone I knew," she said. "Sarah was such a sweet little girl, but so lost and so unhappy. Losing her is devastating to us all."

Pulling out a tissue, she wiped her face. "Martha has been on a drinking bender since the day it happened, and Hank has withdrawn from me. I am afraid he's using drugs again. I'm not sure our relationship will survive this."

As tenderly as she could, Maddy said, "I have a composite sketch of a man who is a suspect, and I'd like you to look at it. It might be disturbing."

"Okay," she said, wiping her eyes.

When she glanced at the sketch, she winced. It was as if she were looking at a dead rat.

"I'm sorry…no, I've never seen that person before?" she said. Maddy took the sketch and got up to leave. "I don't think Hank has seen him either. It would disturb him a great deal to see that face."

Maddy nodded. "I sure understand that," she muttered as she left the house and headed to see Mary Thompson. When she pulled into Mary's driveway, the woman stood next to a fire, holding twigs and small branches in her arms, occasionally dropping a few into the flames. The sight of Mary surrounded by smoke gave the illusion that she was standing in the clouds.

"Can't stop working, can ya?" Maddy said.

Mary laughed a halfhearted laugh. "I thought I'd take advantage of the sun. How are you, Maddy Reynolds?"

"I think a better question would be, how are you?"

"I'm just waiting to exit," Mary said.

Maddy gave her a quizzical look and wondered if she was ill.

"The way I figure it, there are three kinds of people in this world," Mary said. "Some are still waiting to live their lives, and most of those never will." She put another handful of sticks in the fire. "Then, there are those who live every day fully. There's only a few of them. The rest of us are just waiting to exit. Take me. I've lived my dreams already. Now I'm just biding my time, waiting to leave this old world."

"Don't get me wrong," she went on. "I love to see that sun come up in the morning, and the flowers bust through the earth in spring. I love the little children too! Yes, I do, with all their wondrous imaginings and curiosities. But when I see what happened to Sarah, I say to myself, I have lived too long, and I am just waiting for my time to go."

The wind stirred. Smoke swirled around her as rays of sun fell on her worn, purple dress. *She looks beautiful,* Maddy thought, as the unusual woman fed the fire with small wood offerings. Mary was grieving in her way. It was a philosophical way, a spiritual way, and Maddy was hesitant to speak. Finally, in a gentle voice, she said, "Mary, I'm sorry, but I have to ask you to look at a sketch of a suspect. He's pretty fierce."

Slowly, Mary bent down and placed her bundle of branches on the ground. "Let's go up to the porch, dear." They sat on a bench next to each other, and before Maddy pulled out the replica of Jenkins's face, she saw a geometry textbook on the floor next to her. "Catching up on your math?" Maddy asked, kiddingly, as she handed the book to Mary.

"Oh, my," Mary said, "Jodi must have left that here."

"Who's Jodi?"

"She's a young girl who used to live around here. She stops by for a visit sometimes."

"Well, I hope she doesn't walk this road alone until we catch Sarah's…" Maddy was about to say 'killer,' but stopped herself. "The person who harmed Sarah."

"I'm not too worried about Jodi," Mary said with a coy smile. Maddy wondered what she meant, but didn't ask.

Mary opened the folder with the Jenkins sketch and handed it over. She looked at it for a long time. "What do you suppose happened to this man to make his face so filled with hate?" Mary asked. She handed the drawing back and said, "No, honey, I've never seen him before."

After she left Mary sitting on her porch, she spent the rest of the afternoon stopping at grocery stores and gas stations in the area showing people the sketch, but no one recognized Hawk Jenkins. She stopped at the Friendly Bean just before closing time, and, except for Rusty and Artie, the place was empty.

"Strange time for you to be here, Maddy," Rusty said when she walked in. "Would you like something to go?"

"No, I am here on business."

"Oh, what did I do now?" he said as he laughed.

She smiled. "I'd like you to look at a sketch of a suspect in the Sarah Benning case…you too, Artie."

"Oh my, of course…come on out from behind the counter, Artie."

She pulled out the sketch and placed it on a table before the two men. Artie recoiled at the sight, shook his head, and said, "Haven't seen him, thank God."

Rusty just stared. Maddy turned to him for a response. "That's not a face you forget easily," he said. "It's vaguely familiar, but not recently. I can't place where it may have been. I guess I'm not much help."

As she stood to leave, Rusty said, "I'm not sure about the man in your sketch, but I remember something that might be important. About a month ago, a guy was in here several mornings in a row. He acted strangely. He stared at women, and I even had a customer complain to me. She said he made her feel uncomfortable." She pulled out her notebook.

"About a week later, he came back with a young girl about twelve. I remember thinking she didn't look like him and didn't act like she was his daughter. He hasn't been back since."

"You've seen the picture of Sarah Benning in the paper. Did the girl look like her?"

"I'm not sure."

Maddy's interest piqued, and she asked Rusty if he'd meet with a sketch artist, and he said he'd do his best.

"We'll have someone over here in the morning," she said.

When she returned to the department, she told Zep that she had come up empty except for a possible new lead from Rusty. "No one is having any luck," he said. "Tomorrow, I'm sending people to construction sites around the state where iron is being erected. Jenkins was an ironworker; somebody has to recognize him."

As she headed for the door, he added, "By the way, the reports from the medical examiner and lab came in. As we suspected, someone raped and sodomized her before her murder, but no semen."

Shaking her head, feeling emotionally spent, and with her mind on overload, she didn't think she could handle anything more. Just then, Al walked in, plopped himself in a chair, and exhaling a deep breath, said, "Sometimes I just can't believe people. The more I know about them, the less I want to know."

"What's going on, Al?" Zep asked.

"So, I find the name of a guy convicted of raping a seven-year-old girl in Erie County five years ago. The case was overturned because of a Miranda violation, so I tracked his whereabouts since then and found out he's living here in Utica. His name is Randy Ballinger. I do a little more digging and find out he works at Cedar Crest Elementary School as a fifth-grade teacher's aide. Can you believe that shit?"

Al sat up in his chair, more animated than Maddy had ever seen him. "Then I realize, 'Ballinger,' that's the name of the Superintendent of Schools: Miriam Ballinger. And holy shit, guess what, he's her nephew."

"No shit," Zep said.

"Oh, wait, it gets better. Guess where Sarah Benning went to school? You got it, Cedar Crest. Is it me, or has the world gone crazy, putting a pervert like that in with those kids?"

Maddy looked at Zep's reaction and watched as he changed positions from sitting back in his chair to leaning forward with his elbows on his desk, writing in his notebook. When he looked up, he said, "I know Miriam Ballinger. Al, when you go to the school in the morning to interview this guy, I'll be at the Board of Education speaking with his aunt. If we don't handle this right, it will turn into a shit storm."

Then Zep looked at Maddy. "Since most of the ironworkers in New York belong to a union, begin checking a list of unions tomorrow to see if anyone recognizes Jenkins."

Al piped in again, "I've checked every record that I could think of, and I can't find anyone named Hawk Jenkins. It must be an alias."

Maddy went back to her office, grabbed her briefcase, and started down the hallway to go home. Al walked out of his cubicle to do the same. They rode the elevator, and Maddy said, "It's horrifying how many pedophiles there are out there."

"That's one disease I don't think I'll ever get my head wrapped around," Al said.

Each day, the investigation created more questions than answers. Maddy was tired and just wanted to spend a quiet evening with her daughter and headed home.

Chapter 14

Maddy set out to visit unions throughout Upstate New York the following day. Wallkill, her first stop, between Woodstock and New York City, was like a parking lot, with bumper-to-bumper cars. She planned on a three-day trip, working her way east toward Utica, but between the traffic and scheduling conflicts by union business agents, she ended up adding a day.

After a week on the road and eager to get home, her last stop was a Thursday meeting at Local 60 in Binghamton. But with the meeting time delayed, and ending after 8:00 PM, she stayed an extra night. Down in the mouth and missing her daughter, she called Jack. There was no answer. *Shit, Amber has a basketball game tonight.* In her room with nothing to do, she called Zep.

"Hey, Maddy. Any luck?" he asked.

"No one recognized Jenkins, but I left a ton of flyers behind at each stop." She asked what happened when Al interviewed Randy Ballinger.

"Al said the guy had a strangeness about him he'd seen in other child predators. He was cocky and even admitted dodging a bullet in the Buffalo rape case. Although he didn't come right out and say it, he as much admitted that if it weren't for a cop screwing up his Miranda Rights, he'd be in jail. Pretty ballsy, I'd say."

"What about his aunt…the superintendent of schools?"

"She's in total denial," Zep said. "Her nephew has her hoodwinked. She believes that someone set him up, and that everyone is out to get him. Not only do we need to look at him as a suspect in Sarah's murder, but as a threat to the kids in that school." Then Zep shifted focus. "So, what's your plan with Jenkins?"

"I want to give it a few days to see if there's any response to the sketches," Maddy said. "Something's got to turn up; the guy can't just vanish in midair. By the way, did we get the sketch back of the person Rusty saw at the Friendly Bean?"

"Got it yesterday. It's on your desk." Zep's voice trailed off, and he sounded tired. Before they hung up, he said, "Try to get some rest this weekend. Spend some time with your daughter. Don't let her get lost in all this crazy shit."

His words hit her hard. When they hung up, she called Amber again, and this time she answered. "Hi, it's Mom. How are you?"

"I just got back from my game. Mom, you will not believe what happened."

"Tell me," she said.

"We were losing throughout the game and were down by one point with ten seconds left. Coach called a timeout and set a play where Jamie was to take the last shot, but she missed, and the ball came to me. I put it up, and it went in. I can't believe it. We won the game, and everyone came over and hugged me."

"Aww, honey, I'm so proud of you," Maddy said, with her insides twisting. *I can't believe I missed that.*

"When are you coming home, Mom?"

"I'll be back tomorrow before dinner. You'll have to catch me up on everything that's happened since I've been away." When she hung up, the tightness in her stomach developed into a heavy sadness. It was as though achieving her lifelong dream of becoming a detective had the damaging side effect of keeping her from her daughter.

The following day, she drove to Utica and directly into the office. She hadn't slept well the night before, and the day seemed to drag on. Amber sat on the floor, playing cards with Samantha when she arrived home. Her daughter popped up like a jack-in-the-box, ran to her mother and smothered her with hugs and kisses.

"I missed you so much," Amber said. "You won't have to go away again, will you?"

"Not if I can help it."

Chapter 15

After the week-long trip, a pile of papers on her desk awaited when she stepped into her cubicle Monday morning. A note at the top of the stack read, "Call Bernie Pasternack, Albany Business Agent, Iron Workers, Local 12."

Pasternack answered right away. "One of our guys recognizes the face on the flyer you left. Dominick Cavallo is one of my stewards. He's out on the job right now, but I can have him call you when he gets back."

While she anxiously awaited the call from Cavallo, she read through the other messages, separating them into two piles: *crap* and *potential*. When she finished, only one note was in the 'potential' pile. *All these are bullshit,* she thought. Frustrated, she stopped by Al's cubicle. "Are you having any luck with your leads?"

"Three of the four guys are out of contention," he said. "One is dead, another is doing time in Elmira for robbery, and it looks like Randy Ballinger has a pretty solid alibi. He was in the hospital recuperating from hernia surgery on the day of Sarah's murder. This dude, Robert Flack, is still in play, but I can't seem to locate him. Today I'll check into financial transactions. How about you?"

"An ironworker in Albany thinks he recognizes Jenkins from the sketch. It's a long-shot, and if it fizzles, I have nothing."

"Time is working against us," Al said. His phone rang, and he said it was for her.

"I'll take it in my office."

The call came through as she reached her desk. "Hi, this is Dominick Cavallo. I saw the picture of the guy you're looking for, and I'm sure it's someone I worked with a couple of years ago."

"Do you remember his name?"

"He called himself Hawk."

"Do you know where he lives or anything about him?"

"He was quiet. I do not know where he lives. But I can tell you who we worked for. It was the Eastern Construction Company. They're out of Syracuse."

"Think hard. There must be something else about the guy that you remember."

Dominick hesitated. "Let me think." He was silent for a moment, and finally said, "Wait…wait, I know. I saw him walking out of the VA hospital here in Albany about a year ago. He must be a veteran."

Maddy finally had something to go on. When she hung up, she called the construction company, but it had gone out of business. She located the ex-office manager, who explained that a fire had destroyed the company records. "Maybe you should try the IRS. They should have our W-2s."

How the hell does one deal with the IRS on an issue like this? Her next call was to the Veterans Administration in Albany. She got bounced around from one administrative assistant to another until she finally reached the hospital CEO, Marvin Keene.

"Thank you for taking my call, Mr. Keene. I need your help. There has been a gruesome murder of a child here in Utica, and a key suspect was a patient at your hospital. He goes by the name of Hawk Jenkins. We need whatever information you can give us on him."

"I'm sorry, Detective, but we don't give out confidential patient information."

"You don't understand. We think Jenkins will kill again, and we need to speak with him as soon as possible; it's imperative."

"I'm sorry, Ms. Reynolds, we have our protocols."

"Someone raped and sodomized a girl before he killed her. Doesn't that mean anything to you?" At the end of her rope, she felt like she was alone in a real-time nightmare. *Doesn't anyone else care about stopping this guy?*

Keene, unmoved, said, "I suggest your attorney contact our hospital attorney." Then he said goodbye and hung up. Maddy had just hit two bureaucratic brick walls, one with the IRS and the other with the VA. She told Zep, and he said he'd hand both situations over to the legal department for follow up. That was it. The government had stopped Maddy dead in her tracks. Exasperated and with no new leads to pursue, she reverted to the mindless task of looking through old files, trying to identify similarities to Sarah's case.

When she left for home at five thirty, darkness had fallen, and the wind chill factor had reached a negative ten degrees. As she walked to her car, her head felt numb, and her body ached from the rawness of the penetrating cold.

Over the next six weeks, each lead seemed to die before it went anywhere, and with no feedback on Jenkins, Maddy became bogged down with investigating petty thefts and domestic conflicts. As winter reached its depths and the snowbanks climbed as high as the roof of her car, she became a regular at City-Wide Liquors. Three or four nights a week on the way home from work, she would stop. Later in the evening, after Amber went to bed, she'd pour a glass of wine and escape to the bizarre world of *Tempest on the Sea.*

Although she did her best to keep up with Amber's school activities, occasionally she'd forget a basketball game or a band concert, and each time, she would beat herself up with guilt.

Sarah Benning also preyed on her mind. For Maddy, the case was unfinished business and continually crept back into her thoughts. She couldn't shake it. Occasionally, when she worked on *Tempest*, the man in the window reminded her too much of Sarah's killer, and she would have to stop.

Each day, going to work was like swimming against a strong current. One morning she got out of bed, and frost built up so thick on her bedroom window, she could not see out. The wind bitterly howled and rattled the glass. A wave of despair grabbed her, and like the undertow of a mighty ocean wave, dragged her into its murky darkness. All hope drained from her being. She gave up her fighting spirit, threw herself onto the bed, curled into a fetal position, and wailed, "What the hell is wrong with me?"

***

"Mom, I need to get a dress for the Father-Daughter Valentine's Day Dance on Friday night."

"Amber!" Maddy barked as she drove her to school. "Today is Wednesday. Why didn't you just wait until Friday after school to tell me?" Maddy sarcastically snapped, looking over at her daughter's startled face.

"I'm sorry, I wasn't thinking," Amber whimpered. As if remembering why she had said nothing sooner, Amber lashed out at her mother. "And besides, you never have time for me anymore. You're too tired, cooped-up in your room, or reading reports. You missed my parent-teacher conference the other day, and Mrs. Chapman sent you a letter to reschedule. I'm embarrassed."

That hit Maddy hard. She pulled the car to the curb and put her head on the steering wheel. *I can't believe I did that.* She tried to hold back tears, stammering, "I am so sorry. I...I...I..." nothing came out.

"You don't have to say anything. I'll be okay. Come on, get me to school before I'm late."

Sarah's case had brought her into such a dark place, she had become inaccessible to her daughter. It was what she had feared, and now it had happened.

She pulled up to the school. Amber reached over and hugged her before getting out. When Maddy drove off, feeling the sting of guilt, the phone rang, and it was Zep, and he sounded agitated.

"Maddy, that reporter for The Observer-Dispatch, Goldfarb, just called me. Somehow, he got wind of the valentine from Sarah Benning's bedroom. He's going to run a story about it on Valentine's Day. He wouldn't tell me his source, but I need to find out if there's a leaker in the department. Do you have any idea how this could have gotten out?"

"No, I don't." As soon as she hung up, she worried Zep might this she leaked the story. By the time she stepped off the elevator, she had worked herself into a frenzy and bolted to his office. Zep's door was closed, and Maddy watched through the glass office walls as Sheriff Murphy and the Mayor stood by his desk, yelling. Zep sat with his arms folded, looking like a little boy being scolded by his parents.

Finally, the storm ended, and the two honchos rushed out in a huff. She walked in prepared for Zep to light into her, although she knew she had done nothing wrong. If she was going to catch hell, she wanted to get it over, but he wasn't angry. He took the wrath of his higher-ups on the chin and didn't dump it on her. Instead, he got right down to the business of the leaker.

"So, this is what we've got. One scenario is there's a mole in the department. Another is one of our guys had a little too much to drink at Curley's Bar and blabbed his yap in earshot of someone like Goldfarb. The third, which would be a nightmare for us, is that the killer is calling the newspaper directly."

The prospect that the killer might communicate directly with the media took her aback.

"What do we do?"

"We sit tight for a day or two and let things play out," Zep said.

***

The next morning, while the coffee percolated, Maddy walked to the porch for the newspaper. The headline read, Cupid Leaves Sarah Benning a Valentine before Killing Her._ As she stared at the words, the phone rang.

"Did you see the paper?" Zep shouted. Hesitantly, she said she did.

"I'm calling Harald Johnson, the Editor, for a meeting with him, and that Goldfarb guy. I want you with me."

Maddy told Amber she'd have to take the bus to school, then rushed to get dressed. Pouring her coffee into a travel mug, she lumbered through the icy slush to her car, contemplating the explosive situation. Zep was waiting when she arrived.

"Johnson said he'd meet with us as soon as we get there," he said. "Come on, let's go."

Man, he's worked-up, she thought, *I've never seen him like this.* On the ride to Harald Johnson's office, Zep didn't speak. When they arrived, the secretary led them to a conference room with leather-padded chairs placed around a large cherry-wood table. She and Zep sat next to one another. Within minutes, a tall, older man with white, curly hair walked in. A shorter man, half his age, with a boyish face and brush cut, followed. *That must be Goldfarb.*

"Hello, Harry," Zep said. "This is Maddy Reynolds, one of our detectives working the Benning case," Harald said hello and introduced Ben Goldfarb. "Thanks for meeting so quickly," Zep said. The two newspapermen sat opposite Zep and Maddy. "I realize the importance of maintaining the confidentiality of your sources, but if there's a leaker in my department, I need you to tell me who it is. It can undermine our ability to find the murderer."

"Now Zep," Harald said in a dignified voice, "we wouldn't be in business long if we gave the police the names of our sources."

Goldfarb seemed to enjoy the tension his boss created by resisting Zep. He was in his late twenties and seemed to Maddy to be a typical go-getter type. Dressed in a tweed sports jacket, Bostonian wingtip shoes, and a red bowtie that complemented the smartass smirk on his face, she had him pegged as an asshole.

"Harry, you have grandkids," Zep said. "What if they are next on this guy's list? How would you feel if you didn't do everything you could to stop him?" Harald didn't seem fazed by his tactic.

"What I can tell you is that as far as we know, you do not have a leaker in your department," he said.

Goldfarb gave his boss a stare as cold as steel. It was as though Johnson had given the enemy information that would help their cause over his own.

"That means the murderer, or someone close to him, contacted you," Zep said.

"I'm not giving you anything more," Harald said sternly.

"That's all I need," Zep said. He stood up, shook Johnson's hand, and nodded to Goldfarb. Maddy smiled politely and followed Zep out.

When the elevator doors closed and the two detectives were alone, Zep said, "Our guy is calling the paper. He's a cunning son-of-a-bitch. Today is Valentine's Day, and he's going to strike. I can feel it."

Zep's words reverberated in Maddy's head. Cupid's call to the media was an obvious attempt to bring attention to his next killing. Her stomach in knots with the notion Amber was attending a dance that evening at the annual Father-Daughter Dance brought the nightmare to her doorstep.

***

It was almost five forty-five when Jack arrived wearing a black suit with a blue tie that matched Amber's dress. He handed his daughter a white corsage. Although Maddy didn't share the danger that lurked about in the community that evening, she knew her anxiety showed. Amber was to stay overnight at Jack's after the dance and Maddy repeatedly told him he should not leave her alone at any time.

While Amber packed overnight clothes upstairs, Jack asked Maddy if he could discuss something with her, ignoring her concerns. *Here we go*, Maddy thought. *Every time he uses this tone, he wants to talk about taking me to dinner.* That was precisely what he asked about.

"Let's not spoil this moment, Jack. Okay, if you insist on having dinner to talk things over, I will go, but under one condition: Amber is not to know anything about it. She's finally in a good place with our divorce, and I don't want to confuse her."

"Great," he said. "We'll do it on a night when she's at a sleepover."

Amber came downstairs, and before she put on her coat, Maddy asked to take a picture.

"How about one with Dad and me?" As Maddy snapped it, sadness crept in. *This is how I had always wanted our family to be, the three of us, together, and not all crazy the way it is now.*

When she was finally alone, she poured a glass of wine and went to the living room. As she thought about how happy Amber seemed, she grew nostalgic and dozed off. The phone rang, and the clock read 1:38 a.m.… Afraid of what the call might be about, she finally picked up, and it was Zep.

"He did it again," he said. "Cupid took another girl."

The walls closed in on her. Feeling numb, she struggled to grasp the whole of what it meant. Zep continued to talk, but she didn't hear everything. Grabbing a pen, she scribbled down a few notes on a scrap of paper as he rattled off the details.

"Get there as soon as you can," he said and hung up.

For a few seconds, she couldn't move. Then she jumped up, grabbed her coat, and ran out of the house. Barely legible, her scribbled notes were difficult to read. "Female… ten years old. Went missing yesterday at three p.m.… Command center, New Hartford Municipal Building."

She tried to save time by taking the back roads to New Hartford, but the blackness of night and occasional patches of ice made her wish she hadn't. With her mind still dull from the wine, she worried that she might have missed something critical that Zep had said, so she called Al.

"What did you hear, Al?"

"They found a valentine in the kid's coat."

"So, it's the same guy," she shrieked. "Holy shit! Holy shit!"

Her thoughts scattered like bowling pins. "Myers was right. This guy is a serial killer!"

Chapter 16

By the time Maddy arrived at the makeshift command center, the night had taken on a life of its own. The clanking of tables and chairs unfolding, people scurrying to install telephones and computers, and food supplies, pillows, blankets, and cots wheeled in from trucks, created an energy that hung in the air like static electricity. Faces, fixed and purposeful, reflected the seriousness of the situation. Everyone knew a girl's life was on the line.

Zep stood in front of the room and beckoned the crowd's attention. "Take a seat, please." He waited a minute and started in. "Thank you for getting here at this late hour. We have a situation where every minute counts. Chief Ryan and his team from the New Hartford P. D. have been working on the case of a missing ten-year-old girl. It was called in at 3:36 yesterday afternoon by the child's mother."

He paced back and forth in front of the crowd. All eyes homed in on him as he read from a clipboard. "The girl's name is Nancy Miles. When interviewing the parents at their home last night, the officers found a valentine in Nancy's blue jeans like the one in Sarah Benning's bedroom."

A low rumble, like thunder before a storm, rolled through the gathering. Heads turned and whispers grew into loud chatter. Waiting for his audience to absorb the details, he started in again.

"If this is the same perpetrator, he will probably keep the girl alive for forty-eight hours before raping and killing her."

His words brought the full weight of the situation into focus. Faces grew pale. A woman in the back of the room wept, and Maddy tried to grasp the significance of Cupid showing himself a second time. *He intends to unleash hell on this community. It's like Myers said. The guy wants everyone to know he's here.*

"It's now almost four a.m.," Zep continued. "We have less than thirty-six hours to find Nancy alive. We know the route she walked on the way home from school. Based on that information, we have marked off areas for canvassing. You will work in teams of two. When we finish here, you'll pick up your assignments and who you're partnered with at the back table." He stopped pacing, turned, and looked directly at the crowd. "The clock is ticking, people. You are this girl's only hope. Now, let's move out."

Maddy waited in line at the back table and noticed Bud Renshaw was in front of her. He turned, looked down, smirked, and turned back. After he opened his assignment, he turned again, and said "Whew," as though relieved Maddy wasn't his partner. She shook her head and thought, *the guy's an asshole.*

Surprised to find her partner was Allison, Maddy scanned the gym, but she was nowhere. As she headed back to see if there was a mistake, Allison burst through the front door, appearing frazzled. Walking to Maddy, she said, "I got a call from Zep a little over an hour ago. He wants me to start today, so here I am. What do I do?"

"You're partnered with me. We're assigned to the street where the victim was last seen."

"What victim?"

"Oh my God, come on, I'll tell you in the car."

Maddy drove to Beam Street, where Nancy Miles was last seen. It was still dark when the two detectives arrived, and the old amber-colored streetlamps barely made a difference. A heavy mist settled on the rundown, two-story houses, making the street look like it was out of a London murder mystery. It was just past five a.m., and, with the temperature in the forties, they pulled their heavy coats out from the back seat of the cruiser. "We won't make many friends waking people up at this hour," Maddy said.

They agreed to work opposite sides of the street and use handheld radios to communicate. Maddy knocked at the first door, and when no one answered, waited several minutes, made a note, and moved on. An older woman shuffled to the door in a walker at the next house. When Maddy asked if she'd noticed a girl who fit Nancy Miles's description, the woman said, "No. I'm hardly ever near a window. Most of my day is in a chair. But I read about it. Do you have any idea what happened to her?"

"We're working on it, ma'am." After she made an entry in her notebook, she politely disengaged from the conversation. By late morning, she had finished with half the houses on her side of the street with little to show for it. Starting back to her vehicle to check in, she noticed a white pickup parked behind her car with its engine running. The driver, a man with long hair and a ski cap, seemed to stare at her. Slowly, the truck backed up. When she got close, it made a U-turn and sped off.

She jumped in her car, but in her excitement, hit the gas too hard and fishtailed, allowing the truck to gain distance. By the time she reached the major intersection, the guy had disappeared. A bus that stopped next to her at a red light blocked her view. Waiting for it to move, ready to crawl out of her skin, the light finally turned green, and the bus pulled away. A white truck, off to her right, seemed too far away to catch, but she swerved into the oncoming lane and sped, until finally, she had to pull over. "Shit. I lost him," she shouted out loud.

About to turn around, she saw a man with long hair and a ski cap walking out of a paint store. *Son-of-a-bitch, that's him!* She ran to him and flashed her badge. He stepped back, startled. "I'm Detective Reynolds from the Oneida County Sheriff's Department; I'd like a word with you."

"Are you a rozzer?"

"A what?" she asked. She didn't understand what he meant. She repeated herself. The man looked at her, dumbfounded. "What did I do?"

"Were you just on Beam Street?"

"Ah-huh."

Besides being slow-witted, something else seemed odd about him. "What's your name?" she asked.

"Mason Charles."

"Where do you live, Mr. Charles?"

"103 Beam Street."

"I knocked at your front door earlier. Why didn't you answer?"

"I was probably in the basement and didn't hear you." *That's it,* she thought. *He has a slight British accent.*

"What do you do, Mr. Charles?"

"I make things."

What the hell is that supposed to mean? Maddy got him to agree to follow him home and check out his house, and when she walked in the front door, the smell of turpentine nearly knocked her over. Before she took two steps into the foyer, a man in his fifties, bald and rotund, came out from another room.

"How can we help you?" he asked.

She introduced herself and said she was following up with residents about the girl who went missing the day before.

"My name is Donald Charles. I'm Mason's stepbrother, and I can assure you, we had nothing to do with it."

"Oh, I'm not suggesting that you did, Mr. Charles. We're talking with everyone on the block," Maddy said. "Do you remember seeing a girl around ten years old walk by your house yesterday between four o'clock and four thirty?"

"I know who you're talking about. The girl walks by here often. But yesterday, Mason and I weren't here."

Donald's face grew red. "Do you mind if I look around?" she asked.

"Is that legal?"

Maddy shrugged. "I don't have a search warrant, if that's what you mean, so I can only search with your permission. It's up to you."

Donald didn't hide his irritation. Curtly, he said, "Go ahead."

Maddy walked through the first floor and checked out the rooms. Finding nothing, she opened the basement door and walked down. Donald and Mason followed. It was a brightly lit workshop filled with hundreds of model airplanes sitting on shelves.

"Did you build all these?"

"Yeah, I did," Mason responded. "I build things."

"Indeed, Mason loves building his models, don't you?" Donald said, interrupting Mason as though trying to shut him up. With her suspicions heightened, Maddy scrutinized the basement. Looking out a window, she saw a garage out back. "I'd like to look in that garage," she said.

As though she had stepped on his toe, Donald's eyes widened. He hesitated, then said, "Okay."

Outside, he watched with his arms folded. "Help yourself, but be careful; those old doors don't work so well."

Maddy grabbed the two door handles, pulled, and then pushed several times, but they wouldn't budge. Finally, lifting on one with both hands, it broke free. Inside the garage, an old, unusual car, covered with grime and surface rust, looked to be a long time neglected. She wiped the windows and looked inside. Mason said, "It's a Rupert…. It's British."

"Hmm. Can you open it?"

"Sure." He quickly opened the door.

Women's clothing—skirts, blouses, shoes, scarves, and a couple of wigs—lay messily scattered around. *Maybe someone's been using these as disguises*, she thought. "Whose car?" she asked while making a note.

"It belonged to our Aunt Martha," Donald replied. "She willed it to me when she died."

Maddy looked at him with an untrusting eye, closed the door, and checked the trunk, but nothing was out of line. Stepping into the yard, making notes, she asked, "So what kind of work do you do, Mr. Charles?"

"I'm a retired chef. I used to work at a fine restaurant outside of London before I had my accident. Now, I can hardly stand for over ten minutes without being in severe back pain. I am in pain as we speak."

"Oh, I'm sorry to hear that," she said. "I'll just be a few more minutes. You said you weren't home yesterday. Where were you?"

"In Utica at an antique toy and model show. Mason and I didn't get home until after nine o'clock."

"Can you verify that?"

Smiling, Donald put his hand in his coat pocket, pulled out some slips of paper, shuffled through, and held out two torn tickets to an antique show and a parking pass. "This parking pass shows we were there from 9:46 a.m. to 8:36 p.m.," Donald said with a smirk that was pissing Maddy off.

How convenient. A ready-made alibi, she thought.

She eyeballed the house one more time and noticed it had an attic. She was about to ask to see it when Allison's panicked-filled voice screeched through the radio. "I'm in pursuit."

Maddy left the Charles brothers standing in their yard, ran to the street, and saw Allison chasing a man in a baseball hat. Since he was too far to catch on foot, she jumped in her car and rushed to where Allison had disappeared around a house. Maddy ran into the yard where Allison lay stunned, holding the side of her head, and her face covered with blood. "Are you all right?" she asked, as she helped her sit up.

"I think so. The guy hid behind that garage and jumped out when I got close. He knocked me down, called me a bitch, and hit me with the butt of a pistol."

"It could have been worse, Allison. He could have shot you."

"Holy shit, you're right! I could be dead."

Chapter 17

Squad cars filled Beam Street while Allison sat in the back seat of Maddy's cruiser, holding a blood-soaked towel to her head. Zep sat next to her as she explained how it happened.

"I walked to the door of 301 and a guy bolted out, almost knocked me over, and took off. I chased him into the yard, but he disappeared. Then, out of nowhere, he popped out from behind the garage, knocked me down, and slugged me with a pistol, before running into those woods." She pointed to a vast forest behind the house.

"We're not equipped to go after him out there," Zep said. "There are hundreds of acres of woods that run behind these streets. We'll have to call in the K-9 unit."

Maddy sat with Allison in the car as everyone waited for the K-9 team. Finally, an ambulance arrived, and two medics examined Allison's wound.

"She should come with us for some tests," a medic told Zep.

"Aww, come on," Allison protested.

"We don't take unnecessary chances, Allison," Zep said.

"I'll walk with you," Maddy said as she put her hand around Allison's shoulder, helping her to the ambulance. She said she'd check in on her later, before the doors closed.

Within twenty minutes, trucks filled with people dressed in heavy gear arrived. The street was popping with activity, and, amid the clatter of equipment and excited dogs, Maddy heard someone shout out her name. She looked over and saw Trick Diaz. It was the first good feeling she had had the entire day, reminding her of the previous summer when they partnered together.

"Big-time detective now, huh Maddy?" he said through his smile. It was as though Trick couldn't help but smile. He was always upbeat and funny.

"Yeah, and I see you got your K-9 gig too…not bad, Trick."

Diaz radiated positive energy, and Maddy loved being around him. She told a friend once that if you don't like Trick Diaz, you'll like nobody. Although very handsome, he was a loyal family man, with several kids, and never flirted around with the females in the department. Just being near him made her feel better.

Watching the K-9 team unload equipment, ready their dogs, and slowly disappear into the darkness, she felt an uneasiness, knowing the danger her comrades faced.

Law enforcement surrounded the house at 301, as Zep, Maddy, and Bud Renshaw prepared to enter. With their weapons drawn, they crept in, and the first thing she noticed was an overpowering smell of pot and incense. Dishes piled high in the kitchen sink and crumpled up sleeping bags scattered on the living room floor showed that several people had been living there.

The upstairs revealed a more sinister aspect. On the wall of a bedroom hung clippings of child pornography, and on the floor lay scattered child porn magazines. One photo showed a man having sex with a girl about fourteen years old. *Meat!* Maddy thought. *These kids are nothing more than pieces of meat to these guys.*

"Look at these," Bud said as he searched a dresser drawer and found at least a dozen pairs of little girl's underwear stuffed inside. Hearts and teddy bears were on a few, and one had the name 'Dora' written on it.

"Bag those," Zep said. "We need to find out if any belong to Nancy Miles or Sarah Benning."

After they'd cleared the house, the forensics team went in, and while the K-9 unit combed the woods, there was nothing to do but wait. The scene on the street had become as dead as a wake. Cops drifted into small groups and talked among themselves as they tried to keep warm. Maddy and Al stayed near Zep's car listening to information as it came in on his radio.

The temperature dropped, daylight faded, and the more they learned about the guy from 301, the clearer it became how dire the situation was. His name was Benny Bowls. He was a convicted child molester and a recent parole violator, according to Fran Liberatore, his parole officer. When Zep spoke with Liberatore on the phone, she said there was an outstanding warrant for his arrest. He asked if she'd come to the scene. "Gladly," she responded. "I've been trying to track down Bowls for days. He's bad news."

Zep advised the K-9 captain to bring in cadaver dogs. "

Besides doing time for raping a six-year-old girl, Benny Bowls had several assault charges against women. When Fran Liberatore arrived at the scene, she said Bowls, for no apparent reason, just stopped coming to his appointments. "Something was going down with him," she said, "but I did not know what it was. He told me he'd never go back to prison again. I don't think he'll go peaceably."

By five-thirty, it was pitch black, and Maddy could see her breath when she breathed. The steady drizzle and penetrating cold felt relentless. A hand reached out to her with a hot cup of coffee, and when she looked up, it was Al.

"Oh, you're an angel," she said. "Where did you get it?" She took the cup with both hands, savoring a sip, and felt its heat warm her insides as it went down.

"Never mind where I got it, just enjoy. You look like you need it." Al cradled his cup with both hands. "This day is turning into a real cluster fuck, isn't it?" he added, as he leaned back next to her against Zep's car.

"Yeah, and I have a feeling it's not over. Not by a long shot." No sooner had Maddy said the words than the sky lit up with a series of flashes. Beams of light silhouetted the trees toward the K-9 team. Thunderclaps followed. "That's gunfire," Al said.

"Something's going wrong out there," Maddy said. "There are too many shots being fired."

The sounds of men yelling and dogs barking echoed through the woods. "Get a medic out here," a voice shouted from the darkness. Everyone rose to their feet. A man from the K-9 team ran out of the woods, screaming, "We've got a man down; hurry with that medic." Four guys followed, carrying a body across their clasped arms. When they passed by Maddy, a light shined on Trick's face. His head bobbling, blood flowing from his mouth, and his eyes frozen wide. He was dead.

Paralyzed, Maddy watched as they laid him on the ground. A paramedic kneeled and put his hand on Trick's neck. "He's dead." She dropped her head, and her heart sank. Faces, white with shock, looked at each other, unsure of what to do. Finally, his team members dropped to their knees and bowed their heads.

Thinking of the joyful man, Maddy's fists clenched with rage. *This is so unfair. Just a few flashes of light, and he's gone.* Her thoughts went to Trick's wife and kids. *Their lives will never be the same. Those kids will be like me, growing up without their dad.*

The mood among the leadership at the scene turned to alarm. Red-faced and wet with sweat, the K-9 unit captain took off his helmet. "The guy was hiding in a thicket and opened fire when Trick got close," he said. "He didn't have a chance, but got off two shots as he went down."

The captain wiped his face with a towel, and close to tears, continued. "The guy took off into the woods. We pursued him, but he crossed a stream, and it threw the dogs off. He got over to Route 5. When we arrived, a woman was standing on the roadside. She said a man stopped her car at gunpoint, ordered her out, and drove off."

The captain breathed heavily and stopped for a few seconds to take a swig of water. "She said the guy was limping. We found blood on the road." Before he gave Zep the description of the car and the plate number, he said, "The thing is, the guy could have made it to the road without waiting in the bushes. He had plenty of time. It was as though he wanted to kill a cop. We've got to get that son-of-a-bitch."

Zep alerted law enforcement in the area that Bowls was on the run and gave out the description of the hijacked car. Within twenty minutes, a call came in saying someone had seen the vehicle in downtown Utica. Beam Street emptied like a high school parking lot after the last bell.

Sitting in the back seat of a patrol car, Maddy squeezed between Al and Bud, feeling every bump on the pot-holed city street. Zep and another detective sat in front as sirens screamed and lights flashed. Everyone remained silent. Her thoughts were on Amber.

What will happen to her if I get killed tonight? Trick's sudden death brought home that it could happen. She had always avoided dealing with her death, but vowed that if she survived the night, she would make proper arrangements for her daughter, just in case.

When Al made a call to his mother, everyone in the car called loved ones. Maddy got ahold of Jack, explained the situation, and asked to speak with Amber.

"Hi, honey. It looks like I'll have to work late, so you'll need to stay with Dad, okay?"

"Are you all right, Mom? What's all that noise?"

"Remember when I told you there will be times I can't talk about my work with anyone, even you?"

"This is one of them, isn't it?" Amber said.

"Yes."

"Okay, but I'll see you in the morning, right?"

"Yep, see you in the morning." *I hoped so*, Maddy thought. "Love you."

"Love you too, Mom. Be careful."

The cruiser rattled and shook, and within a few blocks of the destination, Zep sent out an order for all sirens and flashing lights to be turned off. Dry in the mouth, Maddy felt a lump in the pit of her stomach move to her throat. She reached down and felt for her father's badge in her pocket. *Be with me, Dad.*

Dozens of police vehicles converged on the stolen car when they arrived. Zep got out and a uniformed cop ran to him. "Someone saw a man running into that building, holding his leg," the guy said.

Everyone gazed at a building known to be a place where lowlifes blended among poor families to avoid the eye of the law. A throwback to Utica's long-gone industrial heyday, the place was four stories of low-income apartments and at street level retail stores. The massive old edifice stood stark against the night, and Maddy felt her number was about to be called. Zep huddled with his detectives and explained the plan.

"The building has two sections with separate stairwells. I want teams of two assigned to each section. Evacuate as many residents as possible, but remember, one of them is Bowls."

Maddy and Bud Renshaw went to the third floor. As she ascended the stairs, the aroma of food cooking in the apartments mixed with the stink of urine in the stairwell created a sickly stench. Her sense of foreboding grew with each step up, and a cruel, unforgiving doubt weakened her resolve. She wondered if all her hours of practice with a gun would make a difference when it mattered. *Targets don't shoot back*, she thought. Again, she looked to her father for strength, reached into her pocket, and held his badge. She whispered, "Please give me courage, Dad."

The third-floor hallway was dark and dismal. Residents scattered like mice into their nests. No one answered at the first two apartments, but at the third, a woman holding a crying baby, surrounded by three kids, opened the door. "Have you seen or heard anyone in the hallway within the last hour?" Maddy asked. Barely able to speak English, the woman became distracted by a weak voice in another room calling for her. "I'll be right back," she said and walked away.

While Maddy and Bud waited at the door, a girl of about four stayed behind and stared at them. She was in pink pajamas, held a stuffed kitty-cat, and sucked her thumb. When Maddy smiled at her, she took her thumb from her mouth and pointed her index finger at the apartment across the hall, two doors down. Maddy kneeled.

"Did a man run into that door tonight?" The girl slowly nodded her head. "Alright, sweetie, now go back in with your mommy and don't open this door, okay?" The child put her thumb back in her mouth, turned and shut the door.

Any fear or doubt Maddy felt washed away. She knew what had to be done, having practiced it at least a hundred times. She whispered to Bud, "I'm going in low; you cover me."

Bud looked at her as if she had lost her mind. "Are you crazy? What about a search warrant?"

"Fuck a search warrant," she said as she pointed at the blood on the doorknob. "That's probable cause. On the count of three, kick the door in. I'll go in low while you stay back and cover me." Bud gave a reluctant nod. Maddy counted with her fingers. Her thoughts were on Trick and as the count reached "three," her last thought was, *I want this bastard.*

The door blew open, and she slid to the floor as Bowls held a gun with both hands. He fired. She heard the bullet whiz overhead as she sent a round into his heart. Bowls stood frozen, still holding his gun, trying to get off another shot. Maddy fired and popped a hole in his forehead. He dropped with a slapping sound to the hardwood floor. Lying on his back, blood gurgling from his mouth, Maddy remained poised for another shot, but it wasn't necessary — the man was dead.

I just killed a man, she thought, sitting with one leg extended, her ears ringing and surrounded by a cloud of smoke. Her mind cleared, and the throbbing pain in her left knee demanded her attention. Grabbing it with both hands, Bud went to her after checking out the rest of the apartment.

"Are you okay?"

"I think so, but I smacked my knee, and it's killing me."

Feet pounding on the stairway shook the walls before Zep, Al, and another detective ran into the room.

"Did you do this?" Zep asked Renshaw, as he looked at Bowls' dead body.

Bud shook his head. "Maddy did it," he said. "Her knee is pretty banged up, but she's not shot." Zep kneeled next to her and asked if she could stand.

"I think so, but I need help."

She felt the throbbing in her knee radiate up her leg as Zep and Bud helped her up. With her arms around their shoulders, she moved with the men into the hallway. Al cleared a path through the crowd of gathering residents.

"How did you learn to shoot like that?" Zep asked as they carefully descended the stairs.

"Lots of practice."

When they reached the street, Al brought a squad car to the front of the building. Together, Zep and Bud lifted Maddy into the front seat. As Al drove to the hospital, Maddy lay back rubbing the banged-up knee and her mind reeling from what she had done to Bowls. A sickening feeling, spurred on by the image of his lifeless body as it hit the floor, began welling up inside her.

Maddy realized the power she possessed. It was a power that she'd worked hard to attain through years of practice with a gun, and it had served her well when she was young. It had allowed her to ward off the dread of the man who killed her father; the man she feared would come back to kill her. *I have the power to take life*, she thought, and at that moment, wished she did not. *Only God has that right.* She knew such thoughts could get her killed against someone out to destroy her, so she pushed them from her mind.

Late that night, she returned home from the E.R. with an ice pack, ace bandage, pain pills, and a monster swollen knee.

Chapter 18

Nigel, 1955, Chicago, Illinois

"Chumps, most people are chumps," Nigel's father said as they flew to Chicago. "And School? Don't talk to me about school. You don't have to go to school as long as you live with me, kid. I'll teach you everything you need to know. You're going to learn ways to hustle a buck, and believe me when I tell you, I know them all." Nigel felt a sense of liberation from prison, and for the first time, he was about to experience life on the other side of the wall.

They landed at O'Hare Airport at 9:37 PM and, carrying their luggage to the cabbie area, an unshaven guy manning a shoeshine stand called out, "Hey Lob."

Nigel's father responded with a gold tooth smile, "What's happening, bro?" He tuned to Nigel and explained his nickname was Louie the Lob. Hailing a cab, Louie haggled the fee down to half price with the driver. "I can swindle an old lady out of her false teeth," he proudly told his son.

The streets slowly grew stark as the cab proceeded to Louie's flat. Abandon cars, burned out streetlamps, and empty streets, except for an occasional person lurking in the shadows, were nothing like in Nigel's London neighborhood. "This area is crime-ridden, and only a few cops come around," Louie boasted. "You can go weeks without seeing a dick among these rat traps."

After a month of living with his dad, Nigel was hooked. Every day was a new adventure. *Sleep until noon, meet up with Dad's friends at Lucky's Coffee Shop and laugh at all those goodie-two-shoe assholes out there stuck in their grinds. I wouldn't trade this for anything.* The afternoon at the pool hall, however, was when the day began. One at a time, guys would stroll in and tell tales of adventures from the night before. The energy slowly grew until the evening, and then the fireworks happened.

By dark, everyone knew what they wanted to do that night. Some guys quietly disappeared to pull off a caper. A trip to a whorehouse was a staple if there wasn't anything better in the offing. Some, though, and it was always the same ones, couldn't get enough of crashing high stakes card games. Then, the next morning, like déjà vu, the whole damn thing started over again. It was a glorious time for Nigel, and he wanted it to go on forever.

Life was like strawberry shortcake every day compared to the fish guts with Mother and Gertie. *And to think, my favorite thing back then was to play with those stupid rocks,* he thought, although he kept Jade for good luck.

"I'm proud of you, son," Louie told him the day he raked in over three hundred bucks after rummaging through the clothes of basketball players while they were out on the court. "That's my boy. He's going to make it big someday," he bragged to his friends.

On his fifteenth birthday, Louie took him to Lady Lila's Men's Club, which he said was the cleanest whorehouse in Chicago. When they walked into the vestibule, the light was low, and a scent of sandalwood lingering in the air made him dizzy. He wasn't sure if it was the pint of brandy he drank or the opium he smoked an hour earlier, but the flowers on the wallpaper danced like the babes at Alfie's strip joint.

A middle-aged woman dressed in a low-cut burgundy gown came out from behind a beaded curtain to greet them. Barely able to keep his eyes off her huge boobs, Nigel wondered how she kept them from falling out.

"My name's Lila," she said. "You must be Nigel. Your father tells me you're ready to become a man. I have just the girl for you. Her name is Tabatha, and she is waiting upstairs."

Louie put his hand on his shoulder and said, "You're going to like this, boy."

Taking Nigel's arm, Lila walked him up the stairs. Looking back, he saw his father's head bob up and down as he chuckled to himself, as though he knew something that Nigel didn't. Stepping in the room, a young girl lay on her side in a nearly transparent silk nightgown. Her milky white skin revealed her age, which was not much older than Nigel's, although she had the body of a woman. Her hair was jet black, and she sweetly smiled at him.

Lila left them alone. He walked to the bed, and Tamatha put out her hand, gently pulling him close, then kissed his lips. His heart pounded, and blood rush to his groin. Without saying a word, Tamatha undid the buttons and zipper on his pants, slid them off, and encouraged him to lie on his back next to her.

Slowly, she unbuttoned his shirt, kissing his chest and stomach. When she put him in her mouth, a violent force came over him. "You fucking pig!" he shouted, jumping up. He slapped her and had to fight off a powerful urge to snap her neck. It took all his effort to restrain himself. Tabatha crawled to her knees, face red and swollen, with tears running down her face, but she did not make a sound. It was as if she had experienced such assaults before and knew better than to make a scene.

Confused by his reaction, Nigel pulled up his pants with a sense of repulsion racing around his brain. *What's wrong with me?* The heat of humiliation pressed against his face as he passed his father in the foyer on the way out the door. *I can never face him again.*

Like broken glass gnawing at his insides, he walked the streets in an icy drizzle. He wished he were dead. *Who am I? Why did I do that? What will he think of me?* Walking in the rain for what felt like hours, he finally stepped into a café. Sitting near a window, he drank coffee, watching cars roll up and down the street.

Hours passed, closing time neared, and he caught a cab home. He walked into the apartment as his father watched television with a beer in his hand. Waiting for his dad to denigrate him like Mother used to do, surprisingly, he simply said, "Don't worry, son, it happens to all of us." And that was it. Nothing more was ever said about the incident, although Nigel remained haunted by his rage and desire to snap Tabatha's neck.

Chapter 19

Nigel, 1957, Chicago, Illinois

"Wake up, Nigel, Johnny Nero's here." Nigel rolled out of bed, got dressed, and went to the next room, where Louie talked with a lanky man. *This guy looks like a pimp.* Dressed in black, he had a gold chain with a black swastika around his neck. The guy sat in the big chair like he owned the place. He lifted what seemed to be a size fourteen boot up onto the coffee table and glanced around the apartment as though he was casing the joint.

He's not here to visit. He looks like a man on a mission, Nigel thought. After some chitchat, Johnny got down to his real purpose. "I have a big job in mind, and I'm thinking about letting you guys in on it." He lit up a cigarette, took a drag, and seemed to look for Louie's reaction. "Liquor stores used to be easy pickings, but now everybody's got a gun. Shit, you never know what you're gonna run into. The way I figure it, if you're going to take a risk, you may as well go big."

Louie sat at the edge of his seat and nodded at everything Johnny said. He seemed impressed by the guy, but Nigel regarded him with a cautious eye. There was something about Johnny that didn't feel right. But when he said, "Bigger than the Lampert Jewelry robbery," Nigel sat up and listened. Everyone knew about the Lampert heist. The guys who pulled it off left town with a boatload of money and were living big in Miami, or so everyone said.

Boy, Dad has bought this guy's line of shit. Despite his instincts warning him about the fast talker, he didn't want to abandon his father to face Johnny's persuasive abilities alone, so he opted to stay silent. "There's going to be a truck full of cash headed to a department store vault. Are you interested?" He smiled, and his huge eyeteeth reminded Nigel of a snake.

"Definitely!" Louie said.

"Good! I got it all figured out, and I know the information is reliable. If we play our cards right, it'll be a piece of cake."

A piece of cake, my ass, Nigel thought.

"It'll only be the three of us…less to split up," Johnny said. "Nigel, you'll be the lookout. Louie, you and me will go in and get the money. I got it all figured out, and it came from a guy who used to work there, so I know it's reliable."

Each morning, the three partners met at Lucky's for breakfast and sat at the same corner table where no one could hear them talk. "Me and Louie will take care of the truck driver, and Nigel will stand in front of the cigar store across the street. If someone comes, Nigel, walk to the alley and start whistling Camp Town Races."

"I don't know Camp Town Races."

"He don't know Camp Town Races," Johnny said as he turned to Louie, laughing. "What the fuck do you know?"

"Take Me Out to the Ball Game."

"Okay, sing fucking Take Me Out to the Ball Game." Johnny shook his head as though talking to an idiot.

Nigel didn't like being laughed at and looked over at his father to see if he was laughing too, but he wasn't. Louie glared at Johnny in his son's defense, and it made Nigel's heart soar. At that moment, Nigel felt more warmth inside than ever before. Despite Louie being taken in by Johnny's bullshit, Nigel realized how much he genuinely loved his dad.

After a week of breakfast meetings, their plan became as smooth as custard, as Johnny liked to say, and the heist was all set for the following Friday. They met at Louie's place early Friday morning and stepped through their scheme one more time. When they finished, Johnny smiled with his fangs protruding, and said, "Are you boys ready to get rich?"

It was a typical summer morning in Chicago: blue sky, comfortably warm, and a refreshing breeze blowing in off the lake. On the way to the caper, Nigel's stomach churned, and when Johnny stopped the car in front of the Cigar Store, he thought he might hurl.

Johnny turned to Louie and Nigel. "We're not fucking around here, right?" *What's he getting at?* The guy slid two pistols from under his shirt and handed one to Louie. "Take this, and I'll keep one. Don't use these on the guy in the truck. We need to take care of him quiet-like," he said as he pulled out a knife and held it in his hand. "We only use the guns if a cop sticks his nose where it ain't supposed to be. Got it?" Louie nodded.

"This isn't what we planned," Nigel protested.

"Never mind what we planned," Johnny said, scowling. "These are our insurance policies."

Nigel didn't like dealing with the unexpected, and the guns showing up at the last second were unexpected. With his anxiety growing, he wanted to back out, but it was too late. He knew others would brand him a pussy, and he couldn't tolerate it, so he took his place in front of Benny's. Leaning on a mailbox, he acted casually, pretending to read a newspaper. Johnny and Louie walked across the street to the alley next to the department store.

According to Johnny's information, the truck with the money was to arrive at 9:17. By 9:16, Nigel felt so conspicuous that he thought every passerby was looking at him. At 9:20, he nearly bolted, and by 9:30, with great relief, he believed the information was wrong, and it was time to pull the plug. As he started across the street to the alley, he heard the rumbling of an engine, turned, and saw the money truck rolling toward him. *Holy shit!* He scurried back to his position.

As the truck pulled into the alley, Nigel noticed two men inside, not one. *What the fuck. That's not what we planned for!* He was anxiously waiting for something to happen when a string of pops, like firecrackers, echoed out of the alley.

"Nigel, Nigel, help." It was his father calling to him. Running to the alley, he saw two uniformed men on the ground. One was face down, his hat a few feet away and blood dripping from his ears. The other was on his back, eyes opened, jaw wide, and looking up at the sky. Both were dead. Louie sat with his legs outstretched, pants blood-soaked at the hip, and clasping his hands over his wound. His gun lay next to him on the pavement.

"They locked the vault in the truck," Johnny shouted, with blood dripping down his hand as he held a gun with the other. "Fuck the money. Let's get out of here."

Nigel helped his father stand, and together they started for the street. Johnny walked slightly ahead, and when an unmarked police vehicle pulled into the alley, he lifted his weapon and unloaded its magazine, blowing out the windshield. Louie raised his gun and fired three times.

The detective had taken cover behind the opened car door. He rose, fired four times, and hit both Johnny and Louie twice in the chest. Johnny fell on his back, and the clang of his swastika hitting the pavement echoed throughout the alley. He was dead.

The thud of Louie's body when it landed sent an ache through his son's heart. His eyes called for help, but there was nothing Nigel could do except watch him moan and squirm. Grabbing Nigel's arm, Louie pulled him close and uttered something. His son only heard blood gurgling in his throat. "Father, what did you say?" Louie looked up, with tears on his face, mumbling unintelligibly. His eyes rolled back, and his body went limp.

Stunned and looking at the detective, he screamed, "You son-of-a-bitch, you killed my father, and I'm going to kill you." He charged, but the taller, stronger man quickly pinned him down.

Police swarmed the area like buzzards on roadkill. Two uniformed cops ran over to help handcuff Nigel. They pushed his face against the hot pavement as he fought to get free. "We're going to have to medicate this guy. Get a medic over here," a cop yelled out.

Four men held him down as a fifth injected him. A tingling sensation spread throughout his body, and all strength drained from his limbs, yet he was conscious. His mind still churned, just more slowly. Lifting him to a gurney, and rolling him through a crowd of cops, he glimpsed the man who shot his father, and heard someone say, "Good job, Jimbo." Repeating it over and over, he burned the name Jimbo into his brain.

Chapter 20

Maddy, 1979, Utica, New York

A loud bang on the front door startled Maddy awake. "That damn paperboy," she moaned. Trying to get off the sofa, a stabbing pain in her knee sent shock waves up and down her leg. *The pain meds from the E.R. must have worn off.*

She edged her hips sideways, sat up, grabbed her jacket from the floor, and took another pill. Laying back, waiting for it to work, trying to piece together the events from the night before, a powerful thought struck her. *I killed Benny Bowls! I feel like the morning after I lost my virginity. There's no going back now.* Years of practice with a gun didn't prepare her for how she would feel if she killed someone.

The pill kicked in, and she limped to the door. The headline on the front page read, "Cop Kills Suspect—Can Nancy Miles Be Saved?" Ben Goldfarb wrote the article. It insinuated, without coming right out and saying it, that by killing Bowls, Maddy had doomed the Miles girl.

"What? This is bullshit." Helpless to defend herself against the public attack, she gimped around the room, agitated, while she read the article aloud. Before she finished, the phone rang, and it was Jack.

"Are you okay, Maddy? The paper says you killed a guy last night."

"Yeah, but they got it all wrong."

"They always do. They always do."

Maddy wasn't in the mood to have a conversation with him, anticipating it would lead to a litany of gripes about journalists dumping on cops. "I appreciate you calling, Jack, but right now, I need to get coffee in me. Can we talk later?"

She made the coffee extra strong, sat at the kitchen table, and looked outside at the gloomy morning. Despite the pain medication she'd taken, she felt a pressure building in her head from the newspaper's account of what had happened. She dialed Zep at home, and a woman answered.

"This is Susan, Zep's wife. He's asleep, but I can wake him if you'd like."

"No, please don't do that," Maddy said.

Then, in a motherly tone, Susan asked, "How are you doing with what happened last night, Maddy?"

"I'm not sure. It hasn't hit me yet."

"Zep had a real hard time when he killed a man. He talked about it for months."

Maddy felt a sudden pang of envy. She, too, had someone to share her troubles with once, but after Jack's affair, all trust went out the window, and she couldn't confide in him anymore. "I think I'll be dealing with it for a long time as well," she said.

"You can call me anytime, dear. I mean it."

After she hung up, Maddy managed her way upstairs, showered, and got dressed. Her knee was double its normal size and throbbing. When the bottle of pain pills fell on the floor, she picked it up and thought how easy it would be to numb not only the pain in her knee but her emotional distress as well. *I better ditch these*, she thought, and flushed them down the toilet. Hobbling to the car, and awkwardly working her way inside, she thought how lucky she was the damaged knee was on the left and not her right, and she could drive.

On the way to New Hartford, she wondered if the cadaver dogs were still searching the woods for Nancy Miles's body.

Maybe Goldfarb is right. Did killing Bowls hurt the chances of finding the girl alive?

The morning rain had stopped by the time she arrived at the Command Center, but piercing dampness ran through her body as she gimped across the parking lot. The bells of St. Michael's Church rang nearby for nine o'clock mass, bringing into focus a strange dichotomy of what was happening in the church versus the high school gym.

Zep called together a small group of detectives, including Maddy, to meet at his makeshift office. They pulled steel folding chairs around a card table he used as a desk and began brainstorming possibilities regarding Nancy's whereabouts.

"Bowls could have buried her in the woods, and we just haven't found her yet," someone suggested.

"He could have her hidden at another location, and she's still alive," was another idea.

Al said, "It's possible that Bowls isn't the perp at all, and it was just a coincidence that we came across another child molester the way we did."

As the team worked on a game plan, an administrative assistant put a note in front of Zep. "I'm going to have to take this, folks," he said. "Let's regroup in ten. Al and Maddy, stick around." When the crowd broke up, a call came through, and Zep put it on speaker.

"This is Harry, Zep."

"Hi Harry," Zep said coolly. "I'm guessing you're calling to apologize for the distorted article you let Goldfarb print this morning."

"No, that's not it. Ben wrote it as he saw it. I'm calling about something more serious."

"I'm listening."

"Just before I made this call, I spoke with Ben. Cupid called him this morning."

Maddy saw Zep's jugular vein puff up.

"Zep," Harry said with a hint of what Maddy thought was fear in his voice, "he told Goldfarb where Nancy Miles's body was."

Oh my God, Maddy thought.

Zep sat up in his chair. "Harry, before you say another word, send that son-of-a-bitch out to New Harford right now, or I am going to have his ass dragged downtown for questioning."

"Calm down, Zep. I'll send him out."

No sooner had he hung up than another call came through. This time, he didn't put it on speaker. Maddy watched as he sat in silence. His face changed from tomato red to plum purple. Finally, he said, "There's something else you need to know, sir. Cupid called the newspaper and told Goldfarb where Nancy Miles's body is." He winced, and during the period of silence that followed, all color drained from his face. "Okay," he said, and hung up. "That was the Sheriff."

Zep turned to Maddy. "When Goldfarb gets here, you and I will talk with him out in a car. There is no privacy in this damn place. It's just our luck someone will overhear the location of the body, alert the press, and they'll be waiting at the scene when we arrive. Wouldn't that look great on the front page? Al, start alerting law enforcement in the area that we may have the location of the body shortly." He paused, shook his head, and said, "I feel another shitstorm coming down."

When Goldfarb arrived, he had lost his swagger. *Maybe he doesn't enjoy being used by a madman*, Maddy speculated. They went to a large police van and Zep said, "I need to know every detail of what Cupid said to you." Maddy had her notebook opened, ready to take it all down.

"At my home, around eight fifteen this morning, he called me and used a filter to distort his voice. He started by saying the police have made a mess of things and killed the wrong guy last night. He said he could prove it. I asked him how. That's when he told me where the body was." Goldfarb paused, put a white handkerchief up to his mouth like he was trying not to barf. "He said the girl is in a sewer on the corner of Genesee and First Street. That was it. He hung up."

"In a sewer?" Zep roared, putting his hands on his head. "Oh, sweet Jesus."

Maddy looked down, shook her head, and felt prickles moving up her arms.

"Who else did you tell about this?" Zep asked.

"Just Harry."

Turning to Maddy, Zep said, "Tell Al to inform the Utica Police. Ask them to cordon off the area." Then to Goldfarb, he said, "You can be at the scene, but absolutely no pictures. Those parents don't need to see their little girl pulled out of a sewer on the six o'clock news."

By the time they arrived at Genesee and First, the drizzle had turned to ice and darkness shrouded the area. A tent covered the sewer to keep the public from looking on. The forensics trucks arrived at almost the same time as Zep, Al, Maddy, and Goldfarb, who stood inside the tented area to watch the forensics team work.

Maddy held her breath as one man used a long steel hook to pull up the sewer grate. Another took a flashlight, kneeled, and shined it inside the hole. His face told the story. Expressionless, he looked at Zep, nodded, then looked down at his feet, shaking his head.

Maddy walked up to the sewer and looked in and saw the white skin of a girl's naked body covered with thick, black sludge. She was face down, and her blond hair floated in the sewage. It was a most unholy sight, and feelings of finding Sarah Benning in the portable toilet came rushing back. *How can anyone do such a thing to a child? He's a fucking monster, a motherfucking monster.* She couldn't look any longer and had to walk away.

The people working the scene appeared lifeless. Each seemed to be in their own hellish solitude, as though it was one of their kids in the hole. Even Goldfarb looked white after looking in. He seemed to have lost his eagerness for the story.

"Who is going to tell the parents?" Maddy asked.

"I'll do it. I'll tell the parents," Zep said. Staying at the scene after the removal of Nancy Miles's body, Maddy waited for forensics to finish their work. Snow fell, and the crowd thinned out. It was almost 5:00 p.m. when she returned to the command center.

Looking around the empty gym, with half-filled cups of coffee strewn on tables, papers scattered on the floor, and all but emergency lights turned off, she thought, *That's it. The search for Nancy Miles is over.* It was as though law enforcement had been puppets on strings, held by a crazed puppeteer. Feeling hopeless as she drove home, Zep called. "Meet me at the office; we need to talk."

Making a U-turn, she got onto the expressway and headed into the city. When she walked into his office, she knew something terrible was coming down. *This will not be good.*

"Have a seat, Maddy." Hesitantly, she sat down. "It's time to look at where we are now," Zep said. "Two girls are dead, and thanks to our friends at the paper, the public believes we're incompetent. They've lost all confidence in us. The murderer is in complete control and playing a very public game. To make things worse, the mayor and sheriff were just here." He stopped, unfolded his arms, put his hands on his desk, and took a deep breath. *Here it comes,* Maddy thought.

"They've started micromanaging us and have ordered me to do something you will not like." Maddy's stomach was in her throat. "They want me to put Hawk Jenkins's composite picture in the paper as a suspect to make the public feel we're homing in on the murderer."

She flew off her chair. "What! That's bullshit! It'll fuck up everything."

"Maddy, sometimes we can't control things, and we have to adapt to the situation."

"But it will drive Jenkins deeper underground and make him harder to find. We're going to be flooded with calls from hysterical people, and they'll suck up all our resources. You know there's no direct evidence tying Jenkins to Nancy's murder. Why would you do this?"

"Everything you're saying is true. But they'll be bringing in other agencies now; the State Troopers, the Utica P.D., and we must face it, we're not in complete control anymore. How do you think I feel?"

She couldn't listen to any more of what Zep was saying. She shouted, "Did we do something wrong? Did we? If we did, tell me, because I don't know what it was."

"You're taking this way too personally. It's political now. Nancy Miles's uncle is a political bigwig, and he contacted the mayor. There's an election coming up this fall, and he's intimidated."

"But there are so many things that can go wrong by doing this," she said, shaking her head.

"I know, but maybe it'll buy us some time," Zep said.

"I just can't believe this," she said, facing away from Zep. She waited a moment before storming out of the room with her knee throbbing.

The next morning, the Observer-Dispatch plastered Hawk Jenkins's face on the front page. The headline read, *'Missing Girl Found Dead. Police Identify Suspect in Murder.'* A sting of betrayal ripped through Maddy, and she tossed the paper in the wastebasket. *Politics, fucking politics,* she thought. *We risk our lives, do all this work, just to have the mayor waltz in and undermine everything for his gain. It's just not right.* At that moment, she lost all enthusiasm for her work.

The Friendly Bean normally boosted Maddy's spirits when she was down. Before work, she sat hidden in a corner booth, alone, sipping her coffee while looking out at the street. Goldfarb was at the counter, chatting it up with Rusty.

"Hey, Maddy, you look like you just lost your best friend," Rusty called over when he saw her sitting alone.

"I'm fine," she said, feigning a perky tone, then quickly got up to leave.

Pushing through the motions of her job, the hours passed slowly. Filling her time with meaningless busy-work generated by countless calls from people who thought they'd seen Jenkins. That evening, at home, Samantha complained that her mother was so afraid she wouldn't let her do anything. "How soon will it be before you catch that guy so I can have my life back?"

"There are a lot of good people working on it," Maddy said. "We'll get him." *That's what I'm supposed to say, isn't it? But we have lost control, and Cupid is in the driver's seat.*

Like everything else in her day, dinner was a halfhearted effort. She fried up a few hot dogs and threw frozen French fries into the oven. As she and Amber ate at the kitchen table, her mind still reeling about the bullshit situation at work, Amber asked to go to a sleepover Thursday night. "There's no school Friday, and Abby's mom doesn't mind." Maddy hesitated, entertaining the same fear about Cupid Samantha's mother had. She finally agreed.

Later that evening, Maddy became suspicious when she overheard Amber on the phone talking about the sleepover with her father. "How did Dad get involved in your sleepover plans?" she asked her daughter.

"It was his idea."

Maddy seethed inside. Her stomach twisted while trying to act unbothered. "Are you finished with your homework?" she asked Amber.

"I just have some math."

"You can finish it in your room."

Once Amber was out of earshot, she called Jack. "I just found out you put Amber up to arranging a sleepover at Abby's. I know why you did it, and I'm so pissed I can spit."

"Come on, Maddy, all I want is to do is take you to dinner."

"It's not what you wanted I'm reacting to, Jack. It's how you did it. You manipulated Amber and me. Don't you realize that's the shit that drove me away when we were married?"

"So, what did you want me to do?" he said.

I can't believe he just asked me that question, she thought. "You could have called me and said there's a day off from school on Friday. If Amber goes on a sleepover Thursday night, would you like to do dinner?"

"I don't feel I can do anything right in your eyes," he said. "I'm sorry."

Even though Jack had stopped drinking, he still thought like an alcoholic, Maddy thought. He'd manipulate people even when he didn't have to.

"Look, Jack, I'm spent emotionally with all that's going on at work. Why don't we just bag the dinner thing for now and try another time?"

After a brief silence, without a word from Jack, Maddy realized she'd hurt him. He finally said, "Okay," and hung up.

The painful incident was reminiscent of similar blindsides when they were married. It was a record playing over and over. She wondered if marriage counseling years earlier would have made a difference, but it was too late now, she thought. *That train has left the station.*

Chapter 21

Another day in paradise, Maddy sarcastically thought, pulling her chair up to her desk to start another day. Ripping a hole in the plastic coffee cup cover, she scanned her desk, looking for a place to start. The phone rang. Lucy, the switchboard operator, said a call from Chicago was for her. "Put it through."

"Is this Maddy Reynolds?" a woman asked.

"Yes, who is this?"

"Joyce Bennett, Bob Bennett's wife."

"Oh, hi. It's been so long."

"I'm at the hospital with Bob. He had a heart attack, but he's going to be all right. The thing is, he insists on speaking with you. I tried to convince him not to call, but he won't take no for an answer. You know how stubborn he can be."

A gruff voice came on the line. "Maddy. It's me, Bob."

"Hey, what's going on with this heart attack thing?" she said.

"Ahh, these damn doctors won't let me go home. But I'm not calling about me. I've been having the weirdest dreams since I've been here, and you're in every one of them. Is everything all right with you?" She couldn't believe he asked her that. She hadn't spoken to him in over a year.

"I'm fine," she said, not wanting to worry him in his frail health. She loved the old man, but he'd be worried sick if he knew what was happening.

"Oh, okay, good," Bob said. He seemed surprised. "We haven't talked in so long. I guess I was worried. You know, because of the dreams and all."

"I'm sure there's a lot we can catch up on, but why don't we wait until you're back on your feet?"

"Sure, sure," he said. "And don't go worrying about me. I'm going to be okay." As she was about to hang up, Bob said, "And Maddy."

"Yeah."

"Are you sure everything's okay?"

"I'm sure, Bob." He was as real a friend as she'd ever had, and she hated fibbing to him. *I'll tell him everything as soon as he's better.*

When she hung up, her eyes rested on a pile of mail. The letter on top from the legal department caught her attention. The attorneys brokered an arrangement with the V. A. Hospital in Albany to gain limited access to Jenkins' medical information. "You may interview his psychotherapist, Dr. Julie Martino, but you cannot access Mr. Jenkins' physical chart."

Maddy immediately called Martino and set up a meeting for one o'clock that afternoon. She swung by Zep's office on her way out. Still pissed at him over the whole Jenkins's sketch-in-the-paper thing, she was relieved to find he wasn't there. She left a message with his secretary and headed out.

Road construction made the two-hour trip to Albany three hours. Her stress level redlined the entire way. *I can't miss this appointment.* She pulled into the V. A. parking lot flustered and ran to the meeting.

"I'm sorry I'm late," she said when she shook Martino's hand. The young, attractive psychologist seemed unbothered. Sitting across from her, she explained the murders of the two girls. "Hawk Jenkins is a chief suspect."

"Yes, I remember reading about what happened," Martino said. "I saw Mr. Jenkins in therapy for about eight months. He's a Vietnam veteran and came to me having depression, anxiety, anger issues, and occasional suicidal thoughts. Explosive episodes caused him to lose several close relationships, which added to his depression. During his time here, he seemed to make significant progress, but a little over a year ago, he suddenly stopped coming. I haven't seen him since."

Maddy looked up from her notebook. "Do you have any idea why he stopped coming?"

"It may have been because we touched on subject-matter he found too disturbing."

"Can you tell me what that was?"

"He came from an extremely dysfunctional family, was often beaten and once almost died. He felt a lot of conflict about it, and we never uncovered the root cause of why."

"We believe he's a heavy drinker and into child pornography," Maddy said. "Did he discuss any of that with you?"

Martino tilted her head thoughtfully and said, "Yes, excessive drinking was a means of self-medicating when depressed."

"And child pornography?" Maddy prodded.

"Near the end of our time together, he shared his difficulty with women and said he read pornographic magazines. But he did not mention child pornography."

Maddy went for the jugular. "Dr. Martino, I witnessed the discovery of the two girls. Someone brutally raped and sodomized them before strangling them and dumping them in the filthiest of places. Do you think Mr. Jenkins is capable of that?"

Without hesitation, Martino said, "No.!" Stroking her chin, she added. "That's just my opinion, of course, but Mr. Jenkins's problem involves reacting in anger to situations where he feels slighted. He might lash out at a woman whom he perceives has rejected him, but not at a child. I just did not see that in him."

Maddy thanked Julie and took Jenkins's last known address from her secretary before she left.

The neighborhood where he lived looked like a war zone. Kids played wildly in the street lined with small, run-down houses. An old man sat on the curbside, clutching a bottle, and a young girl pushed a baby carriage, with a toddler at her side. She pulled over in front of the house, and before she left the car, unsnapped the holster.

As she approached, the curtains move back, as though someone was watching her. When she knocked, no one answered. After a second try, the door unlatched, slowly opened, and a woman spoke through the cracked door.

"How can I help you?" she said cautiously.

Maddy introduced herself and said she'd like to speak with Hawk Jenkins.

"He doesn't live here anymore."

"Can I come in?"

"Do you have a search warrant?"

"No, I just want to talk."

After a moment's hesitation, the door slowly swung open, and Maddy stepped in. A playpen with a child about two stood staring, and an old man with an oxygen mask was asleep in a recliner. The place was small and untidy, but clean.

Moving a stuffed giraffe from a chair, the woman asked Maddy to sit.

"I'm Nicki, Harold's wife. And his name is not Hawk Jenkins; it's Harold Hawkins. He uses Hawk Jenkins so people like you won't come creeping around here, but somehow you found this address, anyway."

"When was he here last?" Maddy asked.

"It's been over a year. But now that the newspapers have covered their front pages with his picture, I'll probably never see him again."

"Do you have any idea where he is?"

"If I did, why would I tell you?"

"Well, it might save his life. Coming with me is the safest thing he can do."

"He didn't do those awful things to those little girls," Nicki said.

"How do you know that?"

"We have three daughters, and he would never harm a child," she said as she ran a hand over her eyes.

"They say your husband has an explosive temper."

"There's a big difference between having a temper and killing children," the woman snapped back.

Maddy paused at Nicki's words, which were consistent with Dr. Martino's sentiments. "I hope you're right," she said.

"Whether I'm right or wrong, he's still a marked man now."

"What do you mean?"

"In case you haven't noticed, child killers don't live too long, whether in jail or out," Nicki said, glaring at Maddy, as though looking right through her. The penetrating words brought back Maddy's anger at the mayor and chief for forcing Jenkins's sketch to be published. She felt a pang of guilt. As she got up to leave, she looked at the woman and could only say, "Thanks for your time."

Driving home, the notion that Jenkins might be innocent hit Maddy hard, and she called Zep. "I think we've gone down the wrong rabbit hole with Jenkins," she said. "I interviewed his psychologist and his wife, and neither thinks he's capable of killing a kid. They both seem like straight shooters, and they might be right. If they are, we've signed the wrong guy's death warrant."

"I started thinking that Jenkins might not be our man recently too," Zep said, with a hint of guilt in his voice. "If it's true, not only have we put his life in jeopardy, but we've got a serial killer on the loose and no clue about who the guy is."

Maddy thought the conversation with Zep was over, when he said, "Maddy, don't hang up. I know you're pissed at me for not putting up a fight about Jenkins, but I want you to know that I felt I had no choice but to do what I did. I was in a battle with the mayor and chief that I couldn't win. All I could do was retreat to fight another day. If they had taken us off the case and brought in an outside agency to run the show, where would we be then?"

She heard humility in Zep's voice and knew it must have been hard for him to speak those words. His authenticity was the quality she most admired about him, and at that moment, she forgave him. "I guess you did what you had to do," she said.

"See you tomorrow, Maddy."

That evening Maddy sulked as she wrestled with her belief that Jenkins wasn't Cupid. After Amber had gone to bed, she sat downstairs in the dark with a bottle of wine and listened over and over to "I Wish It Would Rain" by The Temptations. The bottle slowly emptied, and she had nodded off when the phone rang.

"Turn on Channel 3," Al said excitedly. "Something is coming on about Jenkins."

When the TV lit up, an announcer from a Binghamton news outlet was on a live feed to a local station. He stood at a barricade of cop cars, and in the background, a spotlight shined on a small white house.

"About an hour ago, police got a tip that a man wanted for the murder of two Utica girls is in that house," an announcer said passionately. "Earlier, when police approached, shots rang out. Thankfully, there are no injuries."

In the background, a heavily armed group of men dressed in military gear slowly walked in a formation behind an armored vehicle. "Jesus, what the hell are they going to do?" Maddy said out loud.

"I see canisters of tear gas being hurled into the windows," the announcer said, barely able to control his excitement. After a long pause, he continued. "I can see snipers on rooftops, and police behind that armored vehicle nearing the house."

In her inebriated state, she began talking to the television. "Why the fuck are you people doing that?"

"The vehicle is getting very close to the house now," the announcer said. Suddenly, repetitive popping sounds of automatic weapons rang out, and the nearly hysterical announcer bellowed, "The police are unleashing a hail of bullets. I can see holes in the door and walls, with windows shattered." When the barrage had stopped, only the night and its eerie silence stood alone in a cloud of smoke. A man dressed in fatigues, who had apparently entered the rear of the house, came out and waved his hands, showing that he had neutralized the shooter.

Slurring her words, Maddy cried out, "They just executed the poor bastard!" With the last of the wine on the bottom of her glass, she stood before the TV, and mockingly, held the glass high as though saluting and said, "Here's to you, Sheriff and Mr. Mayor. You just killed the wrong fucking guy." She slugged down the wine, and the negative thoughts that followed edged her closer into despair.

Chapter 22

After the Jenkins debacle, the investigation faltered, and Maddy fell deeper into a funk. Winter had entered its fiercest months, and by the end of February, the smallest tasks felt like a heavy burden. Her liquor store stops increased, and by March became a nightly ritual. She was in sweatpants and a sweater by five thirty, would make a quick dinner for Amber and herself, and after her daughter was asleep, she'd grabbed a good Merlot or Cab for her rendezvous with *Tempest on the Sea*. As Maddy's rut deepened, she wondered why she even bothered to try anymore.

Late one Friday night, as she worked on *Tempest*, and after she'd killed a bottle of wine, Maddy thought she heard tapping on the front window. It was a windy night, and she attributed the sound to the rhododendron in the front yard. But when the sound grew louder and took on a rhythmic beat, she realized only a human could make the cadence. "What the hell," she thought, stopped what she was doing, and tried to grasp what it might be. *Holy shit, that might be Cupid!*

With her mind in disarray from the wine, a shot of adrenaline sent her to the floor. She reached for the light switch, turned it off, and wondered where she had put her gun, but remembered it was in the car. Crawling to the window, she peeked out and saw the figure of a man ducking behind a bush. Ice cold fear ran through her veins as she ducked down. Dizzy, she momentarily lost track of what was happening.

She ran upstairs, grabbed the Beretta from her nightstand, and, in a matter of seconds, was on the front porch. This time, she saw nothing. She sat at the edge of a wicker chair with her eyes glued to the street until daylight. By the time the wine wore off, she questioned herself and wondered if the wine created the figure she saw. *Maybe I didn't see anyone after all.* The next morning, as she nursed a splitting headache with black coffee, Jack came by to pick up Amber for the weekend.

"You look terrible," he said. "I see you're getting back into the red wine."

"Please, save the sermon for another time." She realized the shoe was on the other foot. Jack was sober, and here she was, teetering on the brink of a drinking problem.

When she was finally alone, she went back to bed and spent the entire Saturday hiding in her solitude. At 10:00 a.m. on Sunday, Maddy's feet finally hit the floor. She slipped on a pair of sweatpants and a sweater, went downstairs to the porch for the paper, and glanced at the bush where she thought she saw a man. *A drunkard's folly,* she thought to herself, shaking her head in self-disgust. *I've got to slow down.*

After her third cup of coffee, the caffeine finally kicked in. Feeling a desire to pamper herself, she vowed to stay away from the pantry. *No wine today.* Returning upstairs, she took a long bath while mellowing out to a Rickie Lee Jones album. After getting dressed, she tidied up the bedrooms and changed the sheets on her and Amber's beds. Painting her nails in the comfort of her favorite bedroom chair, she opened the windows to let in the fresh air.

Later, feeling fatigued, Maddy curled up under a throw blanket on her bed and started a Stephen King book. It felt good to be in the comfort of her room. Jack dropped Amber off that evening, and feeling reinvigorated, she was excited to see them both.

"What smells so good, Mom?" Amber asked when she walked in.

"I made your favorite—turkey with stuffing, mashed potatoes, and gravy."

"Wow, this is great. What's the occasion?"

"No occasion. Just felt like cooking today."

After the kitchen clean-up, Amber and Maddy talked in the living room about Amber's friends, school, and her new boyfriend. They went up to bed together, and before turning out the light, Maddy pulled her journal from the drawer.

"Dad, I'm sure you know what it's like to have an investigation go bad. I am trying not to let it drag me down. Today was a good day, got lots of rest. I took care of myself, the home front, and your precious granddaughter. I'll try to keep it up, promise. Love, Maddy."

***

The next morning, Maddy looked forward to starting the first workday of the week with her new attitude, thinking she'd simply do the best she could with what she had.

It felt strange to stop by Zep's office after she had put him on ice for so long. They made small talk without diving too deep into the case, and, as she was about to leave, he said, "Oh, a call came in from Artie over at the Friendly Bean. A woman who lives upstairs keeps calling Rusty, complaining about some kind of noise. According to Artie, Rusty is at his wit's end and wants someone to talk to her. Our police counterparts are short-staffed today, and I told them we'd handle it. Since you seem to know the Bean well, I thought you'd be the person to calm things down."

She hadn't had a cupcake assignment since the Cupid killings started, and it felt good to get her mind on the mundane. When she arrived at the Bean, Rusty wasn't in, but Artie filled her ear with snippets of frequent phone calls from the old woman upstairs. "Frankly, I think she's nuts," he said.

Maddy wrote it all down and started upstairs. A short, eighty-year-old Tonya Petrov came to the door, and she was as sweet as strawberry shortcake. After Maddy introduced herself, Tonya led her inside, gesturing for her to sit.

"I'm so glad you're here, dear. I assume it's about the noise, is it not?"

"Yes. The proprietor of the Friendly Bean said you call several times a day, and he would like you to stop. Can you please explain what it's about?"

"I will, dear, but first, can I get you some tea?"

"No thanks," Maddy said, pulling out her notebook. The woman had her grayish-yellow hair wound tightly in a perfect bun that sat on top of her head. She had an ear-to-ear smile and perfect teeth. *Russian. I think she's Russian,* Maddy thought, trying to distinguish the nature of Tonya's accent.

"Before I begin, let me say that I am glad that you're involved. I hate to bother the people downstairs, and, until now, I had nowhere else to turn."

Oh great, Maddy thought, *now I'm going to get all the calls.*

"To understand the problem I'm facing, you'll need to know a little about my background."

Oh boy, here we go. The lady's a looney tune.

"I was a violinist with the New York Philharmonic, but had to stop performing ten years ago because arthritis in my hands would not allow it. But my ear is still good. It's always been extremely sensitive; in fact, I have perfect pitch," she said proudly. "Although my hearing was of significant benefit in the Philharmonic, it causes me problems now. Certain sounds I find very bothersome."

"Recently, a sound coming from the restaurant below causes me great distress. It is high pitched, piercing, and gives me a headache. I've talked to the proprietor, and he said he does not know what I'm talking about. It's intermittent and occurs only in the morning. I noticed it about a month ago. I am sure that you, with your detective, problem-solving skills, will figure it out and make it stop."

"So, you live here alone?" Maddy asked as she tried to understand more about Tonya.

"I do now," she said. "I used to have a lovely apartment in Manhattan and many friends. But when I left my position, my son, Arnold, made me move here to Utica. He felt it would be safer for me to be close to him."

"Why didn't you just move in with him?"

"With Arnold? Oh, goodness, no. He lives by himself. He's always been a loner and prefers it that way. But he's a good boy. He's taken over my finances for me, pays the rent every month, and makes sure I have enough money to do the things I enjoy."

"And what are they?"

"Well, I subscribe to several journals and periodicals in my field and, from time to time, make contributions to charities that I believe represent worthy causes. Why, just yesterday I sent twenty-five dollars to the local animal shelter."

Maddy suspected her son wasn't the angel Tonya was making him out to be. "How often do you see Arnold?"

"He stops by every week. He's a good boy."

"What does he do for a living?"

Tonya hesitated, looked down and to the side, then said, "I'm not sure."

Maddy wanted to say, *your son sounds like an asshole and a parasite*, but restrained herself. Although Tonya's story about the noise sounded bizarre and she seemed eccentric, Maddy felt sorry for her. In some ways, she reminded her of her grandmother: lovingly gullible. "Okay, Ms. Petrov. I'll try to swing back here and speak with the owner of the restaurant over the next few days. But, please, if you feel the need to call someone, call me and not him." She gave Tonya her card, and as she got up to walk out, the woman asked if she'd like to stay for lunch.

"I have much to do today, but thank you anyway."

It was approaching noon when Maddy left Tonya Petrov's, and instead of going directly back to the office, she drove onto the expressway. A gnawing feeling of being adrift had been growing in her gut all day, and instead of hiding in paperwork, she wanted to drive. Feeling lost in a desert without a fixed point on the horizon to guide her, her mind turned to the most reliable person she knew: Mary Thompson. As if on autopilot, the car headed to Mary's house.

On her knees, planting seeds in a newly tilled garden, Mary smiled when she saw Maddy pull in the driveway.

"Hello there, fine lady," Maddy said when she got out of the car.

"Old Man Winter sure didn't want to give up the ghost this year, did he?" Mary said. "Here it is June, hot as blazes, and I'm rushing to get my tomatoes planted. How are you, Maddy Reynolds?"

"Always better when I see you."

"Come on, let's have some lemonade." Mary got up off the ground slowly, her age seeming to fight against her, and together they walked to the house. Three red padded chairs around an enameled metal table in the kitchen overlooked a lush alfalfa field. Maddy sat as Mary took a pitcher of lemonade out of the fridge and poured two glasses. Caught up in the splendor of an intoxicating citrus fragrance, Maddy asked, "What is that scent?"

"Mock orange," Mary said, pointing to a vase of small white flowers by the window. "Beautiful, aren't they? I wait all year for them."

A hummingbird darted to a red feeder strategically placed outside the window, visible from all chairs at the table. It dashed away when a sudden strong wind blew the feeder sideways. A gust entered the window. "Oh, dear. It looks like a storm's brewing," Mary said, gazing out at a few dark clouds in the distance. The old woman carried a tray with two glasses of lemonade, spoons, and extra sugar to the table.

"I saw you in the paper," Mary said. "You killed a man." She said it empathetically, as though she knew it must have been traumatic. Maddy looked down silently.

"Pretty scary, isn't it?" she added. "You know, walking up to the gates of hell the way you did and looking in?"

"Indeed, it is," Maddy whispered.

"Talk to me, Child. There's more going on here, isn't there?"

"How did you know?"

"I'm not sure."

"Everyone thinks the man killed in Binghamton last week was Cupid and that the danger has ceased."

"But you don't, do you?" Mary said.

"No. The killer is still at large."

"You're right," Mary said. "I can feel his presence. He's very evil and exceedingly dangerous." Mary reached out and put her hand on Maddy's. The two friends sat quietly, looking out at the field, watching life come forth, and enjoying one another's presence. A soft knock at the front door broke the silence. "I wonder who that could be?" Mary got up and returned with a tall, slender girl of about fourteen.

"Let me introduce the two of you," Mary said. "Maddy Reynolds, this is Jodi Novak. Jodi, this is Maddy. She's a detective."

"Oh, hi," the girl said and put her hand out to shake Maddy's.

Wow, she's beautiful, Maddy thought as she shook the girl's hand. Jodi had Asian features: straight, jet-black shoulder-length hair, high cheekbones, a sharp jaw, and milky smooth, dark skin. Yet her eyes were as blue as sapphires, and the freckles on her face made her seem of Irish descent.

"Come sit with us," Mary said. "I just made some lemonade; would you like some?"

Jodi nodded as she sat. Maddy mused at the girl's quiet confidence. *There's a grace about her, and she seems to smile with her eyes*, Maddy thought.

"Jodi and I have been friends for a long time," Mary said, placing a glass of lemonade on the table. "We met at the Holy Ghost Baptist Church. But I don't see her there nowadays."

"We moved to Forestport," Jodi said softly. "My mother dropped me off on her way into Utica today." The girl sipped her lemonade. "I miss our talks," she said, looking at Mary with a smile.

A fly buzzed around Mary's head, distracting her. Jodi snatched it out of midair, placed it in a napkin, and crumpled it up.

"How did you do that?" Maddy asked.

"Oh, Jodi has a lot of interesting abilities," Mary said with a smile. "But you don't get to see them until you've known her for a while."

The young girl seemed embarrassed, smiled timidly, and took another sip of her lemonade. Maddy's curiosity ran rampant, and she wanted to know more about the strange girl but didn't want to embarrass her with questions. Seeming to know what Maddy was thinking, Mary said, "Jodi has an interesting background. Tell Maddy a little," she prodded.

"Am I a suspect?" Jodi said with a giggle and looked at Maddy, her blue eyes all lit up, obviously kidding. "I don't mind," she said. "I was born in Vietnam. My mother is Vietnamese, and my father was an American Marine, or so I'm told. I never knew him. In Vietnam, they called kids like me Children of the Dust, because our fathers were American soldiers, and they considered us as insignificant as dust." Maddy thought she detected sadness in her voice as she said this.

"When I was ten, my mother gave me to a family who ran a work camp because she couldn't find enough food for both of us. People in our village wouldn't swap or give us work because of who my father was. There were lots of kids like me at the camp. They made us work in rice paddies, and if we completed our work, they would feed us and provide us with a place to sleep. One night there was trouble, and I escaped with the help of another kid. Eventually, nuns took me in and an American family adopted me.

When she finished, she looked at Maddy and asked, "What about you? Where did you grow up?"

"I grew up in Chicago."

"Why did you come here?" Jodi asked.

"My parents died when I was young. I moved here to live with my grandma."

"So, we have something in common," Jodi said.

"What's that?" Maddy asked.

"We both got off to a rough start."

Intrigued, Maddy looked at the girl and smiled. Jodi seemed like a lake, calm on the surface, but deep. Though Maddy wanted to know her better, the day was getting away from her. "You're right," she said. "We both got off to a rough start." The wind nearly blew the front door from her hand as she started to leave. "It looks like all heck was about to break loose outside," she said.

No sooner had the words come out of her mouth than a flash of light lit up the sky. Thunder rumbled through the ground, shaking the walls, and the rain came down in buckets, peppering the windows. It was dark as night.

"Come on back in here," Mary said. "You can't go out in this." Maddy stepped back into the house and shut the door. "Now you two go in the living room and relax until this blows over. Jodi, why don't you tell Maddy more about your story?

Believe me, Maddy, it's well worth hearing. I'll go tidy up in the kitchen."

Jodi slipped off her shoes, sitting with her legs tucked under, across from Maddy.

"So, do you have any kids?" she nervously asked.

"I have one. Her name's Amber."

"She's lucky," Jodi said. Maddy looked, wondering what she meant, then noticed how the girl seemed to read her expression. "I mean, to have you as a mother," Jodi said. Maddy noticed her forehead wrinkle as if an unspoken thought caused her pain.

"What about your mother?" she asked.

After a long moment, Jodi said, "All I remember is the day she left me at the work camp. The rest I must have pushed out of my mind. I was ten. She said she'd come back, but she never did. I waited every day for her; every day." Jodi looked down, sighed, and shook her head, as if she were shaking off an unpleasant memory, then looked back over to Maddy and asked, "How did your parents die?"

"A car accident took my mom's life when I was ten, and a few years later, someone murdered my dad. He was a Chicago Police detective."

"Did God send you someone special?"

Again, Maddy wasn't sure what she meant and noticed how Jodi seemed to read her uncertainty. "You know, to help you through that sad time?"

"Oh, my grandma raised me, and yes, she helped me get through it."

"I had someone special sent to me, too," Jodi said. "His name was Cais, and he saved me."

Mary walked in carrying a tray of chocolate chip cookies and a pitcher, refreshed their glasses with lemonade, set the tray down, then quietly left the room.

Jodi continued. "Cais was sixteen and was like a brother to me. One night, another older boy crawled in my bed while I was sleeping. I felt his hands all over my body. He covered my mouth, and I tried to fight back, but he was powerful." Maddy watched Jodi clutch the cushion of the couch, and the veins of her hands swelled as she squeezed tightly. Her face twisted with what appeared to be fear, hatred, and rage.

"You don't need to continue if you don't want to," Maddy said.

"I want to. I do. It helps me each time I tell my story, and there are so few people who I can share it with." She took a deep breath, reached for a cookie, and nibbled at it. Outside, the rain settled into a steady downpour, although the thunder seemed to have moved on.

"It was so dark in that room," Jodi said. "I could hardly see anything. Then, I felt the boy lift off me, and heard scuffling. Something heavy hit the floor with a thud and all the kids woke up. Somebody turned on the light, and Cais stood next to me, bloodied around his neck. On the floor, a boy lay with his eyes open. He didn't move. He was dead."

With her stomach in knots, Maddy wrapped her arms around herself. Jodi changed positions, reached for her lemonade, and took a gulp.

"It was the beginning of the most frightening night of my life," Jodi said. "We ran out of the hut and into a marsh that spread out for miles behind the camp. It was dark, and men with dogs chased us. They got close, and I couldn't breathe. I froze. Cais had to force me into a stream, and we hid beneath the surface. I could see flashlights above, and I thought for sure they'd see us. We lifted our faces just enough to get air and went back down several times before the men moved on. Cais said that if they had caught us, we'd be dead. They had killed other kids for trying to run away."

Jodi paused, held her fingers to her forehead, elbow on a knee, as if in reflection, while simultaneously holding a cookie in her other hand. The rain had let up. *I could probably make it to my car without getting too wet*, Maddy thought, *but I'll be damned if I'm going to leave now*. Jodi reminded Maddy of herself, and she needed to hear her story out.

Putting the cookie back on the plate, Jodi started up again. "When the night had passed, the men were gone. We followed the stream to a road that led to Saigon. Once in the city, Cais taught me how to survive on the streets. Everything matters, he said. Who to talk to, and who not to. He showed me how to steal food and how to fight. He even taught me Sa Long Cuong, a martial art. I got to be rather good at it, too. Eventually, we got jobs and rented a room above a little store. It was the happiest time of my life."

"Enough about me." Jodi seemed self-conscious, as though she had been hogging the conversation. "Let's talk about you now."

"Oh no, you don't," Maddy said. "You need to finish. How did you get to the United States?" Jodi's story was like a magnet drawing Maddy in. Looking at her hands folded on her lap, the girl hesitated, as if unsure whether to continue, and finally started in again.

"One morning, while we slept, a loud banging awakened us. Cais opened the door, and it was the man who owned the building. He was frantic, and we could hardly understand him. When he calmed down, he said the North Vietnamese Army had entered the city, and he was taking his family, locking up the place, and we had to leave."

"We grabbed some clothes, and just like that, the dream was over."

"That must have been devastating," Maddy said as the wind blew rain against the window.

"It was," Jodi said. "We stepped out into insanity. People crowded the streets, pushed and shoved, argued, and fought. It was pure chaos. We knew we had to leave the city. Cais retraced the way we had come months earlier, and by late afternoon we had made our way out. We even found the stream that we traveled before reaching Saigon and followed it to a place where we thought we'd be safe."

"We rested while watching the road from a distance. Masses of bodies flooded out of the city. Every once in a while, the NVA drove trucks through terrified people, leading to some casualties. I'll never forget the horrified looks of the little kids as their parents threw them into the ditches to keep them from being run over."

Suddenly distracted when she looked at a brass clock on a table next to her, Jodi said, "Aren't you worried about getting in trouble with your boss?"

"No. They can do without me for a few hours."

Mary popped in from the kitchen. "The rain is slowing down. I'll be out checking on my plants. You two stay right where you are for as long as you'd like."

When she left the room, Jodi stood up, walked to the front window, and looked out. "You know, people in this country don't know what they have." A glint of sunlight broke through a few scattered clouds, and a deep blue sky showed itself. Returning to the sofa, she said, "That night, when darkness came, an oddly shaped moon hung in the sky and gave off a dim light. The sound of machine-guns in the city was constant, and I knew people were dying. Flashes of light and the rumbling of heavy artillery made everything seem unreal, like in the movies, but it wasn't. It was all happening. The night was alive with death."

As though the hardest part was about to come, Jodi took a deep breath. "Are you sure you're okay?" Maddy asked.

"Yes, I'm okay." She put her feet on the floor and wrapped her hands around her stomach as though she were holding back a powerful feeling, then continued.

"Cais had fallen asleep first, then I found some soft grass and laid down. Looking up at the night sky, listening to the sounds of death around me, I felt safe knowing he was nearby. I fell asleep, but the sound of feet crashing through the water snapped me awake. I couldn't tell where the sound was coming from and didn't know where to run. Unable to move, I froze." Maddy had an impulse to hold and comfort her, but something told her not to, and she stayed put.

"I felt hands squeezing my neck from behind and I couldn't breathe." Her voice quivered. "As I blacked out, the hands suddenly let go, and I fell to the ground. Cais fought the man. He used his skills to knock him down, then shouted for me to run." With her eyes wide and face flushed, Jodi said, "I found a place to hide in the tall grass where I could see Cais. A second man appeared with a gun. The guy on the ground got up, grabbed the gun, took a bottle from his jacket and drank. Then shot Cais in the head. The flash of light broke the darkness and Cais drifted to the ground like a leaf."

Jodi looked at the floor and softly said, "The men went through our things, took what they wanted, and disappeared into the marsh. I stayed where I was, afraid they might find me. I watched Cais's body all night, hoping it might move, but it didn't."

As she sat, a calm came over her, and she appeared serene. "At daylight, a gust of wind shook the surrounding reeds, and I heard a whisper, 'Go now Jodi, be brave and live.' I knew it was Cais speaking to me. I went back into the city, found the sisters of St. Michael's Missionary, and they took me in. When Saigon fell, we escaped on a helicopter to Cambodia. Eventually, I made it to America, and the Novaks adopted me."

"That's quite a story, Jodi."

"Yes, and it's all mine," she said.

Maddy was searching for the right words to say when a car horn beeped, and Jodi's head turned toward the door. "That's my mom." She stood up, stretched her back, and said, "I guess I have to go."

The two women walked to the front door. The storm had left the air clean and crisp. Before Jodi stepped outside, Maddy detected a look of embarrassment on her face. "Thanks for letting me bend your ear," she said meekly, as though concerned she had shared too much of herself.

When Maddy gestured to her with slightly opened arms, Jodi fell into her embrace and put her head on her shoulder. Feeling the warmth of the girl's body, Maddy thought, *The poor thing feels like she's just run a marathon.* "You are quite a person, Jodi Novak," she said. Jodi turned to leave, and Maddy added, "Let's be sure to have Mary get us together again soon."

"Yes, and next time, I want to hear your story," Jodi said. She smiled, turned, and walked to the car.

Maddy headed back to the office feeling uplifted as she drove. It was as though the girl's story forced her out of her shell, helping her see things from a different perspective.

Chapter 23

Nigel, 1957-1961, Chicago, Illinois

Sentenced to Greenville, Juvenile Detention Facility, from the very first day, Nigel feared he might never walk out. It was a prison for troubled kids. None of the residents were older than sixteen, but many looked over twenty-five, proudly displaying long hair, goatees, tattoos, scars, and bulging biceps beneath rolled-up sleeves. The heavy scent of ammonia on newly mopped floors and echoes of basketballs dribbling in the gym made Nigel realize he had entered a world that he knew nothing about. *I hate this fucking place.*

As his world slowly darkened, he felt lost, stayed to himself, and distrusted everyone, especially the counselors. They had a reputation for betraying kids who confided in them. He learned to deal with each day as it came, followed orders, and did what was necessary to stay out of trouble. When he was alone, he would think about life with his father. *No more sleeping until noon, no more adventures with the guys, and no more late-night talks over a beer with Dad. And all because of that fucking Jimbo rozzer.*

Things changed little as time passed, and each day seemed like an eternity. At night, tortured by his father's face begging for help as he lay dying, his thoughts always ended up with that fucking Jimbo cop. His mind, body, and spirit ached, and in time, all he wanted out of life was for it to end. *If this is all there is, I'd rather be dead, but killing yourself is easier said than done.*

As he sat in the game room one morning, staring at the walls as other kids played cards and ping-pong, one kid thundered out, "Hey, check it out." Nigel looked outside, where a laundry truck with its engine running and no one inside, was parked. "How much will you give me if I walk out of here, hop in, and take off?" the kid said.

"You are an idiot," another kid said. "If you took off, how could we give you any money?" Everyone in the room laughed, except Nigel. Instead, he focused on the exhaust pipe that was pumping carbon monoxide into the air. *That's it. That's how I'm going to do it.*

Like all vendors that delivered to Greenville, the laundry truck had scheduled times to arrive each week, and a designated time frame to exit the facility. Laundry deliveries were Mondays, Wednesdays, and Fridays, and for the following week, Nigel tried to calculate the time the truck was unattended. He determined the driver was in the building for a little over twenty minutes, but according to what he could research, dying from asphyxiation in a space the size of the truck would take much more time. To speed up the process, he thought of placing a plastic bag over his head and holding a hose attached to the exhaust pipe beneath it.

On Tuesday, before wood shop class, Nigel secured a length of hose from the scrap heap and, after dinner, stole a plastic bag from the kitchen. The night before he was to execute his plan, he lay in bed, reflecting on his life. He thought about the abuse endured from Mother and Gertie and how he'd freed himself by killing his sister. *It was the best thing that ever happened to me. It allowed me to live with Dad.*

Usually, when Nigel didn't sleep well, he would be short-tempered the next day. But Wednesday morning, he felt good. *Only a few more hours and all this will be over.* He watched the parking lot from the game room and waited for the laundry truck to appear. It pulled in right on time. Waiting until the driver had wheeled his last load into the building, he resolutely walked to the restroom, grabbed the hose and plastic bag he'd hidden in the trash basket, and strolled to the loading dock. Crouching next to the truck to stay out of view, he shoved the hose over the hot exhaust pipe. Looking around carefully to be sure no one could see him, he hopped in the back with the other end of the hose and shut the door.

"All right, almost there," Nigel said out loud to himself. Laying on his side, he slipped the bag over his head, and jammed the carbon monoxide-spewing hose underneath. He took his first breath, gagged, and his eyes burned. He had to cross his arms over the tube to hold it in place. A piercing pain ripped through his head as he forced himself to breathe the poison gas.

Entering a dreamy place, he found himself back in the alley with his father while he died. He looked at his dad's twisted face, eyes filled with pain, begging for help. Unlike before, Nigel understood the words his father mumbled: "Destroy that motherfucker." He looked over and saw Jimbo looking on, laughing, and felt an overwhelming rage. Before he could charge the shooter, Jimbo's voice changed to a woman's voice. *Fuck, that's Mother*, he realized as panic ran through him. Finally, Jimbo's face transformed into Gertie's face, and the voice became Gertie's cackle. She screamed at him, "You killed me, Nigel." He shook with fear. Suddenly, a bright light shocked him out of his dream.

"I've got a pulse here," a voice said. "He's coming out of it." A hand was being held over his face with a plastic mask, and the air he breathed felt like pure spring water, crisp and clean. He heard a siren, saw faces looking down, and a light shined brightly above him.

I fucked up. It didn't work. Despite having a parched throat, burning eyes, and a raw esophagus, he stayed alive. His body shook as the medics held him down. His mind was in a haze, but he remembered the vision of his father and the words that he spoke: "Destroy that motherfucker." At last, Nigel had a purpose in life — killing that cop, Jimbo.

***

After a week in the psychiatric unit that seemed more like a hotel than a hospital, Nigel felt better and had become more sociable. His therapist commented in his session that his progress was remarkable. Smiling, as though grateful for the help he'd received, deep down, he knew it wasn't the therapy that put the bounce back in his step. It was the new sense of purpose his father gave him when he commanded he must kill Jimbo. With lots of time to contemplate his mission to find and kill the Chicago detective, like in chess, he called upon strategy to accomplish his goal.

And to think, I almost killed the wrong guy — me. He made peace with himself and decided not to hide from the person he was, the one whom he once considered his dark side. His father's words changed all that, and he vowed to never again doubt what his inner self told him to do.

Scrutinizing the words from his vision, he realized his father didn't say, kill that motherfucker, but said, destroy that motherfucker. Nigel decided that to destroy was higher than to kill, and he not only needed to kill Jimbo but his entire family, wiping his seed from the earth. *This is going to be the longest chess match ever*, he thought, realizing the enormity of the task. *This might go on for years, even decades. But so what? There's a lot I can do in the meantime.*

After his nineteenth birthday, and a long stint of doing and saying all the right things, the authorities changed Nigel's placement to a half-way house. He was on probation, quickly secured his release and moved into his own place. *Finally*, he thought. *Fuck all those assholes.* He felt like a bird let out of a cage, and not a parakeet either, but a vulture.

A cheap apartment near where he and his father used to live, and a job as a fry-cook-in-training at the Jolly Roger greasy spoon, Nigel was ready to start his new life. About his apartment, he would say, *hot in the summer, cold in the winter, and smelling like rat shit.* He'd laugh, thinking the apartment and job were only temporary. *No fuss, no muss, and off the radar. Perfect.*

I work with a bunch of morons. He laughed to himself one afternoon as he tossed a couple of burgers in the hot, smoky kitchen, listening to his co-workers' senseless chitchat. "Hey, check it out," one of them nudged him. A beautiful girl about fourteen had walked in with a woman that looked to be her mother. She had long, brown hair, skin as smooth as a baby's, and a smile that lit up the restaurant. Her clean presence, pink dress, and knee-high socks that went halfway to heaven froze him in place.

"Your burger's burning, man." Nigel quickly snatched the burgers from the griddle and looked back at the girl's long neck, smooth skin, and a smile that drove him absolutely crazy. He popped a rod just looking at her. When she got up to leave, he ran to the window, hoping to see the silhouette of her body through her dress in the sunlight. *What a babe,* he thought. *Perfection on two feet.*

The very next week, the girl and her mother walked in and sat at the same table. For weeks, the routine repeated itself until one afternoon, her mother left her alone and walked across the street to the department store. Although Nigel hadn't planned on it, he walked by the table, and when she looked up and smiled, he instinctively said, "Hi. I've seen you in here every week. My name is Mark." *Mark? Why the hell did I say that?*

"My name is Patty Bronson," she said warmly, causing Nigel to sit down to conceal the bulge in his pants.

"Oh look," he said, nodding toward the window as a fat lady walked by with a small bulldog on a leash. The woman appeared as though someone inflated her with helium, and the bulldog wore a pink collar matching her dress.

"They go together well, don't you think?" Nigel said dryly.

Patty broke out laughing, put her hands to her face, and blushed. *I think she likes me,* Nigel marveled.

"Well, I have to go, but maybe I'll see you here next week," he said.

"You will. I come here every week after my piano lesson."

When he walked away, the same strange ambivalence he experienced with Tamatha overwhelmed him. It was a sense of arousal yet hostility, a powerful attraction, and a loathing. It bothered him, and he could make no sense of it, so he put it out of his mind.

Over the next several weeks, when Patty's mother left her alone, Nigel came by the table to chat. Finally, he got up the nerve to take the next step. He asked where she lived and when she said near Ashton Park; he asked if she'd like to meet there Saturday for a walk.

"Okay," Patty said with a smile.

He floated home from work with Patty on his mind. Yet deep down, a battle raged between his feelings of titillation and his rage. As he lay in bed that night, he wanted her more than he hated her and imagined she was lying next to him with his hand inside her underpants. Ejaculating without touching himself, in an instant, a dark and little-known part of him reared its head. He became filled with rage. It bothered him that another person had the power to make him lose control like that. Perplexed, he rolled over and ruminated about what was wrong with him until falling asleep.

The next morning, while at work, he tried to think of things to do at their meeting. By ten a.m., he called the whole thing off. *I have a lot of other stuff to do tomorrow.* Feeling relief the rest of the morning, by early afternoon, second thoughts boomeranged around in his head. *Shit. If I don't show up, I'll have blown it with her.* Saturday morning, he rolled over and fixed his gaze on his greasy work clothes hanging on a chair next to his bed. *If I don't go, then all I am is a fry cook. I have to go.*

An unexpected excitement, warmth, and even tenderness welled up within him as the morning went on. He wanted to do something beautiful for Patty. Inside his dresser was a box of vintage Valentine's cards he stole from his mother's room. Handmade and pretty, they made him think of life the way he wished it would be. He went to the drawer, picked out his favorite, and signed it "Mark."

Ashton Park was small, but beautiful. In a glance, he saw several lawns, park benches, clumps of trees and bushes, some footpaths, and in the center, a pond with swans floating in the middle. Patty sat on a bench wearing a blue dress and a ribbon in her hair. "This is a beautiful place," he said when he walked up to her. She turned and smiled the same way as she had in the Jolly Roger restaurant, arousing him as she had before. As he tried to think of something to say, he glanced at the pond.

"Aren't those swans beautiful?" he said.

"Oh my, yes, they are."

"Would you like to walk over?"

"Sure."

They strolled together along a path. Patty put her arm through his, and a warm feeling was like nothing he'd experienced. Further along the way, she laid her head on his shoulder. Rockets ignited from his feet up through to his head. Before them, the trail wound into a wooded area thick with bushes on both sides.

He heard a whisper say, "She really wants it, Nigel. Now's your chance. Don't be a pussy." As they entered the bush-covered area, he felt his heart pound, stopped, turned, and slipped the valentine out from under his shirt. He handed it to Patty. "This is for you."

"Oh, how sweet," she said. As she opened the envelope, he looked around to see if anyone was nearby. There wasn't. Grabbing her shoulders and pulling her close, he kissed her hard on the lips. His teeth bumped hers, and she appeared stunned. Pulling back, she looked at him, confusion and anger in her expression. The heat of humiliation warmed Nigel's face, and he tried to kiss her again, even harder this time. "No, stop!" she said sternly. He put his hand over her mouth, dragged her into the bushes, and threw her down.

The thud of Patty's body when it hit the ground, and the look of shock in her eyes, frightened him for a moment. It was as though he was watching himself from above. *Don't stop. You can't stop now*, he heard himself say, or maybe it was that other voice, he wasn't sure. He forced his way on top of her. The girl fought back, screaming. Putting a hand over her mouth and the other under her dress, he ripped off her underpants, and felt all the places he had fantasized about, but they didn't feel as he imagined.

Unzipping his pants, he penetrated her violently as his lust turned to rage. When Gertie's face flashed before him, he thrust himself into Patty even harder. His erection had become a weapon, and the more he rammed it, the clearer Mother and Gertie's faces became.

Pulling out, making sure he left no semen, Patty squirmed, got free and bit his hand. She screamed high-pitched, and Nigel panicked, grabbed her neck with both hands and squeezed tighter and tighter, trying to shut her up. Her body twitched violently and then went limp. The look on her face reminded him of Gertie when she lay on the kitchen floor.

Standing up, and looking around, he didn't see anyone and didn't think anyone saw him. He zipped up his pants and looked down at Patty's half-naked body. Blood oozed from beneath her dress. Somehow, her death did not seem real. He turned his attention to what he had to do next, which was to get out of the park, but needed to wait for an opportunity.

The sky became dark, and rumblings of thunder were getting close. He crouched down next to the girl and waited for the storm to come. Lightning hit a tree across the pond, and a loud clap of thunder shook the ground. A steady rain fell, and within minutes, people exited the park. *Now is the time.*

Before he left the body, he took the valentine from the mud, wiped it on her dress, and placed it on her stomach. He picked up her torn underpants and tucked them in his pocket as a souvenir. Several people, including Nigel, covered their faces as they scurried out of the park in the downpour that afternoon. No one seemed to notice him as he walked home. For the rest of the day, he listened to the radio for news about what he had done, but there wasn't any.

The incident appeared in the newspaper the next day, but with no mention of immediate suspects. It was business as usual for the rest of the week, but he was on edge the entire time. As the days passed, according to the newspapers, the police had become more and more perplexed. One morning, however, a breakthrough came over the radio.

While he was eating breakfast, an announcer said that they had charged Ramon Sanchez, a maintenance man at Ashton Park, with the murder of Patty Bronson. He had apparently been working the afternoon of the crime and had a prior sexual assault conviction. "Police have reason to believe he entrapped the girl during a rainstorm, raped her, then strangled her to death," the announcer said. *Poor chap*, Nigel thought, *he's being used, I'd say.*

After several months of legal procedures, the court threw out Sanchez's case when they established he was in a car with several co-workers waiting out the storm at the time of the murder. By that time, the story had become old news, and from time to time, only a small article about it appeared on the back pages. His confidence grew that he was in the clear, and put the incident out of his mind.

Chapter 24

Maddy, 1979, Utica, New York

Saturdays were for housework. Maddy lugged a basket of laundry from the basement, sat in the kitchen, and turned on an oldies station as she folded. The phone rang.

"Mom, can I stay at Abby's one more night?"

"Amber, that's two nights in a row. I don't think that's fair to Abby's mom. And besides, you don't have clean clothes for tomorrow."

"Her mom said it's okay with her, and Abby has extra stuff I can wear."

Realizing her hesitancy was because of fear of the serial killer loose in the community, Maddy didn't want to be overreactive, and gave in. After hanging up, she looked at the basket of unfolded clothes, peeked at the sunny afternoon, and took a break. Grabbing a glass of lemonade, she went to the front porch.

Aww, that feels good, she thought as she plopped into a soft-cushioned wicker rocking chair. Watching two boys playing catch out front, the intoxicating scent of a Linden tree filled the porch. Her troubles drifted away as she closed her eyes for a moment, and when she opened them, the boys were walking away.

The phone rang again. She got up to get it, thinking it was probably Amber, but no one answered. When she returned to the porch, a rolled-up newspaper lay on the floor, and wondering what it was, she picked it up. A small, white, fluffy ball fell to the floor. It was a dead kitten.

What the fuck! She looked twice to be sure her eyes weren't playing tricks. Slowly, she kneeled and unfolded the newspaper. It was a recent edition of the Observer-Dispatch. The headline read, <u>Cupid One-Ups Cops Again</u>.

It's Cupid! Thinking he must be watching her, her heart pounded as she looked outside. No one was there. The phone rang again. With her hand trembling, she reached for the receiver. A distorted voice said, "Check Amber's backpack."

Her knees weakened. She dropped the phone and looked for the backpack. "Where the hell is the damn thing?" she yelled as she ran through the downstairs. Finally vaulting up to Amber's room, she found it on the floor near the closet. Emptying the bag on the bed, she prayed no valentine was inside, because if there was, Amber was already in the monster's grip.

Pulling out folders, books, papers, pencils, and gum wrappers, but no valentine. Something white in a side pocket made her heart stop. *Oh my God, no!* She slowly lifted an envelope.

'Detective Reynolds' was written on the outside. Carefully, she ripped an end and slipped out a plain sheet of paper. The note said, 'Unbeknownst to you, sweet dear, I am always near. Cupid.'

Sweat beading on her forehead, she forced herself to breathe. Again, the phone rang, and she ran downstairs as her terror turned to rage. Picking up the receiver, she screamed, "Listen, motherfucker, if you touch my daughter, I'll make you suffer before I kill you."

"Maddy, what's going on!" It was Zep. Leaning against the wall, she slid to the floor with the phone still in her hand. Barely able to catch her breath, she eked out: "Cupid…Amber."

"I'm on my way," Zep said.

Sitting on the floor with her forehead resting on folded arms propped up by her knees, she tried to collect her thoughts. In an instant, it hit her, *Amber! I've got to call Amber.*

"Mom…what's going on?" her daughter said calmly.

Maddy stammered, not wanting to alarm her daughter. Trying to come up with a reason for the call, she finally said, "Are you sure you don't want me to bring you some clothes?"

"No, really, Mom, I'm fine."

"Okay, just checking. Love you." She hung up. *Cupid's trying to fuck with my head.* She ran to the porch with her Beretta, thinking, *Why me? Why is he doing this to me?* An unmarked car pulled in front, and Zep and Al jumped out.

"Working Saturdays, boys?" Maddy said, trying not to act unhinged. Zep and Al didn't smile. They listened as she explained what had happened. Al slipped on a pair of plastic gloves and placed the dead kitten and newspaper into evidence bags. Zep dialed a number to check on arrangements he had set in motion for Maddy's protective surveillance.

"What's that all about?" she asked.

"You're under protective surveillance now, Maddy. There's no way around it. A killer has targeted you. Amber too. Where is she now?" She gave him the address where Amber was, then angrily said, "Great, now I won't be able to make a move without someone in my pocket."

"You'll always have another cop near you," Zep said. "You can work, but not alone. That's the way I want it. No arguments. Amber will have someone assigned to her as well."

"You mean like that?" she said, pointing to an unmarked car pulling up in front of the house.

"Yep, just like that," Zep said.

"Who's in the car?" she asked.

"Bud Renshaw," Al said. Zep looked up at Al, then over to Maddy, and the three laughed.

"Bud Renshaw! How did that happen?" Maddy asked.

"He heard about what was going on and volunteered," Zep said.

"I guess I should feel honored."

"Actually, ever since the Bowls situation, he's been a different guy," Al said. "I suppose we have you to thank for that."

Aware that Al and Zep were taking time away from their families to help her feel safe, she hated to burden them. Yet the close call with Cupid severely shook her and she wasn't ready to let them leave.

"Would you guys like something to drink? I've got Coke, beer, and coffee." When she said 'coffee,' their eyes lit up. She went to the kitchen, started a pot, and brought back a tray with three cups, silverware, milk, and sugar.

"Why did you call me earlier?" Maddy asked Zep as she set the tray down.

"To tell you that you were right about Jenkins. We got into his medical record. Over the years, he had become impotent. The medical experts say there was no way he could have raped those girls." Zep turned his face away sheepishly. Not being a person to rub it in, Maddy said nothing, but felt vindicated.

Al broke the uncomfortable silence. "So, what happens now?" he asked.

With an expression as serious as death, Zep said, "He's about to strike again."

With looks of bewilderment, Maddy and Al looked at each other. "Why do you say that?" Al said.

"Cupid does nothing without a purpose. What he did today sends a message he intends to strike soon. But I don't understand why he's focused on Maddy. He's inviting her into his world."

"Maybe he wants to torture me before he kills me," Maddy said, semi-jokingly. Zep and Al glanced at each other.

"I think it's because she's a woman," Al said. "He hates women."

It was getting dark, and her stomach was still churning. "I can't believe that Cupid got close enough to Amber to put an envelope in her backpack," she said. She couldn't shake the thought.

Finally, she said, "You guys have been great for staying with me this afternoon, but I'll be okay now. I have Bud Renshaw in front of my house and Mr. Beretta at my side," she said, forcing a smile.

Before they left, Zep and Al told her to call them at home if she wanted to talk. As soon as they drove off, Jack called, and she explained what had happened. His ordinarily calm demeanor exploded into a panic.

"I'm bringing Amber to my house tonight," he said.

"Think about what you're doing, Jack. She's safe at Abby's. Zep is assigning a unit to that house; it's probably already out front. All you're going to do is alarm her. Do you really want to do that?"

Jack sighed. "Okay…okay. But I'm going to stay in my car where I can monitor that house tonight, unit or no unit." Maddy knew she couldn't stop him and, deep down inside, was glad he was doing it. *He drives me crazy, but he's a wonderful dad*, she thought.

Before crawling into bed that night, she glanced out at the street and saw Bud in his car eating a sandwich. *How the worm turns*, she thought. She covered up, pulled out her journal, and wrote, *Dad, a serial killer is targeting me, and I don't know why. Please watch my back. Maddy.*

Chapter 25

Nigel, 1964, Chicago, Illinois

On days off, Nigel enjoyed eating breakfast at the Fiddle-Dee-Dee greasy spoon restaurant just down the street from his apartment. As he devoured the Hungry Man's Special, his mind drifted to finding a new love interest.

He had accepted what he once considered an alien force within himself. No longer feeling shame for his violent sexual encounters, he reasoned, *Hey, some guys are fags, and some guys, like me, prefer them young. So big fucking deal.*

Through trial and error, he had perfected an approach to wooing young ladies by taking them to abandoned shacks in the woods, where only trees and rabbits could hear their screams. He always had a location or two available for indulging his every desire and fantasy.

Jojo, his new assistant, was stupid but loyal and aspired to be just like him. Nigel discovered he could manage his exploits more effectively when he had someone he could command. Jojo had a malleable mind, and Nigel was his idol.

As he glanced at a newspaper lying on the counter, a headline caught his attention, distracting his reverie. 'Renowned Detective to Head Bronson Rape-Murder Investigation.' The article mentioned James Reynolds, nicknamed Jimbo, was taking the lead on the stagnated murder.

Oh my, how convenient. I'm on a lucky streak. I'm off probation; the Bronson investigation is going nowhere, and I just made big bucks selling used car parts from a boosted vehicle. Now even Jimbo is at my doorstep. I'll be damned.

Believing the full-court-press the police were putting on the Patty Bronson case could lure his father's killer, Nigel began devising a plan. Jimbo's partner, Bob Bennett, however, was a problem. *He's experienced, tough, and old school, like Reynolds. I've got to get Bennett out of the picture.*

His plan went down as smooth as ice cream. He wrote a letter to the chief of police, pretending to be a journalist working on a story about crime in the city, and the chief took the bait, ordering Bennett to go to the Grand Hotel and meet the fictitious journalist. At about the same time, Nigel contacted Jimbo, and said a man who might be the child killer was at a cabin in the woods north of the city, and gave the location.

On that bleak, overcast morning outside a shack in the woods, Jojo played solitaire, talking to himself as Nigel stared out a window at the road. Every time Jojo made a play, he'd laugh to himself and make a snorting sound.

"You're driving me nuts with that noise," Nigel barked. "You sound like a pig inhaling slop. Knock it off."

He turned back to the window, and a glint of light caught his eye. "Shit, was that a car? See what you made me do." An unmarked Chicago Police vehicle pulled into the front yard.

"Jojo. Get in place. The cops are here." With instructions to shoot the shortest cop, he complied. Jimbo was six-foot-five, and Nigel wanted him all to himself.

Hiding in a closet, Nigel heard car doors clunking shut. *There are two of them. I hope Jojo doesn't fuck this up.*

Through the slightly opened closet door, he saw Jimbo and a junior detective walk up to the house. After three knocks with no answer, the two walked in with guns drawn. Nigel watched as Jimbo went to the left and the other cop to the right, where

Jojo waited. A loud bang rang out. Jimbo darted past the closet toward the sound, and Nigel snuck out, tiptoeing from behind. The young detective lay spread out on the floor. As Jojo aimed at the experienced cop, the detective was too fast, put two slugs in his chest, and dropped him with a crash.

Kneeling next to his comrade, Jimbo felt for a pulse. Nigel came up from behind and plunged a knife into the back of his neck. The big man screamed, stood and arched his back. Enjoying the crunching of steel against vertebrae and bone, Nigel twisted the blade to the left and right. The detective finally dropped forward to the floor. Watching the body twitching as blood pooled around the man who had killed his father, he put his face close to him.

"Fuck you, Reynolds. That's for killing my father. I want you to know I'll be coming to kill your daughter, too."

Like he was dead lifting five hundred pounds, Jimbo made a straining sound, and his face elongated as he struggled to get up. But his body gave way, and his head flopped to the floor. Nigel took out a valentine and placed it on his back.

Grabbing his bag, he ran out the back door. Hopping in a stolen car, he drove to O'Hare International Airport. Satisfaction filled him as he realized he had accomplished a significant part of his father's assignment, despite the task not being fully complete.

Chapter 26

Maddy, 1979, Utica, New York

Rolling with the punches wasn't easy for Maddy, and protective surveillance put her to the test. Each morning, a squad car waited to drive her to work, and in the evening, someone drove her home. Detectives alternated, and although no one complained, she felt like an invalid.

"I guess you're my babysitter today," Maddy said to Allison when she walked out of her house to the car that morning.

"Come on, don't make it bigger than it is," Allison said. "Would you like to drive together or separately?"

"Why don't you follow me?" Maddy said. "I want to stop by the Bean and pick up cinnamon rolls for everyone at the office. It's the least I can do for all my taxi-driver comrades. Do you mind?" Maddy asked.

"Cinnamon rolls? Don't mind at all."

They pulled up in front of the Friendly Bean, and before entering the restaurant, Maddy walked to Allison's car and said, "I want to check in on the old woman upstairs while I'm here. Okay with you?"

"No problem," Allison said.

Maddy came out, laid a box of cinnamon rolls on her passenger seat, and headed upstairs to check on Tonya.

"Oh, what a pleasant surprise. I am so glad it's you," Tonya said when she saw Maddy. "Won't you come in and sit?"

"Not today. I just want to see how you're doing."

"I am just grand. Haven't heard that awful sound in a week."

She started chatting about her trips to the doctor for various ailments and then mentioned how her son had taken her to see a symphony in Syracuse. "I hardly ever get to see him lately. He seems to disappear for weeks at a time, but last Saturday, he was at my door with the tickets. It turned out to be a most enjoyable evening."

"Wonderful," Maddy said. "If you need me, you know where I am."

Al stuck his head around the corner of her cubicle when she reached her desk. "Guess who wants to meet with us in his office?"

Maddy laughed. When they reached Zep's office, he stood with his arms folded and face muscles bulging. Looking like he was about to explode, he said, "I want to get my head wrapped around where we are with the Cupid investigation. I got a call from a bigwig at the State Troopers, and apparently, the mayor requested they send in an 'experienced' detective to help with the case." Al and Maddy sat down.

***

"The Utica police will get more involved now, too." Pacing back and forth, he continued. "My full-time job will involve coordinating information for these other agencies." He sat in his chair and took a deep breath, as though he was resigning himself to being micromanaged.

Lost in reflection, Zep suddenly sat up and said, "Before we have outsiders crawling around, second-guessing everything we're doing, let's look at where we are right now." He stood up and leaned back on his desk. "We've been chasing the wrong rabbit. Jenkins led us down a hole that's gone nowhere, and we've lost the scent of the actual killer. We're back at square one." Scratching his head like he was trying to jog loose a good idea, he finally said, "We need to go back to the beginning and start over. Al, it's back to the record room."

"Maddy, go through the notes of everyone who has worked the case. Look at the interview affidavits and try to find gaps. You know, things that didn't get followed up on; anything. There's got to be something we've missed."

Carrying an armful of folders to her desk, she plopped them down. Culling through the documents was tiresome work. She took several breaks to keep from falling asleep. At lunchtime, she grabbed a tuna sandwich and ate at her desk. By four o'clock, her eyes were falling out of her head, and as she sat back in her chair yawning, Zep burst in wide-eyed.

"We got a call about a missing girl in Oriskany. Al's gone to City Hall to chase down some documents, so you and Allison need to handle it."

Driving out of the city, Maddy cracked open a window as Allison read Zep's notes aloud.

"The girl's name is Candice Bishop," Allison said. "She's ten years old. About 2:40 this afternoon, she rode her bicycle to visit a friend five hundred yards away. After thirty minutes, the mother got a call from the friend's mother asking where Candice was. Mrs. Bishop drove up and down the road looking for her daughter, but there was no sign. I know the road," Allison said. "There's not much on it. A car could have hit her and she could be lying in a ditch."

"This sounds too familiar," Maddy said. Allison asked if she was thinking of the Sarah Benning case, and Maddy nodded.

Arriving at the Bishops' house, a late afternoon breeze blew across an open field. The sound of half a dozen high-pitched wind chimes clamored as they approached the farmhouse. A swing tied to the limb of a tree twisted and turned, as if waiting for someone dear to return.

A tall, lean man in his thirties opened the door. "Come in," he said. Although calm, he couldn't entirely hide the fear in his eyes.

"I'm Tom Bishop," he said. "I'm Candy's father." He led them to a family room adorned with photos from Christmas mornings, birthdays, and vacations. Somewhat out of place was an unusually well done, highly detailed pencil drawing of a dog.

"Who is the artist?" Maddy asked.

"Candice is gifted," Tom said. Maddy made a note.

They entered a large room, where a frail-looking woman with long black hair sat gazing out a window, twisting a handkerchief with both hands.

"Judy, this is Madison Reynolds and Allison Abbott from the Oneida County Sheriff's Department."

The woman got up and gingerly walked to the detectives. "Please find my daughter," she begged. With her head cocked back and eyes half-closed, she whimpered, "She's only ten and has never been away from us…never." Tom put his arm around his wife, trying to console her.

"We'll do everything possible to find her," Maddy said. "Right now, while it's still light, we need to check the road between your house and your neighbors. We'll be back."

Maddy and Allison walked on opposite sides of a five-hundred-yard span of the road between the houses. The sun glowed a pinkish-red as it set over vast fields of corn. Halfway between the houses, on Maddy's side, stood a single tree with branches extending over the road. They walked slowly, inspecting bushes and tall grass. On Maddy's side, near the mid-way point, a culvert with standing water and white waterlilies surrounded the tree.

As they approached, the fully leafed tree branches blocked the sun, making it challenging to examine the ground cover. Stopping to look carefully at each segment of the lily patch,

Maddy noticed a slight disturbance where the lilies seemed uneven.

"Allison, do you see that?" she said, pointing.

"I think so."

Maddy slid down the side of the embankment. Cold, muddy water seeped into her shoes from the muck below as she sloshed toward the disrupted lilies. A glint of light reflected off an object beneath the surface. Passing her hand along the bottom, she felt something hard. Pushing forcefully, it wouldn't move. She grabbed what felt like a steel bar and yanked until a suction-sound of mud releasing, moved the object. It broke free, and up from the depths came a parent's worst nightmare — a little girl's bicycle.

"Aww, Jesus," Maddy moaned, as she held up the pink, mud-covered bike, its streamers dripping with silt. Allison, on one knee, shook her head, looking to the side, as if unwilling to accept what the object meant. Maddy waded toward her and handed up the bike, then climbed back onto the road.

"A car has hit the child," Maddy said. "Her body has to be out here somewhere. We should probably start looking for it."

"Maybe we should let forensics do that," Allison suggested.

"You're right. Of course."

They leaned the bicycle against the tree and returned to the car to call in. Maddy explained to Zep what they found, and that it might be a hit and run. "Maybe so," Zep said, "but investigate as though it might be an abduction."

The two detectives decided it would be best for only one of them to communicate with the Bishops. Allison waited by the car while Maddy trudged up to the house. Tom opened the front door and came out to the porch. After a few deep breaths, Maddy said, "Mr. Bishop, we found a child's bicycle by the oak tree."

Tom turned his head, looking toward a field across the road. A burgundy streaked sky marked the end of the day. When

Maddy described the bike, he looked back and nodded his head, confirming it belonged to his daughter, then looked away again.

Screams rang out from the house where Judy had been listening from the front room. "Oh my God, oh my God, my poor baby."

Tom rushed to her as Maddy patiently waited for the woman to calm herself. "It's important that I gather more information to cover all possibilities," she said. "Would you like me to wait outside for a while?"

Judy pulled away from Tom and shook her head. "No. Come in," she said, wiping her eyes and nose with a handkerchief. Maddy stepped inside, and they sat down together.

She asked them questions about Candy's friends, recent happenings in her life, and any new people she may have met. Writing it all down, she then asked to see Candy's bedroom. Tom led the way. The room had a pastel pink and blue color scheme. Adorned with posters of dogs, cats, and rabbits, a funny picture of a raccoon with sunglasses reading a book hung over a neatly made bed.

"Does Candy have a special place where she keeps things?" Maddy asked.

When Tom said he didn't think so, Judy interrupted, "Check the pink box on the closet shelf."

Pulling a large box from the closet and setting it on the desk, Maddy slipped the lid off and began lifting out items, one by one. A green cloth banner read, "The World's Friendliest Girl Scout." Beneath the flag, a stack of greeting cards, held together with a rubber band, revealed nothing important. When she pulled out a bag of small seashells and emptied it onto the bed, Judy burst into tears.

"Those are from our vacation last summer," Tom said.

Resting on the bottom of the box lay a pink envelope. Maddy's stomach sank. Picking it up, she slid a valentine onto the bed. It looked vintage. On the outside, a little girl walked on a country road, carrying a hand basket filled with vegetables. She flipped it open and it was signed, Mark.

"Is that what I think it is?" Tom said, with wide-open eyes. Judy snapped around, locked her eyes on the valentine, and, like she'd seen a vision of hell itself, wailed frantically.

"I thought he was dead?" Tom shouted.

"Jenkins is dead," Maddy replied, holding herself in check, "but we think Cupid might still be alive."

Tom struggled to keep Judy from collapsing while he stared at Maddy with a horrified expression. As he attended to his wife, Maddy signaled she was going outside and would be back.

"What's going on?" Allison asked when she came to the car.

"Cupid has the girl."

Chapter 27

Maddy and Allison waited by the oak tree for Zep and the troops to arrive. Darkness had fallen, and a warm breeze picked up. They leaned back against the car next to each other with their arms folded, gazing down the road, watching for the friendly headlights to appear.

"I'm not sure I'm cut out for this job," Allison said with her eyes fixed straight ahead. "I mean, I just started, and it's already pulling me into a dark place. It's scaring the shit out of me. How do I even explain any of this to my daughter? Or do I even try?" Maddy asked how old she was.

"She's eight."

"I wouldn't try," Maddy said. "She's too young. All you'll do is make her world dark, too."

"But I feel like I'm lying to her. I've always tried to tell her things as they are."

"I know how you feel. It's like we live in two different worlds; one with our work, which is dangerous, and death is everywhere, and the other with our innocent daughters, filled with hope and beaming with life. Maybe you shouldn't listen to me, though. I'm not sure I'm doing it right. I just remember how hard it was for me growing up, always being afraid. Maybe I shouldn't try to protect Amber so much. I know one thing for sure: I've grown a much harder shell since I've started this job. I worry I'm becoming too insensitive."

"How do you mean?" Allison said.

Stepping away from the car, and putting her hands on her hips, still looking at the road, Maddy said, "It's like when Amber needed a new dress for a dance before Valentine's Day. She asked me to take her shopping. I blew up at her. I said she should have told me sooner, and she cried. The thing is, I wasn't available sooner either. I was so wrapped up in the Sarah Benning case, I couldn't focus on anything else." Maddy sighed and shook her head.

"I think you're a wonderful mom," Allison said as she reached out and put her hand on Maddy's shoulder.

Maddy turned and gave her a half-smile. "Thank you."

In the distance, the road lit up. Tiny lights glowed in the blackness. "Here comes the cavalry," Maddy said. In a few minutes, cars and trucks drove up and pulled over.

Zep got out and looked up and down the road as though he was inspecting lawn damage after the winter snow had melted. "There is nowhere to hide," he said.

Maddy wasn't sure what he was talking about. "What was that, Zep?"

"There's nowhere for anyone to hide. If you're going to abduct someone who doesn't know who you are, you would expect resistance and pick a place where there's lots of cover. But here, except for that tree, there's nothing. I think the kid knew her abductor." At that moment, a technician walked by with Candy's bicycle in hand. Zep looked at it and said, "My kid has one just like it." He then turned to Maddy. "Have you interviewed the Bishops yet?"

"I started to, but the wife lost it when we found the valentine. I'm headed back up there now."

She could see Tom's silhouette on the porch as she walked back up the road. Approaching the house, she asked how Judy was doing.

"She's sleeping now," he said. "Our doctor's a friend. He came by and gave her a sedative."

"Would you mind a few more questions?" she asked.

"Come up and have a seat."

They sat across from one another on the porch. It was dark, and with only the pale light from inside the house to write by, Maddy pulled out her notebook. "Can you try to reconstruct Candy's whereabouts over the last few weeks?"

Tom leaned over, propped his elbows on his knees, held his head in his hands, concentrating. He pulled out a small calendar from his wallet, and he rattled off Candy's activities—Scout meetings, math club, religious education, art lessons, a field trip to the museum with her class, and playdates with her friends. The one that stood out to Maddy was the art lesson because it was the only event Tom mentioned where she might have been alone with an adult.

"Tell me about her art lessons."

"She takes them from Dr. Albright. He's an art professor at Syracuse University and Candy's in his workshop for gifted children. I normally take her on Saturday mornings at ten o'clock."

"How many kids are in the class?

"About ten, but recently she started seeing him individually for an additional hour."

Maddy sat up and moved to the edge of her chair. "Explain that."

"Dr. Albright said Candy is particularly gifted, and he wanted to work with her one-on-one for no additional cost."

No additional cost? That sounds fishy, Maddy thought to herself. "When was the last time she saw him?"

"Two weeks ago, Saturday."

When she finished writing, she asked if they could look in Candy's room again for clues to her recent whereabouts. Tom said okay and led her back through the house. Together they pulled the clothes from a hamper, checking through pockets. Other than gum and a few candy wrappers, there was nothing.

Maddy lifted the top off a toy chest filled with stuffed animals, picked up each one, inspected it, and tossed it on the bed. "Nothing here."

Tom looked through the clothes hanging in the closet, then leaned over and slid a large cardboard box filled with drawings out from under the bed.

"That's some of Candy's work," Tom said as he gently picked up each one by its edges to show Maddy.

The first sketch was a magnificent fall scene of the outside of their house. Fallen leaves gathered around the foundation of the porch, and sunbeams streaming through scattered clouds made perfect shadows of tree limbs on the ground.

"This belongs in a museum," Maddy said. "I can't believe a child her age is capable of such a creation. How did she learn to do this?"

"It's a gift," Tom said. "The people at the university believe she'll be famous someday."

Inspecting each drawing, she stopped at a sketch of the inside of a restaurant. People sat talking at tables as coffee steamed from cups. Half-eaten pastries resting on plates seemed familiar, and Maddy thought the scent of cinnamon rolls seem to be present.

"Is that the Friendly Bean?"

When Tom said it was, she examined the drawing more closely and noticed the back of Rusty's head as he sat talking with a group of smiling customers.

"How often do you go there?"

"Sometimes, when I run errands, Candy waits for me at a table. She'll do homework, read, or draw. Rusty, the owner, is a nice guy and monitors her while I'm gone."

"When was the last time Candy was there?"

"A week ago."

"Do you mind if I take this with me?"

"Only if you promise to return it in its current condition." Tom handed her a special plastic cover, and she slid the drawing inside. As she was about to leave, he asked, "What are the chances of getting my baby back alive?"

An honest answer was less than ten percent, but she saw no sense in causing more anxiety than he was already feeling. "I can't answer that, Mr. Bishop. All I can say is that we have everyone working to find your daughter."

An uneasy, weighty feeling grew inside as Maddy walked back to the oak tree where Allison and Zep waited. Sarah Benning's and Nancy Miles's families came to mind, and she feared that Tom and Judy were next.

"Any luck?" Zep asked when she reached the tree.

"I have some new information."

"Tell us about it in the car," he said.

They piled into Maddy's car and headed to the old Forestport Fire Department, which was being converted into a command center for the operation.

"So, what do you have?" Zep asked.

"Candy, an unusually talented artist, made a drawing of the Friendly Bean a week ago while her father ran errands."

"It seems everyone goes to that place except me," Zep said, chuckling.

"I have the names of two of Candy's friends from school, Kat Banes and Carol Corella," Maddy added. "They might know something. She's also taking drawing lessons from a guy named Albright."

"Well, it's a place to start," Zep said.

When they arrived at the old brick firehouse, Al, who had overseen the command center setup, walked over. They grabbed folding chairs and sat around a card table.

"Let's see the drawing," Zep said. Maddy gently placed the plastic cover on the table and slid out the picture.

"Holy shit! A ten-year-old drew this?" Zep said.

"Yep, and that's the Bean," Allison said.

"It's perfect," Al chimed in.

"Okay, we have four sources of new information," Zep said. "It's after nine o'clock. Let's try to get to one kid tonight. Al, I need you here, so Maddy and Allison, pick one of the two friends and do an interview before it gets too late."

Although Maddy was under protective surveillance, considering the urgency of the situation, she thought she might get Zep to be flexible. "Allison and I can cover both kids tonight if we separate. Time is of the essence, Zep."

He looked at her, squinted his eyes as though trying to decide whether to call or fold in a poker game, then shook his head and said, "Okay."

Allison took the Banes girl and Maddy, Carol Corella.

Chapter 28

Allison and Maddy left the command center in different directions to interview Candy's friends. Darkness had descended on the country roads, and an ominous feeling filled Maddy as a warm breeze and full moon filled the night. The phone rang, and a woman said she had information about the missing girl.

"How did you get my phone number?" Maddy asked.

"Look, I overheard something, and I'm scared. I want to report it. I heard you're one of the chief detectives, so if you want to know what I found out, meet me at Bernie's All-Night Doughnuts on Wolf Road at about ten thirty?"

"What's your name?"

"I'm not giving it. Like I said, I'm afraid, and if you want me to tell you what I heard, I'll be in a blue Honda. I really have to go." Maddy called Zep when the woman hung up and told him about the call.

"Allison's interview crapped out," he said. "No one was home. I'll have her handle it."

When Maddy arrived at the Corella house, a broken chair on the front lawn, a car standing on blocks in the driveway, and two shutters hanging crooked gave her the creeps. She parked down the street and approached the place from the sidewalk. *I hope these people take better care of their kids than they do their house.*

The downstairs lights were on and suddenly went dark. She knocked on the glass front door. A woman slowly came to answer, while a large, bearded man stood close behind. The door cracked. Maddy introduced herself and said she needed to speak with Carol.

"We need Carol's help," Maddy said. The woman stood expressionless. Maddy had to repeat herself. "Your daughter's friend, Candy Bishop, is missing and her life is in danger. Can I speak with Carol?"

The man behind the door suddenly pulled the woman away, stepped in front, and said, "It's late. Come back tomorrow."

"Tomorrow might be too late."

"Carol's sleeping," he snapped. "Come back tomorrow."

Maddy saw a girl sitting halfway down the living room stairway. "I'm not sleeping," she said.

The guy turned and shouted, "Get in bed…I'll be right up."

Alarmed at the guy's tone, Maddy asked, "Are you Mr. Corella?"

"No, I'm Mr. Jones; there is no Mr. Corella," he said sarcastically.

The woman stood nearby with her arms folded, not seeming to like what she heard. The more the guy talked, the tighter the skin around her jaw stretched. Maddy asked a question directly to her. "Would you be able to answer a few questions, ma'am?"

She nodded and smiled, but immediately the guy cut her off. "Not tonight, damn it," he grunted and slammed the door.

Wanting to force him to let her talk with Carol, Maddy knew she didn't have the grounds. Determined to speak to the child, she walked to the pickup in the driveway and took the plate number. *Let's see what happens when we call this in.*

His name was Charles Munns, and as she suspected, he wasn't a nice guy—he had a long criminal record and was on parole. That was all she needed. With a few phone calls, she was talking with Pete Moore, Munns' parole officer. It took little convincing to get Moore to come to the Corella house, and when he pulled up, Maddy explained the situation. "Is that guy the girl's father?" she asked.

"No, he's not even the husband. He is a freeloader who found a cozy little situation here with this mother and her kid."

Pete suggested a plan to allow Maddy a chance to interview Carol. "I'll have Munns come out to the porch to give me an update on what he's been doing. I have a right to do that. Then you can go in and talk with the mother and girl."

"Sounds good."

When Munns opened the door, he snarled at the sight of Maddy and his PO together.

"I'd like to speak with you alone, Charlie," Pete said. "Let's go out on the porch." Maddy felt his hateful vibes as he walked by. The woman, still with her arms crossed, seemed relieved.

"Let's start over. I'm Maddy Reynolds."

"I'm Joan Corella," she said, extending a hand. Maddy shook it, and Joan asked her to come in and sit. The two women went to the dining room table. "How long have you been living here?" Maddy asked as she pulled out her notebook.

"Three years."

"Do I hear a little Texas in your accent?"

"Very good. Yes, I was born in San Antonio. My husband was with the 10th Mountain Division up at Fort Drum. When he died, Carol and I moved here to be close to my sister."

"What about Charlie?"

"I met him when I moved here. He's nice to me most of the time."

Maddy wanted to ask about the rest of the time, but held her tongue. Shifting the subject to Carol, she said, "Candy Bishop's life is in jeopardy. I really need to speak to your daughter."

The woman went upstairs and returned with a black-haired girl with lots of freckles. "This is Detective Reynolds. You're not in any trouble. She just wants to ask you some questions." The phone rang, and Joan said it was probably her mother and left them alone.

Maddy showed Carol a picture of the valentine. "Have you seen this before?"

"Yes. One day, when we were in the schoolyard at playtime, Candy put her jacket on a bench. When she came back to get it, the valentine was on top. We kidded her that Mark Talbert had a crush on her."

"Did you notice any adults around school that day?"

"A lady walked up and down the street in front of the school. I remember because her clothes looked weird, and we made fun of her. She wore a loose skirt and stockings with runs. She was big and walked wobbly in high heels that seemed too small."

Maddy wrote so fast the pen slipped out of her hand and fell to the floor. Carol bent down to get it, and her pajama top rode up her back, revealing black and blue stripes.

"What happened to your back?" Carol clammed up. She looked away, and her face turned red.

"Charlie did this to you, didn't he?"

"Please don't say that I told. Please," the girl begged.

"Don't worry, honey, he'll never touch you again."

When Joan came back, Maddy glared at her. "Stand up, Carol." Maddy pulled up the back of Carol's pajama top and exposed the welts. Joan hung her head, sobbing.

"I'm so sorry," she said.

"Take your daughter upstairs and put something on these wounds. I'm going outside and will be back." When she went to the porch, Munns seemed to have fun dodging Pete's questions, and when he saw Maddy, he smirked.

"Charles Munns, you're under arrest for child abuse," Maddy said as she moved in and handcuffed him before he could respond. Munns looked coldcocked and stood frozen as Maddy read him his Miranda Rights.

"I'll help you secure this piece of shit in your vehicle," Maddy said to Pete. "This asshole has whipped the child, leaving her covered with marks."

After Pete left with Munns, Maddy went back inside and called upstairs for Joan to come down. "Charlie's gone and won't be back. I doubt the court will ever let him come back here again. Carol is going to need a lot of help to heal from whatever he's done to her. You will too. Tomorrow, social services will be here. Cooperate with them, or you'll risk losing your daughter."

As Maddy left the Corella house and started back to the command center, she saw Carol standing on the porch, watching her depart, and felt a pang of sadness. Just then, the phone rang. "Maddy, what's going on?" It was Jack. "You didn't call Amber tonight, and she's worried sick about you."

Aww shit! Maddy thought. "There's been another abduction, Jack. Can you keep her for the next few nights?"

"Yes, but I think you need to break away at some point to see your daughter."

"I'll do what I can. I'm just running on empty."

"Maddy, I told you it was going to be like this."

When Jack started pontificating about the trials and tribulations of being a detective, it would always lead to a pity party, and she hated it. She wasn't in the mood to listen to his sob story.

"Look what it did to me," he continued. "The fucking job cost me my marriage."

That was it. Maddy, still reeling from seeing the whip marks on Carol Corella's back, knew it was the wrong time to dig up the cesspool of shit that preceded their divorce. But there was something about Jack feasting at the table of his self-imposed woes that made her want to reach through the phone and slap him.

"What cost you your marriage wasn't the job, Jack. It was the blonde you were fucking while I was at home thinking you were working late. And it was the DWI and the small fortune we spent so you could save your job with the State Troopers, only to have you lose it anyway by going into work drunk and blowing an investigation. It was the lies and manipulation and the poor-me bullshit you're running to me right now. That's what cost you your marriage."

"But I've been sober now for two years, and it's still not good enough to get you back, is it?"

This night is turning into a real cluster-fuck, Maddy thought, as she tried to fend off Jack's guilt trip. The clock was ticking out Candy Bishop's life, and she had to end the conversation. She took a few deep breaths, and as empathetic as she could be, she said, "Jack, you are doing better now. I'll give you that. You've stopped drinking, and I'm happy for you. But you have to understand, other people are still recovering from the damage you did when you were out of control."

A long pause, and Jack sighed. Maddy calmly said, "Let's not do this now. You've been wonderful lately, and I truly appreciate all your help with Amber since this Cupid stuff's been going on. But I have to get back to the command center, so please tell Amber I'll call her tomorrow. Good night, Jack."

She hung up, and a tidal wave of guilt about not calling her daughter washed over her. Despite her best intentions, there didn't seem to be a way to balance Amber's needs with the requirements of her job, and as far as her own needs were concerned, they didn't enter the equation. There was no time for herself whatsoever. At that moment, she did the only thing she knew to do: push it all out of her mind.

She called Zep at the command center, but there was no answer. *That's weird.* She tried several times and finally resorted to tracking down a temporary command center phone number. She got to an unfamiliar female voice.

"Who is this?" she asked.

"Marcia Dunham. I'm the new assistant. Is this Detective Reynolds?"

"Yes."

"Captain Zepatello said you'd be calling. He wants you to meet him at Bernie's All-Night Doughnuts."

"What's going on?"

The woman reluctantly said there had been some sort of incident but didn't elaborate. Aggravated by her double talk, Maddy demanded to know what was going on. In a frightened tone, Marcia said, "Something happened to Detective Abbott, but that's all I know. I'm the only one here; everyone's gone to Bernie's."

"Everyone is gone?" Maddy felt her heart pound. She made a U-turn and bolted toward Wolf Road. *I was supposed to be at Bernie's, not Allison.*

The doughnut shop was lit up with flashing lights, and a crowd had gathered around an ambulance, blocking Maddy's view. She got out and ran through the maze of people. Zep stepped in front as Maddy looked over his shoulder to see a blood-soaked bandage wrapped around someone's head, rolling by on a gurney.

"Who is that?" she screamed.

"It's Allison."

"Allison!" she wailed. Maddy stretched out her hand and placed it on Allison's leg, trying to follow into the ambulance. Zep pulled her away. "This should have been me!" she cried.

He put his hands on Maddy's shoulders and looked directly into her face. "There's no way you could have known Cupid was waiting here." She wasn't listening, keeping her eyes on Allison.

"How did it happen?" she asked.

"Ambushed, shot in the face with buckshot," Zep said.

"Is she alive?" Maddy weakly asked the medical tech standing nearby.

"Barely," the guy said.

"I'm going with her," Maddy demanded.

"You're not allowed to," the med-tech said.

Zep shouted, "Let her go, it's important."

The tech relented, and she climbed in. A bright light shined down on Allison, and Maddy found a small, out of the way space to kneel. Each moan was like a knife penetrating Maddy's gut.

"Can she hear us?" she asked.

"I think so," the guy said. "Put your finger in her palm and ask her to squeeze if she can hear you."

"Allison, it's Maddy. I am here with you and won't leave you alone. Squeeze my finger if you can hear me." Allison squeezed.

"Squeeze once for 'no' and twice for 'yes.' Did you get a look at the guy?" Allison squeezed twice. "Did you recognize him?" She tightened her grasp once, then tried to raise her head as though wanting to say something, but no words came out, only a raspy-wheeze. She shook, then convulsed violently. With an arch of her back and a loud painful whine, she dropped to the gurney. Her grip loosened around Maddy's finger, and she exhaled a whispered breath.

"She's gone," said the tech.

Unable to believe her eyes, Maddy felt like she was watching a movie. Nothing seemed real. Leaning back against the hard wall of the cramped ambulance, numbness crawled through her chest and limbs. It felt as though an emotional spigot in her brain was off, halting the flow of feelings to her body. Only a heavy deadness remained.

They removed the bandage from Allison's once-beautiful face, now grotesquely distorted by puffy red holes. Maddy had become a lifeless shell, and though she could not feel, she could think, and her only thought was to get out of the tiny space, reeking of Betadine and blood.

Finally, the back doors opened in the emergency room parking area. No sooner than the fresh air poured in than the press swarmed like flies around the ambulance. Questions, photos, pushing and shoving; the scene was chaotic. She stepped out and hid behind two uniformed cops who pushed the crowd back. When she could finally shoulder her way through the throng to the street, a clock on top of an old building ring four times.

Once separated from the bedlam inside the E.R., she became overwhelmed by an intense sense of loneliness. A young man's voice broke through to her. "Would you like a ride home, detective?" It was the voice of a uniformed cop assigned to escort her home.

"Yes, thank you." She stared out the window as they drove. The streets were as empty as she felt inside. It was as if she was twelve again, on the night her father died, but this time, it was Allison whom she grieved.

Chapter 29

Maddy lay on the living room sofa, where she'd plopped herself at 4:37 in the morning. Unable to sleep, her mind raced. It was as if a bomb had gone off in her world, and the fragments of life she had known lay scattered about in her mind. *How can I possibly go on from here?* Her heart ached every time she thought of Allison, but eventually, she slipped into a restless sleep.

Her eyes blurred. Daylight beamed through the windows as the sun rose above the neighborhood. The clock on the mantel read 9:36. She realized the fiasco at Bernie's had derailed the Candy Bishop investigation, yet there was still much to do. Sitting up, resting her head in her hands, she rose and went to the window. There was a patrol car planted in front of her house.

Walking to the kitchen, she stopped to gaze at *The Tempest on the Sea*. The man in the ship's window, surrounded by pandemonium, had become Cupid. "Why have you come to kill me?" There was no doubt in her mind now that Cupid wanted her dead.

Sitting at the kitchen table with a cup of coffee reflecting on the night before, she recognized two new pieces of information pertinent to the case: Candy Bishop had been at the Friendly Bean before she went missing, and an art instructor had met with her alone. Both situations needed to be assessed immediately. Zep called when she was sipping her third cup. "How are you hanging in, Maddy?"

"Just putting one foot in front of the other."

"I know. Losing Allison like that…it just doesn't seem real." He paused as though he were giving Maddy a chance to say something, but she didn't. "For what it's worth, our people are in contact with her daughter's father and her parents. They'll stay involved with the family from now on. It's something we've always done when things like this happen."

"That's good to know," she said.

An awkward silence set in as Zep seemed to struggle for words. He finally got to the point. "I know it's hard to get back on the horse at a time like this, but there's a ten-year-old girl out there who still needs us."

"I know."

They started talking about the case. "If you're up to it, I'd like you and Al to handle following up on Candy's sketch and her meetings with the art teacher."

"I'll make myself be up to it," she said. Again, there was silence. Then she added, "Who's in the car in front of my house this morning?"

"Al," Zep said with a snicker.

Maddy smiled, shook her head, and mused to herself how Zep was a captain through and through. She remained in the kitchen after they hung up, and before turning her attention to Candy Bishop, her thoughts returned to Allison. For the first time since the breath of life left her friend's body, Maddy felt the full thrust of her loss. She bellowed out loud, "I'm so sorry, I'm so sorry," and dropped her head into her arms. She had not wailed as hard since the night of her father's death. When she stopped weeping, face and shirt wet with tears, she forced herself to stand, leave her grief behind and resume the battle against time to save Candy Bishop.

Under the circumstances, she was as ready as she could be to jump back into the case, although she knew she wasn't a hundred percent. After cleaning herself, she went to the driver's side window of the car, where Al waited.

"Looks like it's you and me this morning," she said.

"Yeah, I talked with Zep. It sounds like we have some follow-up to do." Al spoke with about as much enthusiasm as Maddy felt. When they walked into the Bean, Rusty came out from behind the counter to greet them.

"I can't tell you how sorry I am to hear about Allison," he said. They both nodded. Maddy asked if there was somewhere they could speak with him alone.

"Certainly. Let's go to the kitchen."

They entered a brightly lit room where food was being prepared. "Is there a place I can lay this?" Maddy asked, holding up Candy's drawing, still in its cover. Rusty moved two half-made sandwiches from a table and wiped it clean with a rag. She slid the sketch from its cover and laid it down. "Recognize it?"

"Oh my, yes. It's like a photograph."

"A ten-year-old girl drew it right here at The Friendly Bean just two weeks ago," Maddy said. "Her name is Candy Bishop."

Rusty's eyes lit up. "The girl who was just abducted?"

"That's the one," Al said.

Rusty looked confused and seemed hurt, as though thinking Maddy suspected him. He stood looking dumbfounded, then his eyes opened wide. "That was about the time that guy was hanging around here. You know, the one we made a sketch of. He always sat over by the window near where the girl sat."

As though Maddy and Al's brains were operating on the same frequency, their eyes met. They turned toward the door, and before they bolted to the car, Maddy blurted to Rusty, "Don't discuss this with anyone, especially the press."

Back in the car, Al said, "We're running out of time. We should tell Zep that the guy's sketch should go into the paper tonight."

I hate doing that shit, she thought, remembering what happened to Jenkins. But she knew Al was right.

"I don't think we have any choice," Zep said when they called. "Shit, we'll be lucky if the kid's not dead already." Everyone knew they had lost valuable time at Bernie's. "I'll take care of it. In the meantime, keep me posted on that Albright guy."

As they headed to Syracuse to interview the art professor, Maddy asked Al what he found out about him.

"He's a renowned artist, but quite controversial. He's British, working here as a visiting professor."

"What's controversial about him?"

"He specializes in photographing nudes of young girls."

"What?"

"Grab that folder on the back seat and look at some of his work."

Maddy opened the folder. "You got to be shitting me." She was looking at a photo of a girl, about thirteen, lying on a couch with her legs partially open. Every aspect of her blooming womanhood was visible.

"This isn't art. This is child pornography."

"That's exactly what the courts are trying to figure out," Al said.

Maddy shook her head, predisposed not to like the guy. The professor's secretary sent them in when they arrived, and Albright stood behind his desk. He was a tall man in his mid-fifties with a full head of brown hair that he wore combed back. He had a partially gray goatee that made him appear distinguished, and when he spoke, he sounded sophisticated. "Please sit. How can I help you?"

He leaned back in a large leather chair, and behind him hung an abstract painting of a nude woman. Across the room, terracotta wall hangings depicted men and women having sex.

Glass shelves with different colored rocks shaped like male and female genitals stood beneath the wall hangings.

"We understand Candice Bishop is one of your students," Maddy said.

"Yes, she is in the Advanced Child Development Program."

"Have you heard what happened to her?" Al asked.

Albright said that he hadn't heard and asked if she was all right.

"Yesterday, a person who we believe killed two other girls abducted her," Maddy said.

"You mean Cupid." His eyebrows rose.

"We're here because Candy had a private lesson with you two weeks ago. Can you tell us about it?"

Albright glared at her. "I have a few specially gifted students whom I give one-on-one instructions to," he said, sounding irritated.

"Pardon me for saying it," Maddy said, "but I find your preoccupation with photographing young girls nude troublesome."

Unflinchingly, Albright responded. "The female body is a thing of great beauty. There have been many artists like me who have made it a major part of their work. That I focus on girls who are on the brink of womanhood would not trouble you if you understood this genre."

"Have you photographed any nudes since you've been in Syracuse?" Al asked.

"One," he said.

"How old was she?" Al continued.

"Sixteen, and I have all the parental consent forms if you care to see them."

Maddy chimed in. "Have you approached any other subjects since you've been here?"

"Yes," he snapped at her.

"Was Candice one?"

"Absolutely not."

"Dr. Albright, can you provide us with documentation of your whereabouts since your last appointment with Candy?" Al asked.

"Do you have a subpoena?"

"No, but we can get one in about fifteen minutes," Maddy sneered.

Albright stiffened and sat straight up in his chair. "I would like to consult with my attorney before I give you anything."

Al and Maddy looked at each other. "We have little time," Maddy said. "How long will it take?"

"If you wait outside, I'll make some phone calls."

When they left the room, Maddy told Al she couldn't understand why anyone would let their kid have private lessons with Albright. "He's a freaking sicko."

"Maybe they didn't know enough about the guy," he said.

When the door opened, Albright came out and said his secretary would fax over the information. They handed him their cards and left quickly. Maddy and Al were barely back in the car when the phone rang; it was Zep. "Ready for this?" he said. They looked at each other with raised eyebrows, as if to say, *Now what?*

"Someone spotted a woman carrying a box near the doughnut shop last night. I think Cupid is using disguises."

A giant piece of the puzzle from the night before flashed back to Maddy. "Carol Corella said a large woman was hanging around the school about the time Candy found the valentine." As she spoke, something else tugged at her memory, but she couldn't pinpoint what it was.

"That's one more device in Cupid's bag of tricks," Zep said. "What did you two find out about the good professor?"

"We found out that he's not too good," Al said. "He has a preoccupation with girls around Candy's age, and he's into photographing them nude. We think we should put a tail on him."

"I'll reach out to the Syracuse police for that," Zep said.

Maddy had to visit her daughter and thought now was as good a time as any to ask her boss. Resources were thin, and she knew he couldn't afford to tie up another detective, so she just came out and asked. "I really need to spend a few hours with Amber. How about easing up on the surveillance thing for a little while?"

After a long pause, Zep sighed and said okay. "But make sure you check in with me every hour."

Hanging up, feeling a sense of relief, her other concerns still ate at her, so she confided in Al. "Cupid got Allison last night, but was trying to get me. I'm worried because if he succeeds, I've made no arrangements for Amber."

"I had to do that for my mother," he said. "It hit home when a domestic violence dispute put me in the hospital. All I could think about was if the knife had entered above, I would be dead, and she would be alone. You should take care of it," he said. "It'll make you feel better. It did me."

"I'll do it, but I need to start by talking to my ex." Then she asked him a question that had been on her mind. "Another thing I don't understand is why Cupid is preoccupied with killing me. I realize he hates women, but he's singled me out. Why? There must be more to it. There's a missing piece to this puzzle, and I'd like to know what it is."

"Cupid is crazy. What more do you need to know?"

"Something else is at work here. I feel it."

They arrived at the command center and Al walked into the building while Maddy headed to Jack's determined to make her wishes for Amber known.

Chapter 30

Maddy's thoughts wandered as she drove to Jack's on a perfect summer afternoon. The words, 'this was all mine,' entered her thoughts. Unsure of what they meant, they seemed like something a dying person might say when realizing the wonders of life they had taken for granted were ending. *Like Allison, my life can end in an instant, too.* The knowledge made the sun, the sky, and the clouds seem different somehow.

She pulled into Jack's driveway. He sat on his front porch, swinging in a chair with headphones over his ears. When she walked up and sat next to him, he took the headphones off and laid them on his lap.

"What's wrong, Maddy?" he asked, as though he could read her thoughts.

"I need to know what will happen to our daughter if I don't make it through this Cupid nightmare." She looked down, sensing Jack realized her solemn mood. "He's obsessed with killing me, and I'm not sure I'm going to make it."

"What do you want to happen?" Jack said in a soft, understanding voice. For the first time in a long while, he seemed where she needed him to be.

Maddy was looking at the world without herself in it, and said, "I want Amber to stay in the same school she's in now. She's happy there. She has friends and is well-liked. That means you'll have to move. I want her to go to college. You'll need to stay on her about her grades the way I do. And most of all, I don't want her to go into law enforcement."

"I will do these things," he said.

Nodding and looking into her lap as a wave of sadness washed up onto the shore of her soul, she wept. Wiping tears from her eyes, she asked where Amber was, and that she'd like to speak with her.

Jack left to get her, and while he was gone, Maddy realized she wanted to make things right with him as well. *Ours may not have been the most successful family, but we are the only family we have*, she thought.

When her daughter came to the porch, she sat across from her mother, and Jack left them alone. Amber pushed her hair from her face, bit her lower lip, and seemed to know something important was coming her way.

"There are some things I need to explain to you: adult things that I haven't talked about because I didn't want to worry you," Maddy said.

"You mean about Cupid?"

"Yes, about Cupid."

"I hear kids talking in school. They say you're one of the important detectives trying to catch him. Is it true?"

"Yes, but it's extremely dangerous. I can get hurt…even die."

With her eyes squinting, Amber looked at Maddy like she was looking into the sun, and for a moment, said nothing. Finally, she asked, "What will happen to me if you die?"

"Dad will take care of you," Maddy said.

Amber got up, went to her mother, kneeled next to her, and laid her head on her lap. As they held each other, they both cried. Gently rocking back and forth, Maddy ran her fingers through Amber's hair as she did when she was little.

After a long silence, Amber asked, "Why does he do it…why does he hurt girls?"

"I don't know," Maddy said.

"And why does he give them a valentine?"

"I don't know that either."

"Does that always happen? I mean, do evil men always give people they hurt valentines?"

"No, Amber, it's very unusual."

"Then why did it happen when Grandpa was alive?"

"It didn't, honey."

"Yes, it did. I saw pictures of valentines in Grandpa's green metal box in the basement."

Pushing her daughter away, she looked directly into her eyes. "What do you mean?"

"Remember the night you read me the letter Grandpa left you? I asked if there was anything else he left behind, and you said, 'just an old green metal box in the basement with a bunch of work stuff.' One day when Melissa was over, we were playing in the basement, and I saw the green box, so I opened it. Inside were lots of envelopes and some had awful scary pictures. I didn't tell you because I thought you'd be mad at me. A few had old-fashioned valentines like the ones I saw in the newspaper."

"Oh, my God!" Maddy shrieked.

"What does it mean, Mom?"

Not wanting to alarm her, Maddy tried to compose herself. "I am not sure. I'll have to check into it." Her mind raced. *Can it be? Can Cupid be a copycat of the guy my father was after?*

Trying to get Amber's attention off the green box, she told her when the Cupid case was over, they would go on a vacation somewhere fun.

"Can we go to New York City and see *Annie*?"

"It's a date," Maddy said with a smile.

"I can't wait to tell my friends." She gave her mother a hug and excitedly ran inside.

"What's that all about?" Jack asked as he returned outside.

"I told her I'd take her to see *Annie* when this is over."

As Jack walked her to her car, Maddy said, "If something happens to me, remember, keep Amber's life as stable as you can. I don't want her to go through what I did when my father died."

"I promise," Jack said as he opened the car door for her. Before she got in, she turned and said, "I know things haven't worked out the way we had hoped, but I think we've done something wonderful with our daughter. Thank you for that." She put her arms around him. Jack seemed stunned at first, but then hugged her. When the embrace ended, she noticed tears welling up in his eyes.

Driving away, her mind returned to the metal box. Thinking of what it might mean, the phone rang, distracting her. Zep yelled, "Where the hell are you?"

"I'm sorry I didn't call when I was supposed to. I just left Jack's. Zep, I need to stop by my house for a few minutes before I come back to the command center."

"Maddy!" he said sternly. "This is a matter of life and death."

"I'll be okay. I promise I'll be back in an hour."

It was almost six p.m. when she pulled into her driveway. Leaping down the cellar stairs when she ran inside, she searched the messy basement, looking for the box. As she shuffled through a pile of old board games, something green caught her eye. Beneath a wooden checkerboard, the green metal box sat slightly covered with rust. She carried it up to the kitchen where the light was brighter, placed it on the table, and before opening it, realized it could change everything.

Pulling out envelopes of different sizes, some small and white, others large and brown, all contained case notes related to various crimes. At the bottom of the box, she grabbed a package, more substantial than the rest, and emptied it on the table. Black and white glossy photos of crime scenes involving young girls, all dated between 1960 and 1961, slid out. Written on the back of each was the name of the case.

One by one, she scrutinized each photo. They were glimpses into her father's world. In one, a girl around fourteen lay partially naked in the mud. Her dress was torn and bloodied, a valentine lay on her stomach, and the name 'Patty Bronson' was written in pencil on the back. The second case photo was of the valentine's inside, signed, 'Mark.' Icy chills ran through her body.

"Holy shit! Holy shit!"

She remained still and bewildered, unable to make sense of the connection between her current nightmare and the photograph. The name 'Mark' appeared on two other sets of similar images.

How can this be? Cupid must be a copycat. The more she learned, the less she understood. *I have to find out what happened back then.* The only person she trusted to tell her the truth was Bob Bennett. She hadn't spoken with him since he was in the hospital, and though she didn't know how he was faring physically, she called anyway. Bob answered right away.

"Bob, it's Maddy." She could not stop her voice from quivering.

"Talk to me, Maddy. What's wrong?" There was a tone of anticipation, almost like he was expecting her to call.

She explained two girls, ages ten and eleven, were found raped and strangled in Utica, and a third girl was missing.

"We found vintage valentines, each signed 'Mark.' The killer has been harassing me and killed another detective, thinking it was me." Maddy heard a low, barely detectable groan on the other end of the line.

"Bob, I just found out that the murders in Chicago involved similar valentines. How can this be? Do you think this new killer is a copycat?" She walked out to the living room with the phone, sat down, and waited for Bob to give her missing pieces to the bizarre puzzle.

She heard Bob breathe deeply before he spoke, and when he did, his tone was deadly serious. Slow and deliberate, as though he was about to reveal a long-held secret, he said, "Shit, Maddy. I should have told you this a long time ago. I meant to when the time was right, but eventually, I thought maybe I wouldn't have to say anything."

"It's not a copycat. It's the same fucking guy." Maddy was not prepared for that. He continued. "His M.O. was to take kids to an isolated place in the woods, like an abandoned house, or a cabin, where he'd rape and kill them. We always found a valentine signed *Mark*. And Maddy, we found one on your dad, too."

A spear pierced Maddy's heart. Unable to speak, she watched her hands shake as she struggled to catch her breath. Her voice cracked as she asked, "What makes you think it's the same man?"

"I know it is," Bob said emphatically.

"But you told me Dad's murderer died in prison!"

"That was the party line from the bigwigs. I wanted to tell you the truth, but you were just a kid. After your father's death, the city went ballistic. People wanted the heads of the mayor and chief of police. The press was merciless, and there were no clues. The guy vanished like spit in the ocean. All the cops wanted revenge; we loved your dad. That's when things got out of control."

"What do you mean 'out of control'?"

"False arrests, harassment…we came down hard on any low-life we thought might have information. Then one day, we came down too hard. A guy died, and the department started falling apart. Higher-ups tried to hold it together. That's when word came down about this guy in Detroit named Rico Neselli. He had just started a ten-year hitch for Grand Larceny and had bragged to his cellmate that he was the Chicago Child Killer. That was it.

He was a marked man and dead within a month, killed at the hands of other inmates. They hate guys who target kids."

Bob was becoming emotional. She heard his voice tighten. "Then fucking politics took over. It had been ten months after Jimbo died when the Neselli thing came out, and there hadn't been a peep from the killer in all that time. He must have split town, but the public still wouldn't rest easy. The mayor and chief wanted it to be over, so they grasped onto the Neselli story and pushed it with the press. They ate it up. Everyone wanted to believe the guy was dead, so they convinced themselves he was. There were serious consequences for any of us who disputed the party line. They prohibited us from working on the case anymore."

"How do you know Neselli wasn't really the murderer?"

"He couldn't have been. One person got a good look at the killer. It was from the back and a short distance away. She was certain the guy was large, over six feet tall. Neselli was a runt."

Bob sadly said, "I never could accept it. I retired the next year. Your dad was a great man and my best friend. He deserved to have his killer brought to justice, but it never happened, and now the lunatic is back in action."

After a long silence on both ends of the phone, Maddy said, "So why do you think he is in Utica?"

"There is only one explanation. The guy's there to kill you!"

"But why?"

"I don't know. Maybe because he's insane, or he's connected you with your father somehow. Any of a hundred reasons maniacal killers do the crazy shit they do. We may never know. But, Maddy, he's there to kill you. Killing those girls…that's just an appetizer. You're the main course. You're up against one of the most twisted, cunning, and intelligent killers ever. I knew there was something bad going on with you when I had those dreams in the hospital. They all involved you and that fucking maniac. I wish I could be there to help you, but I'm worthless nowadays."

"You have helped more than you know," Maddy said, her mind still reeling from his revelations.

As they were about to hang up, Bob said, "You know, not a day goes by that I don't think about that Halloween night. And now I realize it's still not over for you. I am so sorry. But listen carefully to what I'm going to say. If you come across that bastard, don't give him any chances. Kill him at your first opportunity. With this guy, fuck the law; the law failed with him. Now it's time to think of yourself and your family."

Maddy hung up. From the time that she picked up the phone to call Bob to the moment the receiver clunked back down, her life as she understood it changed. *I feel like I've been on a railroad track, oblivious to a train charging at me, and now it's here.*

Everything she'd understood about her father's death and the man who killed him was false. She couldn't move from her chair. She sat, wondering what to do next. When she thought about telling Zep, something told her not to. Maybe it was what Bob said to her, "Kill him at your first opportunity. With this guy, fuck the law." She wasn't sure why, but for the time being, she would keep it all to herself.

Chapter 31

Racing back to the command center with her mind in a haze, fragments of the new information floated around in Maddy's head. *Cupid killed my father. Allison is dead, and their murderer is coming after me.* It was as though she had entered an alternate reality where anything was possible.

It was 9:09 p.m. when she reached the fire station. Zep was waiting when she walked into the building and looked more worried than pissed. "Oh my God, are you okay?" he asked.

"What do you mean?"

"There's no color in your face. You're as white as a ghost. Are you sick?"

"No, just tired, like everyone else."

"There are several cots in the far corner," he said. "I want you to get some rest. That's an order." He was clearly concerned that the strain she'd been under was too much, and might make her ill. She found a cot, and within minutes was asleep.

Loud guffaws from two young cops joking around woke her up. For a moment, she couldn't remember where she was. Her eyes blurred as daylight poured through a window. Lifting her head, she checked her watch. *Eight-thirty? Why didn't someone wake me up?* Dragging herself to her feet, she went to the coffee table, combing her hair with her fingers. The first sip of high-test gave her the jolt she needed to shake out the cobwebs. She saw Al standing nearby with a grim expression.

"What's going on?" she asked.

"It appears our Dr. Albright has disappeared," he said.

"What happened?"

"The Syracuse police were tailing him last night, and he vanished. That's not all. I found out he raped a ten-year-old girl in the U.K. The guy is more than just a quirky artist. He's a pedophile."

Zep walked over to where they stood and asked Al if he told Maddy about Albright. Al nodded.

"He has friends in Buffalo." Zep said. "According to his secretary, he spends a lot of time there, and the telephone logs show calls just before he disappeared. I'm about to send two of our people to work with the Buffalo P.D."

"So, when do we leave?" Maddy asked, assuming she and Al would go.

Zep turned to Al and said, "You better get moving and make the arrangements. You and Renshaw should leave as soon as possible."

"But Zep..." Maddy protested, taken aback. "What the hell?" Al walked away, leaving them alone. Zep turned to Maddy.

"I'm concerned for your safety, Maddy. There's a lot that needs to be done right here. Check the Call Center about the sketch. Maybe we've had some bites." He turned and walked away.

Feeling as if someone punched her in the solar plexus and knocked the wind from her lungs, she went outside. Pacing around, trying to make sense of what just happened with Zep's sudden change of heart. She felt like he lost confidence in her. Al rushed outside to his car, saw her, and stopped.

"What's wrong?" he asked.

"Zep's got me under lock and key. I can't believe he's sending Renshaw to Buffalo instead of me."

Dipping his shoulder, he sighed. "He's lost Allison, Maddy. He knows Cupid has it in for you, and he doesn't want to lose you, too. Come on, cut him some slack."

He put his hand on her shoulder, and looking her in the eyes, said, "Everyone knows all that you've done on the case. But we have to count on Zep to keep us from getting ourselves killed. That's all that's going on here. Don't take it personally."

Maddy nodded her head and reluctantly said, "You're right." Smiling, he turned away and headed for his car. "Be careful, Al," she said, watching him walk away.

Returning inside, she followed up with the Call Center. The attendant said no calls had come in on the sketch.

"But there was a message for you from a woman named Tonya Petrov. She seemed agitated and wanted to be sure you knew it was happening again. She said you'd know what that meant."

Oh shit, Maddy thought. Tonya's noise was the last thing she wanted to deal with at that moment. "All right, I'll handle it," she said. Tracking down Zep, she told him there were no bites about the sketch, but the noise lady called in and was apparently losing it. "Do you want me to calm her down?"

"You may as well," he said, preoccupied with more important matters. "When you're done with her, stop out to the Bishops. They've been calling, looking for an update."

"What do I tell them?" she said.

"Tell them the truth. We think we have the guy in our sights and are zeroing in on him. Don't give them any more than that."

Zep seemed to have forgotten about surveillance, and Maddy didn't bring it up. She thought he was probably less concerned now that the threat from Cupid had shifted two hundred miles west to Buffalo.

She arrived at Tonya's apartment. With her door unlocked, and the sound of weeping inside, Maddy walked in. The woman sat at the edge of a sofa, hands clasped over her ears, rocking back and forth. She looked up at Maddy, her face twisted, as if in despair.

"It's back…it's back" Tonya said. "Can you hear it?"

Carefully listening, Maddy heard a barely detectable humming sound. Tonya asked again, if Maddy heard it. She was almost pleading.

"I think so. It's extremely high pitched." Standing in the middle of the room, and slowly turning in a circle, trying to locate its direction, Maddy said, "It's in here," referring to a coat closet. "That's strange."

Coats and jackets hung on hangers, stacked up boxes of wrapping paper and sewing supplies, cluttered the small space. One at a time, Maddy checked each item, but nothing made the sound. She emptied the closet and stepped inside. To her amazement, she still heard the vibration.

"What the hell." Placing her ear to the wall on her left and then the right, she heard nothing. Getting on her knees, she put her ear to the floor. She still heard no sound. Finally, she moved to the back wall. *Son of a bitch, there it is.* Scrutinizing the wall, she noticed four screws, one in each corner of a wooden board covering the back. "Tonya, do you have a Philips head screwdriver?"

Tonya had moved to the hallway and shouted back, "Under the kitchen sink." Grabbing several screwdrivers, she started back to the closet. It had been a long time since she immersed herself in something other than the Cupid drama and was eager to tackle the wooden board.

The first screw took a good deal of strength to break free from dried paint caked up around it, but the rest came out with little effort. On her knees, Maddy finished the last screw, and thought, *I wouldn't want to do this for a living. But then again, it's better than chasing a crazy killer around town.*

Once freed from the screws, the board remained wedged in too tight to pull out. With a flathead screwdriver, she tapped into the crack near the wall and pried it loose. She pulled it out, and behind it, four pipes ran parallel from floor to ceiling. Placing her hand on each pipe, she felt a slight vibration on one. *There's the sucker. Now to find where it leads.*

"Tonya, I'm going downstairs and will be back." Maddy tried to approximate the location of the closet relative to the rest of the building. Determining the pipe went into The Friendly Bean's kitchen, she walked to the restaurant. Artie said Rusty wasn't there, but that he'd be glad to help. He led her to the kitchen and to a nook where the pipes came down through the ceiling.

They ran behind a small table where a portable oven and a large coffee grinder rested. She asked him to help her move the still-running grinder away from the pipes. The machine was large and cumbersome. Artie squeezed awkwardly into the cramped area and explained that manufacturers designed it especially for restaurants. Together, they slid the grinder out about eight inches from the pipes on the count of three. Immediately, the humming stopped.

"Ah-ha!" Feeling a sense of accomplishment, Maddy scooched around the side. Sticking her hand behind the grinder, she fished out a pencil. "There's the culprit," she said. "How do you suppose it got there?"

"It probably happened when the grinder was out for repairs a few months ago," Artie said. "Every few days I grind up a lot of coffee. It must have been vibrating between the grinder and the pipe, making that sound."

"Tonya upstairs will be one happy old lady," she said. "Do you mind if I take it?"

"It's yours. We've got lots of pencils."

Walking up the stairs, Maddy noticed the lead in the pencil was a unique shade of purple-red. Stamped on the side was the company's name—Faber-Castell. The color was Falu. She opened the apartment door, and a smiling Tonya awaited. "You stopped it. Oh, thank you," she said, throwing her arms around Maddy.

"This was the source of all your troubles," Maddy said, holding out the pencil.

"Something so small, yet it drove me mad," Tonya said. "Please don't leave yet. Let me make you some lunch."

"No, I need to put your place back together and get moving." She looked at her watch and thought, *I can't believe it's after one, and I still need to get out to the Bishops.*

It was a little past two o'clock when she drove by the tree on the road near the house. Feeling uneasy, she realized it was the spot where Candy had her last glimpse of home. She walked up on the porch, knocked, and Tom came out.

"How is Judy doing?" she asked.

"Not very well. Some of the women from the church brought her to a prayer meeting. I hope it will help."

"That's a good thing," Maddy said.

They took the same seats on the porch as the night before. Tom said, "We read about what happened to Detective Abbott. How tragic." Then, hesitantly, he added, "We're worried about how it might affect our situation. Has there been any progress locating Candy?"

"Allison's death has not deterred us. And yes, we have some new information we're following up on, which leads me to some questions I have for you. What can you tell me about Dr. Albright?"

"Only that he is an outstanding art teacher," he said.

"Mr. Bishop, his specialty is photographing nude women." If Maddy could have avoided telling him what she had to say next, she would have. "He is fond of using girls Candy's age as subjects and..." she hesitated, cleared her throat, and added, "...he has a sexual assault conviction in Britain."

Grabbing his stomach, Tom's face contorted as if a bout of food poisoning struck. "We were tailing him last night when he evaded us. It looks like he's taken off for Buffalo, and we are working with law enforcement to track him down. Right now, we're operating on the assumption that locating him is our best chance of finding your daughter." Maddy pulled out her notebook. "Is there anything else you can tell me about him?" In the back of her mind, she couldn't shake the image of Albright's face, thinking that he was the man who killed her father and came to kill her.

Tom began restating conversations he had had with the art professor. Maddy wrote as fast as she could, and when the lead in her mechanical pencil ran out, she asked him to hang on, reached in her pocket, and pulled out another pencil. "Okay, please continue." There was silence. When she looked up, Tom was staring at her hand.

"Where did you get that?"

"This? This pencil?"

"That's Candy's pencil. Can I see it?"

She handed it over, and he scrutinized it. "Come with me," he said. When they walked into Candy's room, Tom reached under the bed and pulled out a highly varnished wooden box. Inside were dozens of colored pencils. Ordered by color, and held in place in slots, they appeared like a rainbow. Tom took the pencil from Maddy and placed it in the only open slot. The color was slightly redder than the one above it and bluer than the one below.

"These are expensive drawing pencils, and this one belongs to Candy. Where did you get this?"

"In the kitchen of the Friendly Bean."

"What was it doing there? Candy has never been in the kitchen." He paused a moment and added, "Unless it was when I left her alone."

Unsure what to say or think, Maddy stumbled over her words. "I need to follow up on this and will get back to you as soon as I know more." She rushed from the house, pointed her car toward town, and floored it. Black clouds and strong winds whipped themselves into a frenzy, and within a quarter mile, a deluge broke loose. Unable to see clearly, she tried finessing her way through the storm.

Searching her mind for a logical explanation for how Candy's pencil made its way into the kitchen of the Friendly Bean, she came up with nothing, then thought, Rusty! It was incomprehensible Candy's disappearance had anything to do with him and hesitated about calling Zep until she knew more.

The rain forced her to move slower and slower, giving her time to think. An occasional inkling escaped into her consciousness of how she might feel if Rusty was Cupid. Each time the thought entered her mind, she ignored it, despite "betrayal" being the word that best described it.

When she finally arrived, the lights inside the Bean were off. The wind blew hard, and the rain fell at a slant. Someone parked out front in a Ford Pinto, sat with the car running. She couldn't tell who it was. Getting out in the rain, Maddy placed her hand over her weapon and knocked on the driver's side window. When it opened, she saw Artie behind the wheel.

"What are you doing here, Artie?"

"I'm trying to figure out what's going on. I told Rusty about you finding that fancy pencil, and he went berserk. He made me kick out all the customers and close the place up. I don't get it. It was just a pencil."

Her senses suddenly ceased to work. Artie's face became frozen, resembling a picture on a wall, while the sound of the rain receded into the background. The words 'It was just a pencil' reverberated in her head, and Maddy's brain went on full alert.

It's not just a fucking pencil, she thought. *It's the missing piece to the puzzle of my life.* As though someone had put a spotlight on the man on the ship, Rusty became Cupid! For the first time, the monster who haunted her since she was twelve showed himself.

Rusty killed her father, and he came to kill her. Like a fox dressed as a chicken, he pretended to be her friend to destroy her.

"Are you all right, Maddy?" Artie's voice broke through her fog. Realizing she stood unprotected in the downpour; she was vulnerable and had to move. She asked him if he had a key. "I have one for the back door, but Rusty said to never use it unless it's an emergency."

"This is an emergency. Get it out."

The rain beat down, and the wind howled as they walked through the alley behind the Bean. Drenched while waiting for Artie to hunt through dozens of keys, Maddy grappled with the enormity of her situation. *Rusty must have been planning to kill me for years.* His desire for her death was so deep that he had opened a restaurant where she lived and befriended her. She struggled to fathom such derangement.

When Artie finally put the key in the lock, she took out her weapon and thought of Bob Bennett's words: *Don't give him any chances, kill him at your first opportunity. With this guy, fuck the law.*

Artie slid open the steel door and turned on a light. The storeroom was empty save for boxes, cans, and cooking utensils that were scattered on the floor.

"What a mess," Artie said.

They stepped around the debris and walked through the storeroom to the restaurant. "It looks like Rusty trashed the place looking for something," Artie said.

The dining area was empty, and the pleasant aromas that usually filled the place had turned to sickening smells of food going bad. The Friendly Bean had become anything but friendly. It was dark, damp, messy, and it stank.

Half-filled cups of coffee and dirty dishes sat on top of tables. The only thing missing was the people. It was as if they had evaporated. Chairs stood askew, and pieces of bread, scrambled eggs, and bits of bacon from half-eaten meals smeared the floor. Maddy pointed at a picture on the wall in an area where she had never sat before. Printed on a plaque were the words "Rozzer's Roost." "What's that?" she asked Artie.

"Just some old picture Rusty had hanging in a Friendly Bean restaurant he owned in London."

For the second time in twenty-four hours, something tugged at her memory, like an itch she couldn't scratch, and it gnawed at her. "What does it mean?"

"It's a place where cops hang out."

"So, rozzer means cop, right?"

Artie nodded.

Mason Charles! That's it. The day she stopped Mason Charles coming out of the hardware store, he had asked her, "Are you a rozzer?" Another lost memory came crashing through to her consciousness. *The attic! I never checked the attic.* Pieces of experiences that were lost the day Maddy killed Benny Bowls had lingered in her memory, waiting to be found and placed in the puzzle.

"Am I in trouble, Maddy?" Artie asked.

"No, but you're going to have to be questioned. You can leave. I know where you live and can find you. Don't contact anyone about this."

Alone, Maddy stood in the middle of the Friendly Bean, a place she had once adored. It was a sweet façade Cupid had created to mask his nefarious intentions. She recalled friendly conversations with him, and it made her feel dumb and gullible. *I thought he was a friend.*

Filled with self-doubt, she walked out the back door. The rain had stopped, and heat thickened the air, making it sticky. A garbage can blew over in the storm and spilled coffee grounds and remnants of food into a puddle. Drowning maggots squirmed in the filthy water, smelling putrid, and making her gag. *This is how I will remember the Friendly Bean.*

Chapter 32

Maddy drove to Donald Charles's house in her new reality, trying to find her sea legs. For the first time, her life made sense. Knowing the identity of her father's killer gave her a sense of freedom. In her mind's eye, she saw herself at twelve, sitting in an intensive care unit next to her dying father. Her heart broke for the child. Holding her father's badge, she felt he was sitting next to her.

With no intention of telling Zep what she'd learned, she called him. "A lot has happened that you don't know about," she said. "You're going to need to trust what I am about to tell you. I believe Candy Bishop is at Mason and Donald Charles's house. I'm headed there now and will explain everything when you arrive." She hung up.

Parking down the street from the house, she crept to a window and peeked in. The rooms were empty and with no car in the driveway; she surmised no one was there. She went to the back and saw a light shining in the basement. Mason stood at a table, painting a model airplane. When she tapped on the window, he looked up and yelled for him to come to the front door.

"Where's Donald?" she asked when he opened up.

"I...I don't know," he stuttered.

"You must know."

"He's probably with Nigel."

"Who is Nigel?"

"He's the guy that Donald's always taking off with. Sometimes he calls him Rusty. They never let me go with them."

"Show me the attic." Maddy knew she was throwing protocol out the window, but time was running out on a child's life and for her, at that moment, protocol be damned. Mason's body stiffened, and his eyes, filled with fear, glared at her. She knew she'd hit a nerve.

"I can't."

"You have to," Maddy said.

"I'm not allowed in there," he said. It has a special lock. No one can get in. If I try, Nigel said he'd kill me."

When Maddy put her hand on her gun, Mason recoiled, turned, and walked up to the attic. It looked like any other attic, except someone had converted half of it into a room. It had a steel door and a hefty lock.

"What's in there?" she asked.

"I've never been in it."

Maddy tried to open the door by shoving and kicking it, but it wouldn't budge. "Stand back," she told Mason, and shouted for anyone inside to stand clear. Firing three slugs into the lock, the door swung open a few inches. She kicked it the rest of the way, turned on the light, and walked in.

"Jesus," she shouted, standing in Cupid's den of horrors. Trophies of his conquests were everywhere. Pairs of little girl's underwear lined one wall, and newspaper clippings hung like diplomas on another. Among them were Sarah Benning's and Nancy Miles's newspaper articles, the three cases from Chicago, and several from Britain, revealing a long history of Cupid's thirst to ravage prepubescent girls. Most grotesque were photographs of victims in bondage, still alive, and pinned next to them, photos of the same children dead. When she walked to a desk near the bed, the words, "Maddy Reynolds must die," written on a large poster, lay on top.

I've walked up to the gates of hell and am looking in, Maddy thought, remembering the words Mary Thompson spoke to her. Mason's mouth hung open.

"I knew nothing about this," he said.

"Touch nothing, Mason. Just turn around and walk out." She heard Zep's voice calling to her from downstairs.

"Maddy, where are you?"

"In the attic," she shouted. He walked up, and she said, "In there, it's all in there," gesturing at the room.

"Holy Mother of God!" he cried out when he walked inside. Zep looked shaken as he turned to Mason and said he was going to handcuff him. "If you don't resist, it won't hurt." With Mason secured, he moved toward the wall and examined the photos, then the news articles and underwear. He walked to the table and read, 'Maddy Reynolds must die.' He looked at Maddy with disbelief.

Drifting around the room, gazing at its contents and astounded by how perfectly arranged it seemed, she thought about how much pride the serial killer took in his work. Yet it was a cesspool of wickedness, she thought.

Looking at the tortured faces of suffering children who made up the exhibit, Maddy felt a palpable presence of evil. Opening a bottom desk drawer, she pulled out shackles and ropes.

Zep opened the closet door, where woman's clothing and different colored wigs hung on hooks. Taped to the back of the door was an old front-page newspaper article from the Chicago Tribune with a headline that read, "Veteran Detective James Reynolds, Murdered by Child Serial Killer."

"Maddy!" he shouted; his eyes fixed on the headline.

"I know, Zep. I just found out he killed my father. And there's more." She leaned against a wall, her body limp, gazing down at the floor. "I also found out Rusty is Cupid."

Zep's face turned to stone. His lips grew taut, and a cynical grin crept over his face. "That explains how he stayed one step ahead of us all this time. He probably eavesdropped on cops having breakfast in his cozy little restaurant, where he learned everything he needed to know. That son of a bitch."

Then, as if someone hit him with a baseball bat, he looked at Maddy and said, "My God, Maddy, he's come here to kill you." He took off his glasses and let his hands dropped to his side. "I can't let him get to you. You're my responsibility, and I can't let him get to you." It was as though at that moment, he saw Maddy in a new light, not as a comrade but as a responsibility.

"I want you back at the command center," he said. "Now!" Zep seemed frightened. "I'll be there when we finish. And there should be no more acting independently without authorization. I mean it."

As she drove back, Maddy thought about how she had pushed Zep beyond his limit. She worried how hard he might push back. It was just after nine p.m. when she reached Forestport and only a few cars were in the parking lot. With nothing to do but hang around, she tried to get information about what was happening at the Charles' house from an old-timer cop doing paperwork.

"Now that we know the professor is no longer a suspect, Zep has ordered Al and Bud back from Buffalo," the old cop said. "With the Bishop kid running out of time, he wants to organize a big push before it's too late."

"Do you have any idea when he'll be back?" she asked.

"They're going through the Beam Street house with a fine-tooth comb. It will be hours."

Exhausted, emotionally spent, and bored, and knowing that Amber was safe with Jack, Maddy lay down on a cot to rest for a few minutes but fell asleep. When she sat up and looked at her watch, twelve hours had passed. She felt groggy from a sleep hangover and walked out to the main area. The place was nearly empty. Marcia, the new assistant, handed her a note from Zep.

'Don't be upset, but I'm taking you off the case. It's for your protection. I would be grossly irresponsible to do otherwise, knowing what I know.'

Her knee-jerk reaction was to be pissed, but after a few hours of thinking it over, she realized she had gone to a dark place and had abandoned the better part of herself. She had become willing to break the very law that she had sworn to uphold when she considered killing Rusty at first sight.

The note explained they found documentation proving Rusty had recently purchased a cabin in Chenango County, south of Utica. There was every sign he, Donald, and hopefully Candy Bishop traveled there. "It's in a heavily wooded area, and we're afraid he'll kill the girl if he hears a helicopter, so we're assembling a team to hike in."

Finally, he added, 'I know you're close with Mary Thompson. My wife knows her from church. She told me this morning that Mary is dying. If you want to pay her a visit, she's at St. Luke's Hospital.'

Oh, Mary, sweet Mary. Can there be anything sadder than losing you? The thought was almost too much to bear. Now disengaged from the investigation, while everyone else was on their way to Chenango County for the final showdown with Cupid, she visited her dear friend.

After stopping home to shower and change, she drove to St. Luke's. As she pulled into the hospital parking lot, a queasiness grew in the pit of her stomach. *I hate hospitals. It's a place where people go to die.*

When the elevator doors opened on the eighth floor, she found Mary's room and walked inside. Her friend lay in a bed, facing a window, and looking out, deep in thought. Before she spoke, Mary turned to her with a smile. "Hello, child," she said. The light from within was gone, and her eyes seemed dim.. Though her voice was weak, Maddy could still feel love pouring out from her spirit.

"I've been thinking about you," Mary said. "I read in the papers about that poor girl. So sad. Come, sit next to me."

"You're the one in a fight this time, Mary," Maddy said.

"It's my time, dear. It's my time. I'm ready for the good Lord to take me home." Sighing, she lay back in her bed, and explained how she had gotten so sick she couldn't get up.

"I was stuck in the house until my neighbor came by and called an ambulance. I have cancer. They told me I won't be going home again." She worried about her tomato plants, bird feeders, and a stray cat that came around for food. Maddy assured her she'd check in on them.

Then, with some difficulty, Mary shifted position and looked directly into Maddy's eyes. "Tell me what's going on with you."

Familiar with Mary's powers of discernment, Maddy sugarcoated nothing. "I have lost my compass. I've always known true north, but now, when I look up for the North Star, I see only clouds. Mary, I am lost."

"Don't look up there for your true north, honey. You're not in the heavens yet. You're still on earth, and you need to look within yourself. That's how you'll find your way. Trust that."

"Who am I?" The words spilled out of Maddy's mouth like they'd been dangling on the tip of her tongue for a long time. Now, unrestrained by pretense and sitting with a loyal friend, she set them free.

"You're different from the rest of us," Mary said. "Most people avoid fear, but you've lived with it always. For you, running away is not an option. If you do, you'll drown. You're stronger than most, and as strange as it may sound, your fear is your strength."

Maddy knew what she meant. She remembered that at the peak of her anxiety as a teenager, she had to choose between hiding herself or fighting back. Learning to shoot, for her, was fighting back.

"But I'm tired, Mary…I'm so tired."

"So am I, dear."

After a long silence, Mary said, "There is something I want to tell you. I think it might be important." Maddy moved to a chair across from her.

"I had a dream, and in it, you were a mountain lion pursuing a wolf through a forest at night. The wolf was as strong as a tiger and as cunning as a serpent. You were trying to save a kitten he carried in his mouth to devour. As the wolf was about to kill you, the kitten became an eagle and stopped him." With that, Mary's head turned toward the window, and her eyes closed.

Maddy didn't understand Mary's dream, but knew she would always consider her among her dearest friends. Getting up to leave, she went to the bed, leaned over, and whispered, "Thank you for all you've done for me." She kissed her forehead and walked out of the room with her head low, knowing she'd never speak to her friend again.

Chapter 33

The afternoon sun was low in the sky as Maddy left the hospital parking lot. The heat felt more like mid-July than June. A call on the two-way radio disrupted her thoughts of Mary.

"Detective Reynolds. A woman is reporting children lost in the woods. Can you respond?"

"Affirmative." Maddy opened her notebook. "Okay, shoot."

"Nora Novak is the mother, and her address is 312 West Road, Forestport."

"Got it," Maddy said. She headed north on Route 12. *Novak? Forestport? That sounds like Jodi.*

A woman pacing outside a house when she arrived indignantly shouted, "Where have you been? I called you people over an hour ago." Maddy knew it had only been thirty-five minutes. The frantic mother pulled out a pack of cigarettes and lit one up, trying to calm herself.

"I'm Nora Novak," she said nervously. "My two kids, Jodi and Leon, and their friend Toby, rode their bikes to a place called The Deep Woods this morning. They were supposed to be home by four o'clock. It's now almost seven, and I know they're in trouble. Jodi's fourteen and very dependable. If she could be here, she would. Something must have happened. I think they're lost."

So, it is the Jodi I met at Mary's, Maddy marveled to herself.

Nora took a couple more drags and added, "They may have gone as far back as the old Winfield place. It's an abandoned, turn-of-the-century house, far back in the woods. A lot of bad things have happened there, and people stay away from it."

"Is there anyone nearby who knows their way around the Deep Woods?" Maddy asked.

"Clyde Baker. He grew up around here and lives just up the road."

Maddy took down the address and started out for Baker's place. Glancing in the rear-view mirror as she drove, Nora stood in the road with her arms folded, watching. Her empty gaze reminded Maddy of Sarah Benning and Candy Bishop's mothers when their daughters went missing.

She pulled into an opening among a wall of hemlock trees lining the road. A cabin was the only structure around. *This must be it*. The place looked more like a camp than a home.

The sizzling sound of meat cooking and its succulent aroma made her stomach growl when she walked up to the screen door. A tall, slender man in his seventies, wearing a green t-shirt and suspenders holding up his blue jeans, came out.

"Clyde Baker?" she asked.

The old man nodded. Maddy introduced herself.

"Nora Novak thinks her kids are in a place called the Deep Woods, lost. I am going there now. Do you mind coming along to help me find them?" Without saying a word, Clyde turned, went back inside, and returned wearing a green brimmed hat and holding another in his hand.

"What's that for?" she asked.

"It's for you. You don't want to get your hair full of blackflies, do ya? She didn't know what he meant.

Clyde walked to his truck and Maddy to her car. "Can we drive together?" she asked.

"Sure, but that thing you're driving won't get fifty feet into where we're going. Get in." She got into his truck, and on the way, asked him how much danger he thought the kids were in. "Well," he said slowly and calmly, "if Jodi's with them, they'll be fine."

"I met her once," Maddy said. "She seems like quite a kid."

"She's not your average fourteen-year-old, that's for sure," Clyde said, as his hands wrestled to control the bouncing steering wheel.

"I saw her catch a fly right out of midair."

Clyde laughed. "She can do a hell of a lot more than that."

The truck slowed to a near stop, then turned onto a barely visible road lined with high weeds and low hanging willow tree branches that blocked the sun. When it finally broke through, the truck filled with blinding light from a vast open space. "We're here," he said. Clyde got out and looked at the tall trees several hundred yards on the other side of an enormous field.

"Are those the Deep Woods?" she asked.

"That's them, alright. I sure hope those kids didn't go back to the Winfield place."

"Nora said bad things have happened there. What did she mean?"

"Oh, that's a lot of poppycock," Clyde said. "People like to make up stories to entertain themselves. But I'm concerned about what I saw out there last spring. Someone cut a trail to the house from the Black River. It runs about a half-mile behind the place. I can think of no good reason anyone would want to do that."

Maddy wasn't sure what to make of the old man. He was gruff and distant, but considering the circumstances, she was grateful for his help. The height of the trees on the other end of the field seemed daunting, and she doubted that she'd have any chance of finding the kids alone.

"Over here," Clyde called out. He stood by a clump of bushes where three bicycles leaned against a tree. He turned and pointed to a swath of bent grass in the field that led to the woods.

"There. There's where they walked in, and that's where we have to go." He followed the path, and Maddy went after him.

It was late afternoon, and still hot. The sun beat down on the back of Maddy's neck as she trudged through the untamed vegetation. The scent of moisture being drawn from the earth reminded her of Mary Thompson's newly tilled garden in the spring.

Overheated and out of breath, she finally reached the other side. The coolness of the trees felt like she'd jumped into a refreshing spring-fed pond. They stood for a moment, catching their breath and letting their eyes adjust to the darkness, before shouting, 'Jodi, Leon, Toby.' There was no response, only the rustling of leaves.

Moving further into the trees, at the crest of a hill, they came upon red, purple, and orange knapsacks resting on a fallen tree. "What do you make of it, Clyde?"

"They probably had no intention of going beyond this point, but started playing, got lured into the woods and lost their way."

Trees blocked any breeze from entering the woods the further they went. The air was suffocating, and tiny gnats swarmed around Maddy's face. *Now I know why he wanted me to wear a hat,* she thought, laughing to herself. Feeling like a minnow in an enormous lake, hiking in the woods at night felt overwhelming.

Before they started off, Clyde handed her his canteen, and she noticed a tattoo of soldiers raising an American Flag on his forearm.

"Were you at Iwo Jima?" she asked. Clyde gave a slight affirmative nod and turned away with a look of painful aversion. She asked no more questions, but realized there was a lot more to the old man than met the eye.

"I need to call in," she said, as they were about to leave the area. She pulled out her mobile unit, and when she got through, the connection was terrible. Zep's voice sounded crackly and, though barely audible, she understood he had gone with the others to Chenango County after Rusty. She tried telling him she was looking for three kids lost in the woods, but he seemed distracted and simply yelled, "Just go ahead."

It was after eight thirty when Maddy and Clyde started hiking, and night covered the woods like a blanket. "What are the chances of finding them in the dark?" she asked.

"We'll probably meet up with them at the Winfield Place. There's a stream a half-mile ahead that will eventually pass near the house. They'll probably follow it and hole up there."

Prancing over roots, rocks, and puddles like a deer, Clyde's knowledge of the woods gave the impression he wasn't only familiar with the place, but had a deep affection for it. When they reached the stream, he stopped and said, "The water here is fine to drink." He kneeled and scooped handfuls into his mouth before he filled the canteen. "You should do the same. You don't want to get dehydrated."

Tasting sweetly on her tongue, the water felt unusually refreshing as it went down. "How do you know your way around these woods so well?" she asked.

"I used to hunt here with my brother as a kid." She looked at the man's face and, in the moonlight, saw beyond the wrinkles in his skin and his stubbled beard. She realized she had misjudged him. At first, she thought he was a redneck, probably crude and unsophisticated. But he had a sophistication of a different kind, a practical sort, one that could help a person find their way through a dense forest at night. She knew of no one else who could do that.

She noticed him looking out beyond the treetops with a sullen expression. "Are you okay, Clyde?

"That looks like a Gibbous moon," he said. Shaking his head, he looked away and under his breath added, "I don't like it."

"What was that you said?" she asked, unsure of what he meant. When he didn't answer, she looked up and saw an odd-shaped, lop-sided moon. Her stomach turned, and she felt transported back in time to Halloween night when she was twelve. *That's the same moon that followed Bob Bennett and me the night Dad died.*

They left the stream and started moving. The land became steep, and hills came one after another. Maddy worked hard to keep up with Clyde, especially when the terrain changed and the banks left no space to step, forcing them to walk in the water. After a quarter mile of sloshing, with their feet and pant legs wet, they came to a large, flat rock and climbed up.

"Let's wait here a bit," Clyde said. While catching her breath, she looked up, and through an opening in the trees, saw stars shining brighter than she had ever seen stars shine before. *How beautiful.* In that moment, she decided that someday she'd like to live surrounded by such splendor.

"Ready," Clyde said, preparing himself to barrel forward again. They followed the stream to a place where the land flattened out into an opening with no trees. It was a small field where the moon painted a blue hue on the grass. Stopping suddenly, Clyde said, "Quiet!" He pointed to an area beyond the open space. "Look. It's the Winfield house," he whispered. "Someone's in there, and it's not the kids. This can't be good, Maddy."

She looked carefully into the blackness, but saw nothing. Moving her head from side to side, she asked, "What am I looking for?"

"Lights. Over there," he said, pointing.

"I see them," she said.

Out of nowhere, a voice called out.

"Mr. Baker, is that you?"

"Who is that? Is that you, Toby?"

"Yes. It's Leon and me." The two boys came out from behind a clump of trees. They looked scared and cold.

"Where's Jodi?" he asked.

"She went up to that house hoping the people inside would help us find our way home. She made us hide here until she knew for sure that it was safe. Two men came out. One grabbed her by the hair and dragged her inside. That was an hour ago."

Maddy's heart raced. "Can you describe what they looked like?" The descriptions fit Rusty and Donald to a T. "We have to move these boys further back away from that house," she said.

Maddy's mind stirred, thinking about how destiny had led her to Rusty. There was no doubt in her mind that before the night was through, one of them would be dead.

When the house was out of sight, she called Zep. Sounding exasperated, he said, "We hiked all the way back to the damn cabin, and the place was empty. No one's lived there for years. It was another well-crafted Cupid ploy, and we took the bait. Son of a bitch."

"Listen carefully, Zep. I am within seventy-five yards of Rusty and Donald right now. They are in an old house in the woods outside of Forestport and have taken one of the three lost kids, a girl of about fourteen. I have two boys and Clyde Baker, a neighbor, who knows the woods very well. He helped me find the boys. I think Candy Bishop is probably in the house, too."

After a long silence, in a high-pitched voice, he said, "Did I hear you right? Cupid and Donald Charles are where you are?" The terrible irony didn't escape him, and almost sarcastically, he added, "I took you off this case to keep you safe from that monster, and now you're facing him alone?"

During the long silence that followed, Maddy noticed the boys' faces frozen with fear. They had overheard the name 'Cupid.'

Zep's voice rang out clearly as he said in a monotone, "What are you planning to do?"

"I'm going in there," she said.

"Maddy!" he shouted.

"Zep, listen to me. He's going to kill both kids unless I do something."

He didn't respond, and Maddy thought, *He knows I'm right.* "I'll leave the boys with Clyde about a hundred yards from the house. He'll have my hand-held unit. If I don't come out in thirty minutes, Clyde will call, and you can send in help. But no helicopters before then. Agreed?"

"I don't like this."

"What else can we do?"

Zep sighed, and in a low, barely audible voice, filled with resignation, said, "Okay." Before Maddy headed back up the hill, she gave Clyde instructions on what to do, shook his hand, and said, "Wish me luck."

Clyde stood and put his hand on her shoulder. "You're one of the brave ones, Maddy Reynolds."

Chapter 34

Walking up the ravine, Maddy felt Cupid's presence growing with each step. The tortured faces on his wall flashed through her head. *It all comes down to this*, she thought. *An entire lifetime, and it all comes down to this.* The place was lit with lanterns, and light from the abandoned house flickered through the trees, coaxing her closer. She pushed all thoughts from her mind except one; *The man who killed my father is inside.*

The pale moonlight helped her navigate fallen tree branches, roots, and rocks. Reaching fifteen yards from the house, she saw movement inside, sending her into the shadows. Waiting for the movement to stop, she crouched, then scooched her way to the house. Leaning her back against an outside wall, she slid to a window and heard Donald Charles's voice. Peeking inside, she saw Jodi tied to a chair, appearing roughed up — hair messy, face red, and her left eye swollen. A missing pane of glass allowed Maddy to hear what Donald was saying.

"You are a pretty one, different from the others," he said. His enormous belly hung over his belt and sweat dripped from his face. "You seem so sweet. I can make things easy for you if you're nice to me. Cupid is very rough with his girls, but I promise to be gentle." Aroused, he didn't hide the bulge in his pants while Jodi, expressionless, kept her eyes locked on his every move.

Where the hell is Rusty? Maddy wondered, not wanting to make a move until she knew where he was. On the ground, near her feet, a light from a basement window shined. She bent down and looked inside. Candy Bishop lay on the dirt basement floor, not moving, face down. Her eyes were closed, and Maddy couldn't tell if she was alive. She returned to the window and heard Donald say, "Cupid doesn't understand me. I try to get him to be nice to the girls, but he wants to be so brutal."

"If you free me from this chair," Jodi said, "I'll go with you into the woods where we can be alone and away from Cupid." Donald's face lit up, and his excitement grew larger. He smiled tenderly and reached out to unbutton her shirt.

"Not here," Jodi whispered sternly. "Cupid might see us."

"Just a little taste," he said after he loosened her top button. He began rubbing her chest with his fingers. Revulsed, Jodi turned her head. He loosened a second button, and this time, rubbed the skin closer to her breast. *How far do I let this go?* Maddy wondered, pulling out her weapon.

Donald loosened a third button and placed his hand on her breast. Jodi lunged her teeth into the flesh of his wrist, clamping down. He screamed, pulling his arm away with blood dripping from his hand and splattering on the table. Enraged, his eyes bulged. He reached for a wooden board the size of a baseball bat leaning on a nearby wall. As it descended toward Jodi's head, Maddy's first shot entered over his right eye, popping his head back. He stood frozen in place, eyes blank and staring into space. The second shot tore a hole in his throat, and his large body crashed onto the table, with blood gushing from his mouth.

Rusty still didn't enter. *He's watching from the other room.* An object flew in and crashed into the lantern. The room went dark. The shadowy image of a man running into the room quickly disappeared. Pushing her way around the side of the house through bushes, by the time she arrived in back, two people disappeared into the trees. Her instinct was to follow, but she returned to the house for Candy Bishop.

Running to the basement, she gagged at the smell of urine and feces. Candy was still alive, and placing her face close, Maddy whispered, "You're safe now, we're going to get you home to your mom and dad. Just be calm, sweety."

She returned upstairs, and rushed to the front of the house, shouting for Clyde to come quickly. "There's a girl in the basement barely alive," she told him when he walked in. Clyde acted quickly. He covered Donald's body with a blanket to keep it from the boy's view, then carried Candy upstairs to a cot where Leon and Toby waited. While he and the boys attended to the child, Maddy tried contacting Zep.

"What's going on?" he shouted.

"I made contact," she said. "Donald is dead, and Rusty took off into the woods with Jodi. Candy is alive, but not in good shape."

"I'm sending a unit in right now," Zep shouted.

"No! Damn it. Don't do that! If he hears them coming, he'll kill Jodi," Maddy said emphatically. "I'm going after him myself."

"Son of a bitch," Zep shouted. "Let me talk to Clyde."

Maddy handed him the phone. He nodded every few seconds while listening to Zep, and finally said, "He's headed toward the Black River. It's about a half mile from where we are. He could have a boat there."

There was another pause, then Clyde continued, "If you're asking me what I'd do if I were him, I'd head downstream to the reservoir. If he's smart, he'll have a car hidden somewhere around the shoreline." Clyde handed the phone back to Maddy.

"Maddy," Zep said. A long silence followed that seemed like an eternity. "Don't get yourself killed. We'll be nearby, but out of sight. Keep the phone with Clyde. Once you are far enough away, he'll have to guide a medevac unit in to take Candy, Clyde, and the two boys out."

"If anything happens to me, Zep," Maddy said, "Promise you'll try to explain all this to my daughter."

"I promise," he said.

The boys seemed distracted from their physical discomfort by helping Clyde care for Candy. When Maddy was ready to set out after Rusty and Jodi, Clyde looked at her and said, "Godspeed, my friend." Maddy reached out and gently grasped his arm. Then, turning, she hurried off into the darkness.

Chapter 35

The moon lit the way as Maddy proceeded into the night. A vaguely visible path soon disappeared into a marsh. She had no choice but to advance in a straight line, hoping Rusty and Jodi did the same. A guttural sound echoed in the distance. She stopped, stood perfectly still, but it didn't repeat, and she continued.

When the river was in sight, Maddy followed it downstream, believing it was the most logical direction for Rusty to go.

I'll move in as close as I can to get a kill shot, she thought. *But if he hears me coming, Rusty will kill the girl for sure.* Her brain was in high gear. If a fish jumped, she'd snap around. If the crickets stopped chirping, she'd stop and listen for footsteps. Everything mattered. Her and Jodi's lives were on the line.

An open area lay just ahead, and she moved into it. Slow and silent, she hoped to get a glimpse of her prey. *Nothing.* A hundred or more yards away, the Black River moved purposely, glittering in the moonlight. She stayed in the open, but near to the trees.

Startled by another loud noise, this time she recognized the sound of a motor straining to start. "Shit," a man's voice echoed across the open space. *That's him. I'd know that voice anywhere.* She followed just inside the tree line toward the sound, keeping the river in sight. The image of a boat emerged in the darkness, and she edged in as close as she could. *There he is!*

Chilled when she saw Rusty move about in the boat's front, bullying the controls. He shoved a throttle and slapped some buttons. *He looks like he's losing it.*

Sitting motionless in the back of the boat, Jodi appeared tied up. Each time the motor moaned, Maddy's heart skipped, knowing Jodi was a goner if it started. Rusty was too far away for a clear shot. Feeling helpless, Maddy considered making a charge, but the fifty yards of open space put Jodi at risk.

Jodi began squirming about each time Rusty's back turned. *What the hell is she doing? She's going to get herself killed.* She seemed to stretch out her leg, push down on something several times, then snap back into a sitting position before Rusty turned around. Then he caught her. "What the hell are you trying to do? I'll crush your head like a plum if you're not careful." He locked his gaze on her, then turned back to the console.

The motor moaned more slowly each time Rusty tried to start it. To Maddy's amazement, Jodi kept up the strange movement. The motor would almost start up but coughed as though flooded. *Damn, she's flooding the engine.*

Frustrated, Rusty finally let the starter run continuously until the battery was nearly dead. A loud backfire, followed by an erratic sputtering, brought the motor to life, and it started.

"All right!" he shouted.

Alarmed, Maddy stepped out of the woods, ready to charge the boat. She waited for Rusty to look away, but when he went to the bow to untie a rope, the motor stopped running. She stepped back into the cover of the woods.

"Fuck!" he yelled, hurrying back to the console, but the battery was dead. He ran to Jodi, pulled her up by the hair, pushed her to the shore, then tied the rope around her neck. The two disappeared down the river.

The thought of Jodi heading for a horrible fate turned Maddy's stomach. Mary's words came back to her, and she hoped her friend was right about the girl's special skills.

Several minutes passed before she followed. A mist settled on the river as the night air cooled, and, despite her constant movement, Maddy felt cold. *I'm probably dehydrated. I wish I'd brought Clyde's canteen.*

As she moved forward, the sound of feet trudging through mud just ahead startled her, and she stopped. *I'm too close.* She waited, then continued.

A fallen tree blocked her way. She crawled over its branches and noticed a light glowing in the mist about a hundred yards ahead. Cautiously, she moved toward the glow. The muddy, fishy smell of the river and the strange, shining moon created a surreal feeling. She was entering an alien world where nothing was familiar and anything could happen.

Nearing the illuminated mist, she saw what seemed to be an open area ahead. Moving within the cover of a thicket, she approached the lighted area. A stone quarry was before her, empty, without a soul in sight. The substantial open space had a dirt hardpan and several forty-foot piles of stone scattered about. Amber lights on top of four telephone poles cast a dull glow on the dirt as the Black River flowed in the distance. Front-end loader machines lined up near a blue steel building in the center of the quarry. The building had two entrances, and no windows. Nearby, six white portable toilets stood side-by-side like tiny houses.

An empty parking area and two sets of wet footprints led to the building. Maddy knew only Rusty, Jodi, and she were present. She broke into the open and ran to the shadows of the building. Sweat beaded up on her face as she leaned her back against its wall. Pulling out her Beretta, she slid toward the door. A sign read, "Closed Until Further Notice." Maddy stepped inside.

The room was thick with gasoline fumes. It was a machine shop, and two partially disassembled earthmoving machines stood inside. Holding the gun with both hands, ready for anything, she inched her way around the enormous contraptions. Something moved to her left, and instinctively she snapped around, prepared to shoot. Nothing was there. *Man, I'm jumpy.*

When she was sure the shop was clear, she moved toward the double glass doors on the other side of the room. Beyond them was a hallway with offices on both sides and a gray steel door at the far end. Although the office lights were not on, the florescent lights in the hallway illuminated the rooms. She checked them out. They were clear.

Standing at the gray door, she thought, *I can feel him.* Quivering, she called on her father for courage. Using the weight of her body to nudge the door open, Maddy slipped inside. Except for a dim light on the opposite end of the large room, there was darkness. Unable to see the floor, she had to slide her feet to avoid bumping into something and giving her position away.

The room reeked of body odor. When her eyes adjusted to the darkness, she saw rows of tall, thin metal cabinets and realized she stood in a locker room. Moving toward the dim light, she got near, and two bodies sat on the floor. *That's Rusty!* Her breathing quickened, and her heart raced.

He held a rope tied around Jodi's neck as she leaned back against a wall. Rusty sat across from her, appearing deep in thought. *He's trying to figure out a way out of the mess he's in.*

Releasing the safety on her weapon, she took aim, but did not have a clear shot at his head. Moving to a different angle, her foot hit something hard. The sound of breaking glass cracked the silence. Rusty jumped up, pulled Jodi close, and put a knife to her throat. "Who's out there?"

Maddy stood frozen in the shadows. Her options were gone. Rusty moved the knife to Jodi's nose. "I'm cutting this pretty nose off if you don't come out where I can see you." Blood drip onto Jodi's shirt, and Maddy moved into the light.

"Oh my, my, my, look who we have here," Rusty said in a high-pitched voice. "I guess this isn't such a bad day after all." He centered Jodi in front of him, blocking a clear shot.

"Let the girl go, Rusty. The entire Oneida County Sheriff's Department is almost here. You can't get away."

"Maybe so, but I know two people who won't be alive when they get here. Now put that gun down and kick it over before I damage this pretty bitch."

Rusty cleverly covered a clear shot to the vital parts of his body with Jodi. Maddy kicked the gun over. Rusty picked it up and put the knife in his back pocket, as Jodi watched his every move.

He talked rapidly in the third person like a madman, and Maddy had to strain to understand what he was saying. "Everybody wants the big prize. Cupid is the big prize. But all you people are too small to have such a big prize as Cupid."

With the gun in his right hand pointed at Maddy, he put his left arm around Jodi's neck and held her to his side. As he rambled on, Jodi, with both hands still tied behind her back, managed to slip the knife from Rusty's back pocket sliding it into her own.

Maddy said, "You're pretty good at hurting helpless children, but let's see what you can do with someone who can fight back. Let the girl go, then it'll be just you and me."

"Brilliant. There's nothing more I'd like than to rip you apart with my bare hands, but the answer is no. I kind of like this girl, and when I'm done with you, I'll be having her for dessert." He pointed the gun at Maddy's heart and said, "Before you die, there is something I want you to know. Your father killed my father, so I killed him. But that doesn't make everything even, not by a long shot. I'm going to wipe his seed from the face of the earth. After I kill you, I'm coming back to kill your precious Amber."

Filled with rage, and about to lunge at him, Mary's dream popped into her head: "As the wolf was about to kill you, the kitten became an eagle and stopped him."

Jodi jerked the rope just as Rusty pulled the trigger. The bullet went off its mark, smashed into Maddy's left shoulder like a sledgehammer, and knocked her to the floor. She lost consciousness for a few seconds, and when she opened her eyes, she felt a burning pain in her chest radiating to her ribs.

Jodi broke free from Rusty's grip, twisted her body in a circular motion, and thrust her left knee into his groin. He screamed, squatted, and held himself. As he struggled to regain control, she whipped her body in the opposite direction. Using her momentum to drive her right knee into his kidney, Rusty collapsed with a thud. The lockers rattled, and the big man couldn't move. Jodi disappeared into the shadows.

The gun flew from his hand and slid beneath a steel cabinet. Maddy saw Rusty watch it vanish and drag himself to where it disappeared. He reached for the weapon, unable to extract it.

Slamming the metal locker with his fists, he yelled, "Shit, shit, shit!" Maddy had all she could do to slip out of the room into the quarry. Barely able to hobble across the yard, she left a trail of blood to the high grass where she hid.

Within minutes, he limped into the yard screaming, "Cupid is going to unleash hell on both of you bitches!" He followed the blood trail into the high grass and thrashed about haphazardly. When he turned his head, Maddy grabbed a stone and hurled it at the steel building, and it hit with a "clank." He snapped around, dragged himself back into the quarry, and began checking anywhere a person might hide. He examined the earthmoving machines, then the stone piles, and finally, he headed to the portable toilets.

Where is Jodi hidden? Creeping closer to the quarry, Maddy found a baseball-size rock to use as a weapon. *You bastard, now the tables have turned. I can see you, and you can't see me.* She thought of the years he had stalked her without her knowing. *It's him or me. One of us is going to die tonight.*

As he checked the portable toilets, Maddy hid behind each one he finished with. Hoping to get close enough to crush his head, she watched him sneak up on each toilet and rapidly open its door. He'd look in as though ready to destroy whoever might be inside.

A wave of wooziness, and Maddy had to stop to collect herself. She put her head low to the ground and waited. Hearing Rusty say, "Got you!" she looked up. He had his hands around Jodi's neck.

"You little bitch! Cupid has had enough of your shit." Jodi turned her head from side to side, gasping for air. Only fifteen feet away, Maddy hobbled. It felt like a mile. Using her good hand to prop herself up, she prepared herself to deliver a crushing blow to Rusty's head with the rock.

Although losing the battle against the monster's grip, Jodi seemed to regain strength when she saw Maddy. Arching her back, she twisted her body, and with both hands still tied behind her back, flung the knife from her back pocket in Maddy's direction. It fell halfway between Maddy and the killer. Rusty saw what she did and turned. Looking at Maddy, he smiled. He whipped around back to Jodi, smashed her face against the portable toilet, and knocked her unconscious.

"Now it is just you and Cupid," he said, grinning.

Stretching for the knife, a bolt of pain arced across Maddy's chest. She grabbed it and held it with all her strength, knowing it was her only hope. Rusty stood over her, trying to take it, and in the struggle, the knife catapulted several feet away. As he raced for it, Maddy stuck out her hand, hooking his toe with her fingers. He stumbled beyond the knife and landed on his stomach.

She tried reaching for the weapon, but Rusty grabbed her leg and reeled her to him. In a headlock, his vice-like grip tightened around her neck. In desperation, she reached in her pocket for her father's badge, freed the pin with her thumb, and jammed its spike into Rusty's elbow. He screeched and immediately released her. Barely conscious when she hit the ground, she whispered, "Dad, please help me."

Forcing herself to get up, she turned, lowered her good shoulder, and like an offensive guard, smashed into Rusty's stomach, driving him backward. He fell into a slippery pool of leachate from an unmaintained toilet. The stink was horrendous. Trying to stand, he slipped and fell.

She grabbed the knife and lunged, shoving the blade deep into his lower back. He let out a groan and fell face down into the sludge. She climbed on his back to finish him, but he bucked violently and shook her off. Landing on her back, she nearly lost consciousness, but still clutched the knife.

Covered with blood, Rusty struggled to get to his feet while in the sewage, but Maddy got to her knees first, leaned over, and stabbed the only body part she could reach—his calf. He jolted, and in agony, screamed, "Cupid is going to fuck you while he cuts your head off, you bitch!" Climbing on his back a second time, under her weight, he collapsed. As if aware he was losing the battle, he made a last-ditch effort to shake Maddy off. She shifted her weight and used her legs to keep him pinned down.

Rusty's stamina waned. In his weak moment, Maddy thrust the knife into the back of his neck, feeling the steel rub against bone and vertebrae. Like a pig being slaughtered, a high-pitched squeal resounded throughout the open yard. His body stiffened, then collapsed into the sludge.

She rolled off, and although barely conscious, felt an overwhelming sense of relief. *Thank you, Dad.* She crawled several feet away from the reeking body and collapsed on her stomach. Exhausted and in pain, she looked up from the ground and began scanning the quarry for Jodi, but there was no sign. As she looked, the shadow of a man moved over her.

Oh, my God! He's still alive!

She couldn't get up, so she rolled to her back as the deranged killer stood before her, with his pained-filled face covered with black filth and blood. *He looks like a demon from hell.* While reaching around, trying to pull the knife from his neck, Maddy, with all her remaining strength, lunged the heel of her foot upward into his groin.

His eyes filled with disbelief. Looking at her with unmitigated hatred, he lifted his head skyward and released a thunderous roar filled with a lifetime of pain. His body drooped, and he helplessly staggered backward, glaring at Maddy. Collapsing into the leachate, the weight of his body forced the knife through his neck, leaving the blood-covered blade shining in the moonlight.

His eyes remained opened, and even in death, they seemed filled with contempt. Barely conscious and with great effort, Maddy slurred the words, "Cupid is dead!"

The man who had brought so many people so much suffering lay sprawled out in reeking filth. Her thoughts went back to how he had left Sarah Benning and Nancy Miles. He had killed her father and her best friend. Cupid was the destroyer of over ten girls; but now, finally, he had found his reward adorned in sewage.

Trying to get up, trees and lights converged into a blur, and she collapsed. Dizzy, she lay on her back with her eyes closed and heard a sweet voice.

"It's me. Jodi." The girl's face, swollen and bloodied as she applied pressure to her wound, appeared like an angel's. Maddy faded in and out of consciousness as a loud chop, chop, chop sound of helicopters vibrated through the ground, and soon shadowy figures hovered over.

She heard Zep's voice. "Thank God you're alive."

Drifting between black silence and swirling light, her head spun like she was on a carnival ride. Before being lifted to the helicopter, all sounds and smells muddled together, and she nearly vomited. When whisked away into the air, a soft hand found hers. *It's Jodi's.* With her other hand, Maddy clutched her father's badge before everything went black.

Chapter 36

"Good morning, Ms. Reynolds," a nurse said as she walked to the bed, holding a tray.

"Breakfast?" Maddy asked.

"No, not yet. More meds."

"Again?" She gulped down a cupful of pills. "The doctor said he thought I might go home today. Have you heard anything?"

"No, but I'll ask," she said. Leaning over, the nurse helped her prop up with pillows. "Would you like me to help you clean up?"

"No, I think I can handle it," Maddy said.

"Ok, just be sure not to get your wound wet."

Oh my God, look at me. She gazed at herself in a hand-held mirror, and primped herself as best she could before returning to the bed.

"Hey, Maddy." Zep and Al stood smiling in the doorway.

"Hey guys, come over and have a seat. Sorry, I look like a giant hairball." They laughed. Zep held up a bouquet of yellow lilies, and Al clutched a box of chocolates.

"How are you feeling?" Al asked.

"Still a little sore, but I might go home today, so I feel great."

"You've been through quite an ordeal, Maddy," Zep said.

"I still haven't put all the pieces together. It's going a take time."

"Take all the time you need," he said.

The nurse returned, saw the flowers, and said she'd find something to put them in before taking them away.

"I got your favorites," Al said, holding up a box of Godiva chocolates. "You probably need a fix."

Maddy sensed something more was going on than met the eye. "Aren't you two supposed to be out catching bad guys?"

"You caught them all," Al said. "Now we have nothing to do."

She noticed a heaviness in Zep's eyes and finally came right out with it. "Okay, what's going on with you two?"

They looked at each other, then Zep said, "It's the noise-lady."

"Tonya? What about her?"

"She's dead."

Maddy grimaced. "What happened?"

"Breaking and entering gone bad," Zep said. Some kids got in her place, and when she tried to call for help, they shot her. The boy who did it is fifteen.

Looking down, she shook her head, hardly able to speak. "Did she suffer?"

"No. She went quickly."

"She was so happy to be rid of that annoying noise," Maddy said. "If it weren't for her obsession with it, we may never have connected Rusty to Cupid." She was silent for a moment, and added, "I'm not sure I can do this anymore."

"You've been through a lot. Take your time and think about it," Zep said.

Reaching out her hand, Zep took it, and she said, "Thank you."

Al pointed to a blue and pink card with a dragonfly. "Wow, that's beautiful. Who's it from?"

"It's from Jodi."

"That girl was amazing," Al said.

"Jodi saved my life," Maddy said. "She said in her note she needed facial surgery, but the plastic surgeon thinks there will be no visible scars when she heals.

"By the way," Zep said, "I spoke to Tom Bishop about Candy. She's in a special hospital unit at Albany Medical for traumatized children. He said it's going to be a long recovery. The emotional and psychological scars will be the most difficult to heal."

The nurse returned carrying a plastic water pitcher with the flowers and placed them next to the bed. "That's the only thing I could find to put them in," she said, "but they're still beautiful." Turning to Maddy with a smile, she said, "It looks like you're going home today. Your husband called a few minutes ago and asked how you were doing. I told him he will need to speak with you."

"He's my ex-husband."

When the nurse left, she said to the men, "Everyone wants us to get back together, but I'm unsure. Amber has finally come to a good place with our divorce and I hate bringing her into more turmoil." Looking at Zep, she said, "I know you won't want to hear this, but she doesn't want me to go back to police work."

A man in blue scrubs walked in, looking at a chart.

"We better get going," Al said.

Zep got up to leave, started for the door, stopped, and turned. "Remember, take all the time you need to decide about what you want to do."

"Thanks," she said, thinking that she'd never go back.

When Zep and Al walked out, Maddy lay back, reflecting on all that had happened. Her eyes rested on her father's detective badge lying on the table next to Jodi's card. She thought of the monster he had pursued for years but who ended up killing him. Shaking her head, she said, "We got him, Dad."

The End

About the Author

John Netti is an award-winning author. In the early years of his career, he worked as a rehabilitation counselor, offering help to people in need. Some accepted it, and John was privileged to share their journeys.

From them, he learned of human suffering, tragedies, and life's victories, but most of all, he realized we share a never-ending quest to be known. John tries to make his characters known to his readers, even if for a little while. He enjoys writing fast-paced fiction that draws readers into a story, allowing them to experience it as though they are there.

Other Titles by John Netti

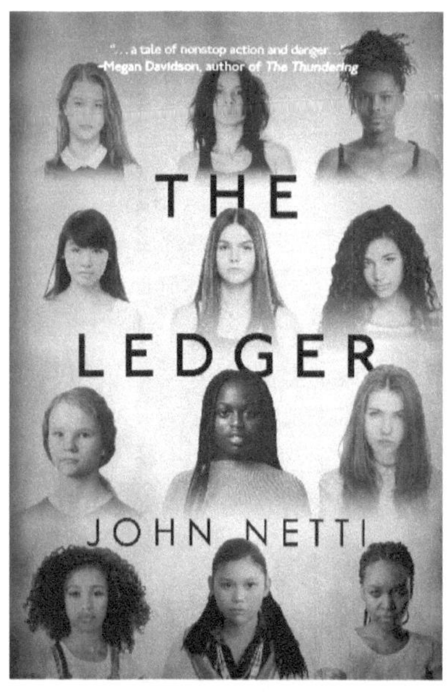

Note from John Netti

Word-of-mouth is crucial for any author to succeed. If you enjoyed *Deranged*, please leave a review online — anywhere you are able. Even if it's just a sentence or two. It would make all the difference and would be very much appreciated.

Thanks!
John Netti

We hope you enjoyed reading this title from:

www.blackrosewriting.com

Subscribe to our mailing list – *The Rosevine* – and receive **FREE** books, daily
deals, and stay current with news about upcoming
releases and our hottest authors.
Scan the QR code below to sign up.

Already a subscriber? Please accept a sincere thank you for being a fan of
Black Rose Writing authors.

View other Black Rose Writing titles at
www.blackrosewriting.com/books and use promo code
PRINT to receive a **20% discount** when purchasing.